"TURN AROUND, SHOUTED TRAIN.

He would see that this was a fair fight.

He saw the flash of Nair's gun as it whipped up. Then he raised his own revolver and fired.

A heavy weight struck Train's left shoulder, tore it with mangling pain, and twisted him violently in the saddle. He lost his balance and crashed to the ground.

He heard the yell of triumph. Nair was erect in the saddle, firing again and again, thundering his exultation in the victory. Another blow struck him with sickening effect; it ripped his thigh from hip to knee. A third bullet spattered dust and gravel in his face and half blinded him.

And in that way, lying on his back, Train forgot his pain, drew his bead with solemn care, and pulled the trigger. . . .

STEVE TRAIN'S ORDEAL
was originally published by
Dodd, Mead & Company, Inc.

STEVE TRAIN'S ORDEAL *by*
Max Brand

PUBLISHED BY POCKET BOOKS NEW YORK

STEVE TRAIN'S ORDEAL

Dodd, Mead edition published 1967

POCKET BOOK edition published November, 1968

2nd printing...................November, 1974

Standard Book Number: 671-75847-0.

Front cover illustration by John Duillo.

Printed in the U.S.A.

STEVE TRAIN'S ORDEAL

◈

The town consisted of two parts. Up on the hill where the eucalyptus trees had been taught to grow, were the homes of the well-to-do ranchers and miners who, for mysterious reasons understandable only by the natives of the great Southwest, had retired from active life, and built their houses in the "city." They led dreary lives up on the hill where the eucalyptus trees grew thick enough to make a show at a distance, but not thick enough to make a shade. The sun upon the brow of that hill was as hot as it could be in any part of that hot State. But it had become the fashion to retire to San Lorenzo, and therefore the ranchers and the miners continued to come to it regularly as soon as they found that they could not stick in the saddle on a real pitching pony.

John Rainier, leaving this gloomily sunburned region behind him, advanced down the hill to the second section of the town.

It crouched by the river with scarcely a single second story in the whole list of its houses, like a dog at the feet of its master. This was the Mexican village from which the servants were recruited for the domestic establishments of the whites. It was so humble that it could find shelter even under the willows that stood along the river banks, their delicate green branches showering down like water from the bowl of the fountain. The willows grew even at some distance from the very bank of the stream, for the soil was porous, and allowed the water to seep far in.

Moreover, every spring when the heat of the sun melted the snow in the upper mountains, far away, a great brown tide swept down the San Lorenzo River, crowded above its banks, and washed through the Mexican quarter of the town. There was a dyke to prevent the inundation, but though it was built up every fall, it was made either too frail or too low, for the good-natured inhabitants always waited for the work to be completed in some happy *mañana* when plowing and scraping would be a pleasure and not disagreeable work. Every spring saw the destruction of the dyke; every spring the brown waters rushed about the Mexican quarter; every spring some houses crumbled under the pressure and the dissolving action of the river against the dobe.

But still the town was never moved, and the dyke was never made perfect. Indeed, the yearly excitement and the nights of painful watching as the San Lorenzo grumbled and began to rise in its might made half the fun of living in that sunburned valley.

Down the hill, on this hot day, came a pudgy little man who walked with the hurrying step of a great city, not the lazy stride of a cowman. He was in a perspiration before he reached the easy, level valleys which twisted through the Mexican quarter. Once among them, he advanced with greater leisure. It was impossible to continue hurrying when such an audience lingered near.

Every doorway was occupied by loungers smoking cigarettes and staring into the profound blue sky of the dreamer; every doorway gave tantalizing fragrances of cooking food, for the afternoon was wearing late, and through every doorway he had glimpses of the hard-packed, clean-swept dirt floors.

There were children innumerable. There were dogs of twenty breeds. Here and there a pig wandered and paused to root out some hidden treasure of a dog. The chickens clattered and scratched in the bright heat of the sun; the white-washed dobe walls glistened in the light and turned smoky blue in the shadow, and in the warm air stirred a whisper which said that every day was worth living for the contentment which it brought and which need not be labored for.

For his own part, John Rainier profoundly believed in leisure, but a nervous temperament kept him active. It kept him, now, from pausing to chat with any of the lounging

2

ease-takers in the doorways, for though he smiled at and greeted every one, he went on and on as though he expected to find some better chance a little in advance. Presently he heard the thrumming of a banjo in the hands of an expert, and a mellow baritone, softened with languor, began to sing:

O Mollie, O Mollie, it is for your sake alone
That I leave my old parents, my house and my home,
That I leave my old parents, you caused me to roam—
I am a rebel soldier, and Dixie's my home.

Jack o' diamonds, jack o' diamonds,
   I know you of old,
You've robbed my poor pockets
   Of silver and gold.

Rainier, chuckling, hurried around the next winding of the alley and came upon a slim, soft-eyed Mexican girl standing in a doorway. She smiled at a white cloud drifting down the sky, but plainly her heart was at her feet, where the singer lounged.

He was dressed in the luxurious height of Mexican fashion, from the long, spoon-handled golden spurs upon his heels and the bright silver conchos which ran up the seams of his trousers, to the wide sombrero which sat on the ground beside him, all weighted and covered with gold medallions. But the face which looked up to the girl as he sang was the face of a white man. Though the desert sun had burned it as rich a brown as the backs of his hands, though his hair was the deepest black, and the brown of his eyes well-nigh black also, yet one felt the Anglo-Saxon in his blood—perhaps in his smile, or in the strong modeling of his forehead.

In age he could not well be past his early twenties, but it was plain that here was no son dependent upon a father's will and pleasure. One might have traveled ten thousand miles without finding so handsome a picture of mischief and indolence.

He strummed his banjo again through a soft interlude, and then began another verse of his song:

My foot's in the stirrup, my bridle's in my hand,
I'm going to leave sweet Mollie, the fairest in the land.
Her parents don't like me, they say I'm too poor,
They say I'm unworthy to enter her door.

3

But it's beefsteak when I'm hungry
    And whisky when I'm dry;
Greenbacks when I'm hard up.
    And heaven when I die.

Then memory, which had been struggling in the mind of John Rainier, found what he wanted.

"Steve Train!" he cried.

The handsome youth in the doorway sat up and yawned. Then he gave his hand to Rainier as the latter rushed up to him.

"John Sullivan!" he said.

"Rainier!" said the other a little sharply.

"Of course," replied Steven Train, grinning. "John Rainier, of course. Honest John! What are you doing in these parts?"

"I'm a valet," said Rainier.

"A which?"

"A valet."

"What gag is that?" asked Steve Train.

"Not half bad. I'll tell you later. What you doing yourself?"

"Doing?"

"Yes. What's your job?"

"I've stopped working," said Train, yawning again. "Stopped working three years back. Work ain't what I'm cut out for. You wouldn't believe it, now, but I got a weak liver. Work plumb raises the dickens with it."

John Rainier chuckled. "I guess it does," he said. "You showed signs of it coming on the last time I seen you. But," he went on, with a sudden interest, "I think you're the very man I'm looking for."

"Maybe," said Train, turning an impatient glance away from Rainier and penetrating the shadows of the house into which the girl had retreated when the stranger came near.

"I got *the* job for you, old son."

"Maybe."

"A job without no work in it."

"A which?"

"No work and all pay. Does that sound—"

"Queer," said Train calmly. "Sounds like a catch."

"I mean it, Steve."

"Coin or credit."

"Coin. Hard cash right on the nose."

Mr. Train rose, unlimbered his lithe body, stretched him-

4

self, catlike, so that every muscle was tugged at, and then allowed to relax. Then he turned to the door and hissed softly. Instantly the girl appeared, regardless now of who should watch her. The cavalier whispered words in quick Spanish which Rainier could not follow. Then, kissing the tips of his slender fingers to the señorita, he turned away at the side of Rainier.

"Still at it?" asked Rainier, half in admiration and half in envy. "Still busting hearts, Steve?"

"I'm one of them unfortunates," said Train, still trying to yawn away the inexhaustible sleep which tingled in his body, "I'm one of them unfortunates that can't go no place without being took advantage of. The girls see that I'm plumb simple, and that I'll follow a smile like a bull chases a red rag. That's me, John."

And he turned his large, melancholy eyes upon his companion.

"Confidence!" snapped out John Rainier. "That's what you're cut out for. If I could keep my face like you, I'd be on Wall Street, Steve. They'd have a value for you back there."

"There ain't nothing on Wall Street," stated Steve, "except money. And money's dirt. Elbow room and a good time. That's all I want."

Mr. Rainier seemed to have other opinions of this modest desire, and he began to chuckle softly to himself.

"What's the valet game?" asked Train, and, having reached an old willow, he sat down with his shoulders against its broad trunk and whistled to a roan-colored dog, one of whose ears was ragged from a recent fight. The cur lingered a suspicious moment and then sneaked up to him and submitted to the caressing hand.

"Dogs and horses are easy for you, Train," said his companion. "Them and the ladies, eh?"

"But valets," said Train, "I never had no luck with. What about 'em?"

"It's a funny gag," said Rainier. "Two years back a flatty grabs me in Denver. He soaks me in the calaboose. I pry a way out with my fingernails, you might say, and flag it for the railroad. Beat the rattlers to El Paso, got kicked off by a fresh shack, and spent the night wondering whether I'd better wait for another train or hike into town. You'd of sat it out."

"Sure."

"You've got more patience, but I walked. On the way I

come across an oldish fellow riding a mustang that was turning itself inside out. Pretty soon it threw the old bird out of the saddle; one of his feet hung in the stirrup. I says to myself: 'This sap has a barrel of the long green stowed in his pocket. Why should a horse get away with it?' I managed to grab the head of the horse and stop the fool. Then I untangled the old fellow, who was all dust and blood. His face was a smear, and I thought at first that he was out for the finish. I took a peek at his wallet; it was as flat as the palm of my hand. His watch was silver plate—hardly worth packing along to town to hock. Even his pocketknife had nothing but a plain bone handle. There wasn't enough loot in that job to give me three squares.

"I decides I'll have to be a hero and get a reward that way, if the sap don't cash in on my hands. He didn't cash in. I brought him to, tied him together, and strapped him on the back of his horse. I bundled him into a hospital, and about a month later, when he could sit up in bed, he asks me what he can do for me to reward me.

" 'Nothing,' says I. 'I want no reward except to see that you're straightened out, sir.'

"He fell for that line. Fed me some questions. I told him that I'd been a grocer, and that bad debts had ruined me, and that I had fifteen hundred dollars standing out against me, and so I had to quit my business and go West. Old Patrick Comstock—that was his name—thought it over for a while. Then he gave me that fifteen hundred dollars in cold cash, along with another thousand for expenses. He told me to get myself some good clothes, buy a ticket to my home town, pay off my debts, prove my honesty to all the tradespeople in the place, and then if I couldn't think of another business that I wanted to go into, I could come back to him and go into his service.

"I got as far as Chi. There I dropped the whole wad at black jack in Three-fingered Louis' dive. You know that place?"

"Sure. The bouncer in that dump taught me how to throw a knife."

"I was cleaned. I turned around and rode the rods back to El Paso. Found out that Comstock had bought a ranch at San Lorenzo. He didn't ask me no questions; just looked over the clothes I was wearing, and then he says that I can start work whenever I get ready.

" 'What shall I do?' says I.

6

" 'Look around the house and see what's to be done,' says he.

" 'I'm no good inside,' says I.

" 'Are you much good outside?' says he.

" 'I can bear a hand,' says I.

" 'Can you rope a cow?'

" 'Nope.'

" 'Can you ride range?'

" 'What's that mean?' says I.

" 'You'd better stay inside,' says he.

"I sat around the house a while. He had two Chinese boys that done all the work. All I could think of doing was to dust the books in the library, but that pleased the old man a lot.

" 'Jack,' says he, 'I've plenty of people to take care of my ranch and my house and my business, but I want somebody to take care of me. Will you be the man?'

"So I took the job, and it turned out a cinch. I see that his clothes are always pressed and brushed, though I don't have to do the pressing and the brushing. I watch out for the saddling of his horse, the looks of his saddle, the shine of his boots. That's about all. That's why I'm getting so flabby."

"You look like a mushroom," said Train critically. "I'd hate to step on you. Where do I figure in on this party?"

"Well, kid, if you've listened to me chatter, you know that I'm something big in the house up the hill, yonder. I go over with a bang. I'm the guy that saved his life, and that's now prolonging it. That's me. D'you get it?"

"Yep."

"Well, old Comstock is now hunting for a brave man and an honest man to do a piece of hard work for him. Something important, where he'll have to be trusted with big stuff, and that's where you come in, Steve. You're that same honest and brave man!"

2

This suggestion was received in silence by Train, but finally he turned to his friend and showed his white and even teeth in a smile which was quite without mirth.

"That's good enough for the stage," said Train.

His companion, however, continued in all earnestness.

"Just what the big play is, I dunno; but it's something hot. There'd be a haul in it, I know."

He told the story in much detail. Mr. Comstock had announced that he must secure a man who possessed both courage and honesty. The first man he tested proved to be lacking in the first quality. The second had fallen short in honesty. He had then come to Rainier and asked him to do his best to find a man possessing both these qualities.

"Why didn't he use you, John?" asked Train.

"Because I'm a boob with a gun; I never could do anything with a Colt, and this job needs a crack who can't miss. That's where you'd shine again. Besides, the old man says that he can't risk losing me."

"A risky job, is it?"

"According to him. Does it sound good to you, Steve?"

The languor of Steve Train was gradually diminishing. He actually sat up straight as though his back no longer was in need of a support.

"Begins to look like there might be something worth while," he admitted. "When do I see Comstock?"

"Right now—pronto, if you want to."

They went up the hill to the big house of Patrick Comstock; they passed under the gate and came into the patio itself, and there Steven Train had a first sight of the rancher. He sat half in sun and half in shadow, a man with young eyes in an old face, and a mist of white hair stirring above his forehead. He was very thin, very fragile in appearance. The book he was reading seemed too thick for the hand which was supporting it. He laid aside that book and regarded the two.

"Here's a man I know, Mr. Comstock," said Rainier. "Name is Steven Train. I think he might be the right man for you."

"How do you do, Mr. Train," said Comstock, making no movement toward shaking hands. "Does Train know about the work?"

"A little," answered the valet.

"Then you may let us talk here alone."

Rainier disappeared, and Steve Train was waved to a nearby chair. The sun was hot, but Train loved its heat. He stretched himself in the blaze of that intolerable light, almost forgetting the man beside him for the moment.

"You're a Westerner, Train?" asked Comstock.

"That's what," replied Train, still drinking in the heat of the sun.

"But Rainier is an Easterner. I wonder how he came to know you?"

"I forget where we met up," answered Train. "I remember his face. My memory ain't the best," he added, turning to Comstock with his peculiar, lazy smile.

"That outfit of yours," said Comstock, "is almost too good to work in."

"Sure," said Train carelessly. "Work ain't my line."

"No?"

The sharpness of this query recalled Train to himself, but having committed himself, he now shrugged his shoulders.

"What *is* your line, Train?"

"Oh, I hunt a bit, trap a bit, loaf a bit," he answered, smiling again.

But Comstock was frowning. "A Westerner," he said, "except for a gun."

"Why," said Train, "sometimes one gun out of sight is worth two on the hip."

Mr. Comstock sat up. "You do carry a weapon?"

"Sure," said Train. "A gat comes in handy now and then."

"For what?"

"Rabbits," said Train.

Mr. Comstock smiled, but he shook his head. "But you keep it out of sight?"

"Yep. A lot of game is gun shy, you know."

For an instant the rancher hesitated, stirring uneasily in his chair as though he were on the verge of terminating this interview by dismissing his man. Finally he decided to probe a little deeper.

"In the work before me," he said. "I may need some one who is an excellent shot. Would you qualify, Train?"

"Well, I'm medium good."

"For instance, there's a sparrow yonder."

It perched on the twig of a rosebush, tilting up and down in the breeze.

"I never shoot nothing except on the wing," said Train, and with a gesture of such astonishing ease and speed that Comstock could not be sure from what place it was produced, he brought out a long Colt, which balanced in his hand as lightly as the sparrow flirted on the twig.

It exploded at the same instant. The twig, shorn in twain,

dropped to the ground, and the sparrow darted into the air with a frightened chirping. A second bullet missed that elusive target, but hummed so close that the bird dodged with whirring wings to the side. Before it could straighten out its flight, the third shot tore it to bits and cast upon the ground a mangled body, upon the air a flutter of small feathers.

Voices cried out in the house at this sudden fusillade, in which the explosions had followed each other almost faster than thought. Two men rushed out into the patio.

But they found the master unharmed, and beside him a gayly dressed and handsome stranger was rolling a cigarette with no sign of a gun in view. Mr. Comstock dismissed them with a gesture and then turned to his companion with an enthusiasm which he could not restrain.

"How have you learned to handle a gun in that fashion?" he asked.

"It's easy," said Train.

"Then tell me how to learn, and I'll begin at once."

"Work a couple of hours a day for ten or twelve years," said Train simply.

The rancher laughed, but he sank back in his chair with a sigh of disappointment.

"Of course," he said, "one is always looking for a miracle to happen. But most miracles are explained in the same fashion—they're simply the result of hard work and lots of it."

"Work?" said the other. "Handling a gun ain't work. It's fun; it's a game; that's all."

And he made a quick, muscular gesture with his fingers which seemed to bring the heavy Colt into existence again. Plainly the rancher was now willing to take him more seriously.

"I suppose," he said suddenly, "that you're not very flush, Train?"

"Broke."

"Not a cent?"

"Flat busted."

"Tell me," asked Comstock curiously, "how you would have provided yourself with a dinner tonight."

"I've got salt in my pouch," said the other, "and bullets in my guns. And yonder is my dinner, taking exercise."

He waved to the brown hills of the desert, rolling away to the north and the east.

"I gather that you are not afraid to trust yourself to the hills?"

"Not a bit."

"But why?"

"There ain't no part of the desert where something doesn't live. Where something else lives, a man can. If there's enough green stuff to keep a rabbit running, a man can live off the rabbit. That's all."

"But if you miss the rabbit?"

"That's it," said Train. "You mustn't miss."

"Well," said Comstock, "I'll see that you have your supper tonight without shooting it. After that, I hope you'll stay on with me for a time, until I have a chance to talk business with you. In the meantime, your pay is—what?"

"Fifteen a week?"

"Thirty," said Comstock.

So Train moved into the big house on the hill and took his place in the establishment.

"But," said Comstock, "where's your horse?"

"Yonder," said the other, and pointed down into the distance, where a thin black cloud was trailing above a swiftly moving train.

"I understand," chuckled the rancher. "But in the work you do for me, you may need a horse. Look through the ones you'll find in the corral and in the stable. I have some beauties, Train, and you may take your pick."

Horses being the pet hobby of the rancher, he had brought up some of his finest stock for use of himself and his men at the town of San Lorenzo. He now sent for his head groom. This was a man of middle age, but with the starved face of a jockey. The harsh diet and regime of exercise with which he had vainly attempted to keep himself down to weight in his youth had made it impossible for him to put on flesh in later life.

"This is Train," said the rancher. "He is to do some work for me, and I want to lend him any horse of mine that he takes a liking to."

"*Any* horse?" asked the groom, with a marked emphasis.

"Any horse, Thompson," said the rancher severely. "Mind that he has a look at them all!"

Thompson surveyed the brilliant and outlandish garb of Train with manifest dislike. Then, with a shrug of his shoulders, he led the stranger to the corrals. There were seven

11

or eight fine animals there, with heads as finely made and eyes as gentle as deer. They crowded along the fence to nibble at the hand of Thompson and snort at the stranger.

"Beauties!" cried Train enthusiastically.

"You know what stuff that is?"

"Good stuff, I'd say."

"Thoroughbred," said Thompson curtly. "Mostly thoroughbred. A little dash of mustang, but I been breeding that strain thinner and thinner every year. Not a loafer in that gang. Not a one that would let you down in a pinch. Not a one that wouldn't run itself to death without being touched with a quirt. You got spurs, I see?"

He added this with a long look of disapproval at the heels of Train.

"Spurs for looks," said Train, "and sometimes for mustangs."

"Well," muttered Thompson, with a sigh, "the boss says that you ride anything you want to ride. You'll weigh in around a hundred and seventy."

He ran his appraising eye over Train.

"To a pound," answered Train.

"There's a neat filly for you. She has the foot, too. She's a charm, I tell you. Shall I call her yours?"

"A bit light in the loin, ain't she?"

"Light? Not a bit! Can't have perfection. Know what that mare is? That's out of Mischief, by Sir Arthur. She's a trick, I tell you!" And he rubbed his hands in his enthusiasm.

"She's a trick that I don't take, I guess," drawled Train. "Lemme see the rest."

"There they are. If you want strength, there's a colt that's turned four. He'll last all day. He's honest—that's all!"

"It ain't enough," answered Train. "He ain't cut for speed."

"You want the world with a fence around it," snapped out Thompson. "Take a look at the brown horse, then. That's—"

"They're all fine," said Train, "but let's have a snoop around the stable."

He received a black look and a muttered oath from the groom, but he was taken next to the stables. There, in a double row of box stalls, were six horses, each with its head thrust out to greet the visitors. And by their heads alone he knew them.

"This," said Train, "is more like it."

He felt the surprised glance of Thompson turned upon him, but he was too busy with his survey to take any heed of that.

"This is more like it," he said again. "That gray is a winner, and what's the black colt down yonder?"

Disregarding all the rest, he went straight to the door of that stall and looked in upon a rangy three-year-old with a skin like velvet and the finish of a statue in polished black marble. Train gave it his hand to nibble. It was affectionate.

"If she was a year or two older—" sighed Train.

He turned upon Thompson. "What's the filly?" he asked.

"Out of Folly, by Tiger," said Thompson.

"Folly belonged to Mr. Comstock, eh?"

"Yep. The old mare died last spring."

"Old?"

"Nineteen when she passed out. Not old for her, though."

"Did you raise her?"

"I did. She was out of Caprice, by Samson. We'll never have the like of Folly, God bless her!"

He spoke with a sad enthusiasm, rubbing the nose of the filly.

"Well," said Train suddenly, "if you raised her and she was seventeen when this filly was foaled, then you have something else by her on the place. You've got an older brother of this filly, here. Lemme see it, Thompson."

The dark blood rushed into the face of Thompson.

"No brother of the filly on this place," he asserted violently. He changed his tone. "Look here," he said, "you know a horse. I seen that right away. If there'd been a brother of the filly, I'd of showed it to you. I could see that kind of a horse was to your taste—good head—plenty of speed—disposition like silk—heart as big as an elephant's. But there ain't any brother. No, sir; I'm sorry that the filly ain't a four-year-old, for your sake!"

"She has a sister, then," said Train, as convinced as ever.

Thompson had grown pale.

"She's sick," he said huskily, "Whimsy's sick. Mighty sorry, but Whimsy's sick."

"Too bad," said Train, swallowing a smile. "Lemme see her, though."

"Can't do it," said Thompson. "Sorry, captain. Like to see a man that knows horseflesh have his choice. But Whimsy is so darn full of nerves that it upsets her to have strangers around. I keep her quiet, and—"

13

"Just a look," broke in Train.

Thompson hesitated.

"What's in the end stall?" asked Train.

"Nothing. Just a—"

But Train had already gone to explore, and, when he opened the end door of the barn, he saw that it was as he had surmised. The window of that stall had been drawn shut, and the reason was that the inhabitant of those quarters did not need that ventilation, for a second door of the stall opened onto a pleasant little paddock on the brow of the hill, where the cool of the breezes would sweep, and where a broad-limbed tree gave shelter from the sun. In this shadow stood Whimsy.

He knew her at once, and he knew, also, why Thompson dreaded to part with her as a miser dreads parting with his gold. She was big—perhaps an inch over sixteen hands—but the fine quality of the two-year-old filly, compared with her elder sister, was like a clay sketch beside a polished bronze. And when she turned her head, with the wind riffling through her thin mane, her large and gentle eye met that of Train with almost the shock and the thrill of a human glance.

"Sick?" said Train. "Sick?"

"I was joking with you," stammered poor Thompson. "Matter of fact, that's Comstock's own pet horse, my friend. I didn't want you to see her, because I knew that she was the only one he wouldn't let you have. Let you have her? Why, you'd better ask him for ten thousand dollars."

Train laid a hand upon the rail of the fence and vaulted over, and Thompson, watching the alert and eager step and the raised head of the young fellow, groaned with despair. He had done his best, but he knew that Whimsy was lost to him.

3

Whatever the work was which lay in store for Train, he had no word of it for two days. During those two days he spent nearly every waking moment with Whimsy, until Mr. Comstock, on the third morning, exclaimed with wonder when he saw his new employee approach the paddock and saw Whimsy toss her head and whinny a greeting.

"No wonder," said the jealous Thompson. "I don't mind a man that's fond of horses. But when it comes to treating them like they was women—why, Mr. Comstock, he don't come near her without sugar or an apple or something. Any horse'll neigh when it sees feed in sight."

Comstock smiled faintly, but made no reply.

"What would you say, Thompson, of a man who's so very fond of a horse?"

"All depends. Might be called foolish, I'd say."

"But such a man—he'd be honest, Thompson, don't you think?"

"Never can tell," said the surly fellow. "I've watched them that follow the ponies. There's something about a horse. Worst man in the world—the hardest and the crookedest—will love a horse. Can't tell nothing about that!"

The rancher turned the conversation, and, early that afternoon, receiving a message by telegraph, he suddenly sent Rainier about the work of packing a bag and straightway sent for Train.

He was called away for a matter of a few days, he told Train, and most inopportunely, for he expected the visit of a man who was coming to receive a quantity of cash that was being held for him in Mr. Comstock's private safe.

"I could leave Rainier," said the rancher, "but I'll need him with me, and I must trust this affair to you, Train. Here," he went on, giving Train a slip of paper, "is the combination. The drawers in the safe are all labeled except one. In that blank one you'll find eleven hundred dollars in cash. The man who will come for it is a short, stocky fellow, about forty years old, and with a very bald head. You can't mistake him. His name is Gregg. Take his receipt and give him the money."

With those instructions, he left in the company of Rainier, who had only one opportunity to draw his friend to one side.

"It's a plant, Steve. It's to try you out. He's risking eleven hundred in cash to prove to himself that you're honest. Stick tight, for God's sake. Something a lot bigger is coming along behind all this. Stick tight and play the honest man. Later on, we'll have something worth while to split. Will you do it?"

"Eleven hundred is chicken feed," returned Steve. "Leave it to me, old-timer!"

The servants were given the day off, now that the master was away; and when they trooped down to the Mexican

15

quarter of the town, Train found himself alone. There was not even a dog for company.

Accordingly, he went first of all into the strong cellar room, where the safe was kept, and tried the combination numbers which had been given to him. The door opened easily, and in the little dark crypt which was exposed he saw, as had been described, a number of little drawers, each labeled correspondence, mortgages, and so forth. There was only the one blank drawer, and in this he found the money. There were twenty-two fifty-dollar bills, a stiff little sheaf secured by a brown-paper wrapper around the middle.

Train flicked the ends of the bills and counted them with a swift dexterity. And, as he did so, he turned the problem slowly in his mind. It would be simple enough to shove this money in his pocket, go to the corral, saddle Whimsy, and gallop off into the desert. He knew that desert, both the plain and the mountains, as a man knows a book. And with such a horse as Whimsy beneath him, it would be hard if he could not avoid all pursuit. Moreover, pursuit must necessarily be delayed because the master of the house and the servants were away. He could lock the safe after him, and no one would be the wiser concerning the theft until Comstock returned. As for Rainier's advice to wait for bigger game, many things might intervene. Something of his long past record might come to the ears of the rancher and make him see that he was trusting fortune too far.

But he returned the money to its drawer, and then went up to the room above, from which the narrow flight of stairs led down to the safe. And, as he sat there, he smiled to himself when he thought that he who had faced death half a dozen times for a tenth of this sum, should now sit calmly by with eleven hundred dollars his for the taking.

Evening came, without a sign of Mr. Gregg. He went into the kitchen to eat the supper which the Chinese cook had laid on the table for him there. Then he went back into the little room where he had been sitting. Long watches, however, were not to the liking of Steven Train. He was capable of great feats of endurance, but only when there was danger to hound him; in dull times of peace, as the camel accumulates fat on the hump, so he laid up a store of rest. There was no couch in that chamber, but this was a small inconvenience to one whose bones had been jostled many a time as he lay curled on the rattling floor of an empty box car. He folded a rug for a

16

pillow, stretched himself on the floor, and, as the evening was warm and he needed no covering, he was instantly oblivious of the world.

He wakened, at length, out of the soundest sleep and with a suddenness that had him fully alert before he had sat up.

It was a small thing which had disturbed him just as it needs only a small thing to make the wolf leap to its feet and bristle with anger and alarm. But, somewhere in the house, there had been a light creaking. He listened intently. The sound was not repeated, and now he grew wary. For, had it been the noise made by one of the servants entering the building, it would have come again. There would have been a stir of some sort from some corner of the old place.

In the meantime, he looked cautiously around him as he rose to his feet. It was night, now, and the window, glistening in the light of the lamp which he had lighted, was like a slab of highly polished black marble. But still there was no whisper to alarm him in the house.

Another would have laid aside all apprehension at this moment, but Steven Train was not like others. He stripped the boots from his feet. Even in them he could move quietly enough, but in his stockings he was noiseless as a stalking cat. In this fashion he crouched by the open door for a moment, waiting, until, though there had been no sound in the approach, he was aware of something standing in the hall outside, breathing softly. He reached for a gun. Then he remembered that the weapon was in his coat, which he had taken off because of the warmth of the night. He could not regain his Colt without rising and crossing the chamber. But to rise and move about would be, most certainly, to alarm the man who now stood outside the door. He could only trust to his hands. And, resigning himself to this difficult fate, he tensed and unflexed his fingers to prepare them for the grip of the struggle.

Before, in fact, he had time to come to a decision, the door began to swing cautiously open, as it might have moved if a weak draft of wind had been pressing against it. But Train knew that it was the careful touch of a man's hand.

He raised himself a little, poising himself on hands and feet, with one knee lowered, like a sprinter on his marks. One heel was jammed against the wall behind him. He was like a bent spring, full of gathered power. The door opened a little wider.

17

A man appeared in the dim and shadowy gap. Straight at him leaped Steven Train.

The impact was too sudden to allow the other to defend himself. He was driven a staggering pace back across the hall, struck heavily against the opposite wall, and then crumpled to the floor.

The intruder had only time and strength to gasp out: "Shoot, Bill!"

And Bill fired.

The flash of the gun enabled Train to make out two things —the place where the second assailant stood, and the glitter of the revolver of the first, lying within reach of his arm. For this Train reached. He had no time to turn it, catch his finger over the trigger, and fire. For the first shot having shown the assailant just where the enemy was, the second was fairly sure to be driven immediately to the mark. Train flung the heavy weapon at the man who stood in the darkness. The other's Colt exploded, the bullet flying wild. The next instant the iron-hard fist of Train was at him.

Then a shout boomed from the outdoors. Some one in the stables had heard the firing, and was coming on the run.

"Run for it, Bill; the game's up!" shouted the first assailant, and setting a good example, he bolted.

The second hardly needed advice, however. With pain to spur him, he ran like a deer, leaped sidewise through the door, and so gained the patio.

Steve Train did not pursue. To be sure, his own uncanny speed of foot might well have served him to overtake these secret enemies, but he did not like to risk himself in the face of danger when he was unequipped except with his bare hands.

He went slowly back into the room from which he had sprung for his counterattack. There he was found by Thompson, pulling on his boots and whistling a gay air. As for Thompson, he came in with his lean face flushed with excitement and a pump gun swinging in his right hand. The instant he saw Train, he instinctively covered the latter.

"Why, Thompson," said Train, "you look all heated up. What's wrong?"

"Wrong?" shouted Thompson, his eyes glittering. "There's maybe murder—that's what's wrong. There's been gun play around here! Where have *you* been?"

"Asleep."

"Through all this?"

"I thought I heard something, so I woke up."

"There's blood on your hand, Train. Whatever's happened, you've been in it. By the heavens, I knew that there was something wrong with you!"

"I scratched myself on my own spur," said Train contemptuously. "Now, get out! I need rest. A couple of gents like you would ruin the nerves of an army."

"And your shirt's torn—"

"Sure," said Steven Train quietly. "And here's a couple of guns that I didn't have before. Ever see 'em before this?" He extended two big Colts.

"They ain't your own?" asked Thompson, amazed.

"My own?" said Train. Then he shrugged his shoulders. "When you see a gun of mine as dirty as either of these, you'll know that I'm ready to have somebody put a slug in me and no questions asked. Why, these here guns are so far off their feed that you couldn't shoot a pig with one of 'em!"

After this, he refused to say another word about the encounter. But, when others came in from the stables, they were able to dimly reconstruct the struggle. They found a spot of blood against the wall just opposite the door of the room in which Train had been sleeping, and a slight indentation, such as might have been made in the plaster by a man's head as he fell violently backward. In the patio they found two pairs of boots, without the owners. And when the hands of Train were washed and it was seen that the blood was not his own, they made sure that two miscreants had attacked him in the night, and that he had routed them both.

Thompson came back to apologize. "I made a mistake," he said. "I got rattled and excited. I'm sorry, Train."

"Tell it to Whimsy," said Train cruelly. "I'll get on without your apologies."

So, very bluntly, he got rid of both questions and congratulations at a single blow, and the others retired to their own quarters again over the stables, where they had their rooms. They might have discovered that the new member of the household of the rancher was a very brave and dangerous man, but they also were convinced that he was the most unsociable fellow in the world. How could they be blamed, since he seemed so distinctly to prefer the society of horses to that of men?

No Mr. Gregg appeared, but early the next morning the rancher returned, announcing that a message from El Paso had made his journey unnecessary. On his arrival, he listened to the excited reports of the attack on the house which had taken place during his absence and the singular gallantry of Steven Train in repelling it. The courage and the battle prowess of Train lost nothing through this relation, it may be taken for granted.

Since he refused to give a minute description himself, the vivid imagination of Thompson and the other servants was called upon, and they made the best of it. The tale which Patrick Comstock heard was that five gigantic desperadoes had entered the house, and with their guns attacked Train, and that Train, with nothing but his bare hands, had disarmed and routed them all.

Afterward the rancher drew Train aside and asked for the truth.

The answer of Train was astonishingly blunt.

"I fell asleep like a flathead," he declared. "A couple of gents nearly got at me, but I surprised 'em in the dark of the hall. I had 'em licked by luck before they could see me, you might say. That's all there was to it."

"Enough!" said Comstock quietly. "I should say that it is quite enough. Train, I want to see you in front of the house in half an hour, ready to take a ride with me. I have something to say to you."

When Comstock was gone, John Rainier came, fairly panting with eagerness.

"How did those two crooks happen to get on the job?" he asked. "Can you guess that, Steve?"

"Comstock hired 'em."

"How do you get at that?"

"They fought like hired men."

Rainier shook his head in hearty admiration. It was exactly as Train had surmised, for the two had been picked up and given money by the rancher for the assault upon the single guard in the house. Two directions had been given to them—the first was that they must not stir until they were sure that Train did not have his gun with him; the second was that they themselves must under no pretext use firearms. It was simply to be a test of Train's nerve. The two had apparently made sure that Train was unarmed by spying through the window and seeing that he had laid aside his coat. As for the second, the tigerish attack of Train had made them fight for their lives, and they had drawn their revolvers, though to no purpose.

"And you saw the coin in the safe—and let it ride?" questioned Rainier in conclusion.

"Eleven hundred iron men," replied Steve Train. "I used up more muscle in putting that long green back in the safe than would of moved a ton of hay."

"It'll be worth while," Rainier assured him. "The old boy thinks that you're the only hundred-per-cent honest man west of the Mississippi. He'll tell you what he wants to use you for when you're out riding. Understand? It's so important that he won't trust walls to keep the secret. He wants to have you out by himself!"

That proved to be the case. By the time Train had saddled Whimsy and ridden the mare to the entrance of the patio, Thompson was on hand with the tall gray gelding which Comstock used, and they cantered off together down the hill, across the valley, and then Comstock slowed the pace to a walk and led the way up the brown bank of the San Lorenzo. It was not until they had gone on in this fashion for ten minutes of silence that he began to talk.

"I've been turning this thing back and forth in my mind for some time," he said. "The best way, I think, is to tell you the whole story, Train. I begin with my young manhood and a little boy who lived in my home town. The boy's name was

21

Jim Cartwright. I was in the last grade of the school when he entered the first, and before he'd been there a day, I had to take a hand to keep him from being bullied, because he came from the far Southwest with a Southwestern drawl, you see, and clothes like a miniature cow-puncher.

"That was the beginning of our friendship. When he grew older and went into business, I helped him again, but after he was once on his feet, he needed no help. He bought a farm. In five years he paid off the last bit of mortgage, and he was ready to expand. He bought more land, and was ready to buy still more when I persuaded him to buy certain stocks which I was interested in. He took my advice. The stocks dropped out of sight. Two dry, dead years followed, one after the other. Cartwright was wiped out, and went West before I did, and I have every reason to believe that he entered into a most illegitimate business out here. In a word, Train, I suspect him of being identical with that celebrated criminal, Jim Nair!"

The nerves of Train were hardly existent, so perfectly were they under his control, but at this point he started a little and Whimsy, as though her body reacted only to his mind, started also, and began to dance in excitement. The rancher regarded man and horse with a side glance of the profoundest admiration. He was one of the many who envy physical adroitness, physical strength and endurance.

"Jim Nair!" exclaimed Train.

"I'm sure of him. The full name of my friend was James Nair Cartwright, you see."

"Is that all you have to judge him by? Just because the name sounds the same?"

"Isn't that enough?"

"I'd say not. You knew an honest man, and he was a friend of yours. But Nair is a red-handed devil. He talks with bullets. He's got about twenty men on his record. It ain't talk, either. I could name a dozen of 'em offhand. When in doubt, the trumps he leads is bullets. Doesn't sound like a man that had worked hard at a farm."

"When a hard-working man is broken by hard luck," said the rancher thoughtfully, "my experience is that he may become a worse criminal than the weaklings who ordinarily go bad. He's a man of brains and system. He has force of character. He can organize his confederates. He knows how to use patience and care. And that is just the description of this Jim Nair who has made such havoc during the past five years. He's an exceptional man. He always was, and his criminal record is as unusual as his business record was in the old days. No, I'm certain that the two are one and the same man!"

To this argument Steve Train replied by shaking his head. Then he shrugged his shoulders.

"Do they look the same?" he asked.

"According to the descriptions I have heard of them, they do. Cartwright was a big fellow, rawboned, very powerful, with a strong face and a loud, harsh voice. All those details fit in with what I have heard of Nair."

At this Train nodded. "I guess that makes it sure," he said quietly. "But I've always thought, once a crook, always a crook; once honest, always honest!"

"By no means," said the rancher. "Consider, as I do many times, that there might come extraordinary temptations which would shake my virtue to the ground. I never read of the fall of some man who has long been unchallenged in society as a man of perfect integrity, without trembling to the bottom of my boots. I might have done what he had done. I still may do it. By Jove, it haunts me at night! Although I suppose that an outright young fellow like you never will think of such possibilities."

"The old gent is a boob," said Train to himself. But all he did was to make a noncommittal gesture.

"Now to get back to the story," said Comstock. "I told you that the stocks in which I had induced Cartwright to invest dropped out of sight. I felt very guilty about it, of course. It was a group of speculations, but I had been sure that they would go through. I was convinced that I was making Cartwright a rich man, while I myself expected to become many times a millionaire. We were both disappointed. I was hard hit—so hard hit that I had to give up all speculation from that time forth. I planned to come West and go into the cow business, and as you may perhaps have heard, I have been fortunate in my choice. But Cartwright was wiped out, and when I offered to give him enough to recover his farm, he told me that he wouldn't take charity. He used to have a theory, in those times, that every man was good for just one start, and no more. He felt that he had his fling, and that he could never have another.

"That was the theory he lived by. Rather a despairing one, wasn't it? In the meantime, as I said, he disappeared in the

West. Then wild tales came of the doings of Jim Nair; finally, I heard details which made me suspect that Nair and Cartwright were one and the same.

"I tried twice to get in touch with him. I was prepared then, just as I'm prepared now, to help him out of the country and support him in another place, if he will go. He is too clever not to know that the life he has been leading can lead to only one end—death with a noose around his neck, or with bullets in his brain. I tried to reach him, but I always failed. Then a sheriff got hold of a message I had tried to send to Jim. That got me into real trouble for the time being. I saw that I could not use careless methods unless I wished to make trouble both for Jim and myself.

"Since then, I have found a new reason for wishing to reach him. At first it was a mere friendly desire to help him. Now I have to find him for the sake of my own peace of mind. I told you those were speculative stocks I had invested in with Cartwright. They were worse than that. They were oil stocks, and in every one I had been swindled by wildcatters. However, it turned out that even the wildcatters had made a mistake in one affair. They thought they were cheating us. As a matter of fact, oil was there; it has been found. The well was running big. The old worthless stock had suddenly become of some value. Every day increased it. Finally it soared to a high point which I felt would never be reached again. I sold my stock and Cartwright's at that time, for all of his papers had been placed in my hands before he disappeared in the West. My own profits were large from that sale. For Jim Cartwright I secured no less than fifty thousand dollars! Enough, in a word, to support a single man with its interest!"

"Fifty thousand!" echoed Train, and whistled.

"And now, Train, you will understand my proposition. I had to convey that money to Nair. But how could I reach him? Certainly he has no fixed address; he dodges here and there through the mountains. The work of a hundred posses has not been sufficient to run him down, but I felt that one brave, intelligent, well-mounted man who knew the country might be able to reach Nair. I want that man to carry with him on his expedition fifty thousand dollars in greenbacks."

He paused and looked straight at Train, but all that Train could see was the fat face of John Rainier. How the little pig eyes would pop out when that sum was mentioned. Fifty thousand dollars—twenty-five thousand dollars apiece.

24

"You, of course," said Comstock, "are the man! If you'll undertake the commission, Train, with all of its dangers, I want to give you the fifty thousand and send you out to find Nair."

"Why not?" asked Train. "Why not?"

"Remember, it will be dangerous work. On the one hand, you'll be hunting Nair, and perhaps in such a way that he will think you an enemy. And those enemies who hunt him are apt to be hunted in turn. He'll think you an enemy until you get close enough to give him that money?"

"That's plain."

"Not only that, but you will be apt to have the law against you. Certainly if the officers of the law knew that you were trying to carry fifty thousand dollars to an outlawed man, they would do their best to capture you and the money also. That money would be confiscated as soon as they got their hands on it."

Train grew silent for a moment. "Having the law against a man is a pretty serious thing," he suggested.

"Of course. More than serious. I don't want to hide any of the difficulties of this thing from you. I want you to realize everything, my young friend."

"If they nab me, I'll get the pen for this! Every man that helps an outlaw gets the ax. That's the way they run things."

"They do. And I suppose that they are right. God knows that I've done my best to think out this matter and get to the right and just thing which must be done. I only know that if I keep money which really belongs to poor Jim Cartwright, who was ruined through me once, I'll never be happy the rest of my life. The fifty thousand has to go to him. And you, Train, are the man to take it?"

"Are you sure I will?" asked Train curiously.

"I'm certain of it."

"Thirty a week isn't big pay for such work."

"As for the pay, I'll be glad to make it whatever you wish. You have only to name your wish. Speak out, Train. But I don't depend on the money to get you to do the work. It's the bait of excitement and danger, I think, which will make you carry on with it. It's the game for the game's sake. Am I wrong?"

And Train, feeling that he had resisted long enough, nodded his head.

"We've made the bargain, then?" cried Comstock eagerly. "My dear boy, I'm delighted!"

And, turning in his saddle, he stretched forth his arm and shook the hand of Train violently.

5

Train had kept his handshake more or less sacred through all of his spotted career. His signature of his promise might be of small value, but a handshake was something which, he felt, peculiarly put an obligation upon him.

The very ceremony had something about it which was impressive to him. For, during it, the gun hand was surrendered to the gun hand of another man. It might last only a second, but, during that second, one was placed at the mercy of another human being, if there were treachery in the mind of the second person. He would gladly have escaped on this occasion, but his hand was taken before he could well avoid it. And now he gritted his teeth.

Not that he would live up to his contract. Of course, he told himself, a plum of fifty thousand dollars which only had to be divided between two people was too much of a good thing to allow a few silly scruples to spoil the profit. Twenty-five thousand dollars! That would be his share, and it would give him what he had always wanted—a sufficient capital to enable him to become a real, bona-fide gambler. He could already make the cards talk, but without some fat thousands behind him, even the best card manipulator cannot run any long career. It is the weight of money in the purse which will most effectually empty the pockets of other men. He had seen it exemplified over and over again.

They turned back toward the house, now, and the final details were discussed, but not before the honesty of Patrick Comstock had forced him to confess that the events of the night before had been devised purely as a test of Train. There had been no Mr. Gregg; the two assailants had been hired men, but it had been necessary to fully test both the fighting courage and the honesty of Train before the great sum of money was entrusted to his keeping for the difficult and long trip on the trail of Jim Nair. To this frank narration, Train listened with wonder which almost became awe, but, as he listened, he pacified himself by a terse thought: "There have to be easy marks in the world, and this is just one of them."

In the meantime, he heard all that the rancher could tell him about Nair. The strange and cruel story of Nair had been many times repeated through the West, but perhaps no one had heard it more often and with more details than Train. A man with whom he had traveled for a month had actually been a member of the gang of the great bandit, and had been expelled for some offense against the leader. Yet, even though he were at a distance of a thousand miles from Nair, he still feared to talk too much about his former chief, such was the dread with which Nair had inspired all of his followers. To Train he confessed only scattering details of the appearance, the habits, and the prowess of the outlaw. Above all, Train knew from this informant that Nair repeatedly returned to the Banton Mountains as an ideal hiding place, for their ragged defiles, their heavy forests, their wilderness of rivers, creeks, and dry cañons made a perfect hole-in-the-wall country for any one who was familiar with the ground.

But Train was not familiar with it. It was an untramped country to him, and therefore he would be at a double disadvantage in it if he ever went there. He had no intention of carrying his ruse that far, however. His mission gave him plenty of time. He need only start for the north, and then, when he saw fit, branch off to the side. He would make the agreed split with Rainier wherever the latter chose to meet him. After that, he could wing east or west, according as a fancy of the moment led him!

In this happy frame of mind he reached the ranch, put up Whimsy in her stall, bedded her down with the greatest care, saw to her feeding, and then went into the house itself.

There he met Rainier, with disaster written in his face.

"The devil has taken a hand against us, Steve," groaned Rainier. "Who'll you guess has come to town?"

"I dunno. Who?"

"A friend, Steve. An old friend."

"Well?"

"Gresham!"

Steve Train folded his arms, and the inside hand dipped inside his coat and seemed to grip something beneath his arm.

"Gresham?" he repeated.

"The old man himself!"

"What the devil brought him here?"

"Not you."

"After you, then, Jack? Has he something on you?"

"He doesn't know me, even. Not under this name. Nope, he come along on another trail, hit San Lorenzo, and the first thing he heard was something about you. That's the worst of you, Steve. Can't disguise yourself. People can describe you always so's a blind man could spot you in a crowd. When Gresham heard something about you and your togs, he put his nose down and trotted up the hill to the old man's house. He's there now. He's talking to the old man right this minute!"

"Talking to Comstock?"

"He is."

"Couldn't you sidetrack him?"

"Not Gresham. He's a fox. I'd of tapped him on the napper and put him to sleep if I'd had a chance, but he sits in corners and watches out for himself. I couldn't get at him. He's a detective, pal. He ain't a bum!"

They confronted each other in dismal silence for a time. While they waited, one of the Chinese servants came hurrying with a message that Mr. Comstock wanted to see Train "plenty quick."

"He's got his knife in you already, Steve," said Rainier, with a groan. "Which way are you going to blow?"

"You think I'll drift because Gresham is here?"

"Unless you're batty."

"Listen, Jack. This ain't a penny-ante game. It's high stakes."

"How much?"

"Fifty–thousand–fat–round–iron–men!" said Train slowly, with an accent on every word.

The valet turned pale with excitement. "As good as in our hands," he breathed.

"It was all over—we had the deal sewed up. I was to get the coin tomorrow morning and start for—Nair!"

"Nair? Jim Nair?"

"Yes. This gent Comstock is a nut on honesty. Some old stock in his hands made a turnover for Nair. Now Comstock is eating his heart out to get the profits to Nair. Can you lay over that?"

"Crazy!" said the valet, tapping his forehead.

"Sure. Crazy he is. Now I'll go have a talk with Gresham."

"A talk with him! What you mean, Steve?"

"What I say."

"Will you—face him?"

"Why not? He only saw me in one town, under a different name."

"I tell you, pal, if Gresham gets his hands on you, you're done."

"Maybe. This is worth a chance."

"What's he got on you?"

"I dunno. I can't figure just what. That's what I want to see."

"Steve, you got the nerve. I hand it to you for that. You're cool. I'll say that in court!"

"Save it till I need it," answered Train calmly.

He was told that the rancher waited for him in the library, and to that room, accordingly, he went. When he tapped at the door he was bidden by the strong voice of Comstock to enter, and coming into the apartment he found the old cattleman sitting in the farthest corner of the room with his face in shadow and the smoke from a newly lighted cigar swirled in slow drifts about him. He evidently was reflecting.

"Ah, Train," he said, "I have an important matter to speak to you about. Take a chair, will you?"

"Right," said Train, and accordingly moved to the chair facing the judge and sat down in it. He had hardly settled into it, however, when a ringing voice called from behind him:

"Curry!"

He felt the eyes of Comstock grow keen and pry sharply against his own.

Even though he was forewarned of what he must expect in the interview with Comstock, it took all his self-control to keep from some movement of eyes and voice. But just as he had taught himself to move as the cat moves with inescapable and convulsive speed, so also he had schooled himself to endure the shocks of just such sudden nerve strains. He had learned how to sit passively at the card table when some carelessness had half revealed the crooked trick which he had thus performed; he had learned how to meet hostile and cunning glances before, and the training served him in good stead now. He met the stare of Comstock with perfect steadiness, and then turned slowly in his chair toward the detective.

The latter had started out from behind the door, and now

he met the eyes of Train with a stiffly extended right arm and an accusing finger pointed.

"You, Curry!" he cried again. "I've found you at last! This has been a long trail, but I've landed you now!"

Those artful fingers of Train could not resist one twitch toward the gun which was hidden in his coat beneath his armpit, but he restrained himself again.

"Is this a game, Mr. Comstock?" he asked his host.

The rancher was considering the two of them with an intent glance and a frown, as though he had not yet decided what to make of this situation.

"That remains for this gentleman to prove," he said. "You do not know him, you say?"

"This gent with the loud voice?" asked Train, unable to resist the opening for such a taunt.

"Leave him to me, Mr. Comstock," said the detective. "I'll refresh his memory. I expected that he'd forget me. Birds of his feather have a convenient memory that way; but I'll wake him up!"

6

Mr. Gresham was a little man. He did not have piercing black eyes, nor raven hair, nor a long, lean face, nor the enormous brow of the thinker. He was not quiet nor sinister nor subtle. Instead, he had little pale eyes, and blond, unnoticeable eyebrows. He was quivering now with energy and determination, like a bull terrier shaking with eagerness for a fight. He thrust one hand deep in a trouser pocket, spread his feet wide, and he barked his statements, he drove them home with hammer blows of his clenched right fist delivered into the thin air.

"Your name," he said, "is Curry, or that was the name the last time I spotted you in St. Louis. Am I wrong?"

"Go on," said Steve Train. "I like to hear the way you do it. You listen, too, Mr. Comstock. This gent aims to frame me, I guess."

"I intend to listen," answered Comstock gravely and dryly.

This was a heavy blow to Train. He had counted upon more enthusiastic backing from the rancher, but that he should be doubted so quickly and so thoroughly went to prove that Comstock had already been induced to put more than half faith in the integrity and wisdom of the detective.

"Go on, friend," said Train. "We're set to hear you. What's your name, partner?"

"You know that I'm Gresham. You know me only too well," said the man of the law, "but I intend that you'll know me still better. You know that I'm Gresham, and that I can prove what I'm going to say about you. When you were Curry, in St. Louis, the string of the fiddle you were playing was gambling. You were working with the Doctor, that old confidence man, green-goods expert, and poker cheat extraordinary. He was rounding up the fall guys, and you were the one who cleaned them out."

"Go on," said Train. "I'm listening."

"I'll go on, all right. You don't have to tell me. Before you hit St. Louis, you were the Harmony Kid that put into your pockets the whole pay roll of the Carver Ranch in one night's black jack. You were packing a banjo around with you—"

"That's mighty queer, Mr. Comstock," said Train thoughtfully; "I *do* play a banjo."

"H'm!" said Mr. Comstock. "Go on, Gresham, if you please."

"Before you were the Harmony Kid, you worked Hamilton town as Paul le Blanc. Before you cleaned up Hamilton, you were the fellow they called Lazy Jim, in Butte City. And, long before you hit Butte City, they knew you in Tucson and called you Two-gun Chalmers."

He waited after this stroke, which he apparently felt would be crushing to Train. The latter, however, was now smoking, and he flicked the ashes from his cigarette before he replied: "I've been in Tucson, too. But that and the banjo is the only two things you've said that's true."

And, as he said it, he looked full in the face of his accuser. Mr. Comstock regarded them both with the wistful eyes of a man in the deepest doubt. He shook his head.

"Look," said Gresham to the rancher. "Give me five days to get my evidence. I'll prove to you that this lazy-looking youngster is as bad a fighter and clever a crook as Jim Nair himself."

At the mention of this name, both Comstock and Train looked quickly at one another.

"That's a large order for so young a man," said the rancher to Gresham.

"I tell you, it's the truth!" answered Gresham. "It isn't age that makes a good crook any more than it's age that makes a good opera singer. They're born with the talent or else they never can develop it. You can't raise a ten-sack crop on bad land without rain. This fellow you know as Train, this man here, is one of the kind that's born with too much brains to go straight. His hand is too quick to do anything more honest than pull a gun or juggle the cards. A two-gun man, Mr. Comstock. That's his size, and you know what that means?"

The mind of Comstock drifted back to the scene in the patio, and the pitiful drift of little gray feathers which was all that remained of the sparrow. He turned with a more pronounced frown to Train.

"Train," he said, "I understand that most people who can handle two guns at once are crooked. They've been forced to develop that rare talent because they live in daily fear of their lives from enemies. And most men who have such enemies are those who live outside the protection of the law. I don't wish to jump to conclusions; tell me if I am in error?"

"He'll tell you," said the detective, sneering, "that a two-gun man is the right hand of a sheriff. He'll tell you that a two-gun man is better for a town than a courthouse. Go on, Curry. Tell your fairytale!"

But Steve Train, who had been thinking hard and long, decided that he must not follow the line which the detective laid down for his rebuttal. Accordingly, though a pair of guns even at that moment weighed down his coat from the inside, he shook his head quietly.

"Knew some of these trick gun fighters here and there," he declared, "and maybe some are square. Some kids take up gun play for the fun of it. But the real two-gun men that I've known—the ones that could hit two targets with two guns— have been pretty hard characters."

"Ah?" said Comstock.

"But where this all gets," said Train, "I don't know. Here's a man that says he knew some crook in St. Louis called Curry. Maybe he knows a lot of crooks and maybe he knew one named Curry, and maybe Curry packed a lot of other aliases. What's that to me? I'm Steve Train. I never saw St. Louis. I never saw Butte City, neither. Where I've hung out has been here in the south. Gresham, here, has followed a wrong steer. He talks about two-gun men. I never wore two guns in my life; I aim to take care of myself with one!"

Comstock nodded, as though the exhibition of snap shooting which he had seen in the patio not many days before had been enough to convince himself on this point. But Gresham stabbed the air with an indignant forefinger again.

"Never wore two guns!" he cried. "Why, Comstock, I'll lay ten to one that he's got two on him right this minute!"

Train inhaled a breath of smoke. Only a bluff could help him here. He considered it for a fraction of a second. Then he said: "Take a look, Gresham. I'm willing."

He added: "I'll take that bet, too. Ten dollars to one, Gresham. I'll do better. I'll lay you evens!"

Gresham scowled. Then he shook his head in a way that brought gloom to the heart of Train; for Gresham had never been bluffed in his life, and he did not intend to begin bad habits now.

"I take you," he said, and advanced to make the search.

"I've lost twenty-five thousand dollars," said Train to himself. But, like a good loser, he smiled straight into the eyes of Gresham.

"Search me if you want to," he said, "but whether you find two guns or one, I'll be the last man you'll ever search."

"You hear that?" said Gresham to the rancher. "When you get 'em cornered they're all alike. They can't help showing their teeth."

"And I strongly advise you to take his word for it," broke in Comstock. "I think it would be decidedly worth your while!"

Gresham merely laughed. "I've had 'em threaten to get me for fifteen years," he said, "and I'm still doing business. From the yeggs to the green-goods experts, they all swear that they'll knife you in the back, some bright day."

With this, he laid his hand on the lapel of Train's coat. And, with that touch, the gun fighter and gambler bade farewell to his brightest dream.

"Wait!" cut in the voice of the rancher.

Gresham turned a scowling face. "Well?" he asked.

"You needn't search him, Gresham."

"What?"

"I mean it. I've made up my mind."

"You've made up your mind to believe him? Rather believe him than me?"

"I'm making no personal comparisons. What I finally decide to do is my own business. In the meantime, I fully appreciate that you have taken a great deal of trouble to be of help to me, and I shall not forget what you have done, or tried to do. However, I have to ask you to step out of this affair, now."

"Of all the—" began Gresham.

But then, being a man of sense and a true ornament of his profession, he shrugged his shoulders and made a gesture of resignation.

"It's your business, as you say," he admitted. "If you want to cut your throat, you're free to do it, but some day you'll be sorry for this. I give you my word for that!"

He turned to Train. "You're a cool devil, Curry," he said. "But don't think that you've shaken me off. I'm not that kind. I stick worse than a burr; you'll find that out. Worse than a damned burr. So long, everybody!"

With this, he walked out of the room. His heavy, quick step went down the hall. His heels clicked on the flagging in the patio. Then he was gone, and the silence pressed in on the two who sat in the library.

Finally Comstock, who had bowed his head to study the pattern of the carpet on the floor, lifted his wise old eyes to the face of the younger man.

"Train—"

"Well, sir?"

"I have made up my mind that you—that you will carry that money of which you have been talking with me this afternoon."

A load of a ton's weight slid from the mind of the gambler.

"Mr. Comstock," he said simply, "I'm glad that you know a man you can trust."

To himself he was murmuring: "Twenty-five thousand flat! That for a starter. Maybe, too, I can bunco Jack out of part of his share. Why should the fat face get as much out of this as I do?"

"When do you start, Train?"

"The minute I get the money."

Comstock turned, opened an unlocked drawer of his desk, and drew out a long, stiff, brown-paper envelope.

"Here are fifty one-thousand-dollar bills," he said. "And here is a receipt. And here is two hundred dollars in cash for your expenses on the trip. Sign the receipt, Train."

And Train, dazed, moved his pen through a cloud of joyous wonder and placed a signature at the foot of a slip of paper which acknowledged that he had received fifty thousand dollars in money from Patrick Comstock and that he would, to the best of his ability, deliver that money to the man known as James Nair, unless he should discover that James Nair was not one and the same man as James Nair Cartwright.

He finished the signature. Then he received the envelope and slipped it carefully into an inner pocket.

"Is there anything else, Train?"

"Not a thing, sir. Good-by."

"Good-by, Train. Good luck to you. Do everything except lose your life. But I'm sadly afraid that the last thing is exactly what you'll do!"

Train waved his hand carelessly and started for the library door.

"Train!" called the rancher.

The heart of the gambler sank into his boots. But, when he turned, he saw that the latter was sitting at his desk with a faint smile of quizzical amusement upon his lips.

"By the way, Train," he said, "I have really been surprised."

"How, sir?"

"That a man who could manage one gun as well as you do, could not manage two at all."

In spite of himself, color poured into the face of Train, and though he fought against it, he could not prevent the spread of that guilty flush.

"We all got our limits," he said clumsily. "Ain't any way of stepping over a fence, sir."

Comstock placed a hand across the lower part of his face and hurriedly looked down. "That's all," he said. "Good-by!"

7

When Train reached the outdoors again, the hot perspiration was standing on his forehead. Unquestionably the rancher had been smiling at him and had raised that hand to cover the smile. Why, then, could this have been? It presupposed a knowledge of all that Train really was. In that case, the stiff brown-paper envelope could not contain real money. In that case, all of this was merely a part of a complicated trap for Steve. He conned the matter back and forth on his way to the barn. In any case, the thing for him to do was to mount Whimsy and make his get-away, and if he carried off from this affair no greater spoils than the beautiful mare, he was assured that this was more than a balance for the cash concerned.

At the barn he wasted not a minute, for he opened the container and looked at the contents. There was no doubt about the genuine character of that money. He was too old a hand with the "queer" to be taken in. This was the real stuff. He scrutinized only one corner of the middle bill of the well-compressed stack. That was sufficient to reassure him, and he heaved a great sigh of relief. No matter what had been behind the smile of the rancher, it was a poor jest which, at the same time, threw away a fortune of fifty thousand dollars.

As he put the money back into his pocket, he was forced by a sudden prickling in the small of his back to turn sharply around, and there was the detective standing directly behind him—his broad jaw set, and his nostrils flaring with disgust and with rage.

Train shuddered, as he had shuddered a few times before when he had been confronted by the passion of a truly honest man. For there is something in honesty more terrible to the dishonest than the fear of death. The devotion to truth is the greater mystery because they can understand death, but not the desire to be true. So it was with Train, as he confronted Gresham.

"You've got the stuff, then," said Gresham.

Train looked around him. There were far too many walls, and the possibility of far too many ears in closest proximity to him.

"Come outside," he invited.

So he and the detective went into the open, where Whimsy came to listen to their tales with her sharply pricking ears.

"We're alone," said Gresham. "There's nothing here to be a witness. Now tell me the facts. You're Curry?"

"Sure."

"You're Harmony, too?"

"Right."

"You did the work in Tucson?"

"Of course."

36

"And now, with me standing by to warn him, Comstock puts that stuff into your hands?"

"Looks like it." And Train pressed the breast pocket which contained the subtly rustling mass of wealth.

"Well," said the detective, "I'd say that he has it coming to him—no matter how much he loses! But—what's in his head? What's in his old fool head?"

It was the very question which had been obsessing the mind of Train, so that he started a little.

"Can you guess?"

"I wouldn't ask, if I could. But he stumps me. What popped into his mind and made him stop me like that? You didn't pass him any sign. I was sure of that!"

"Not a one!"

Gresham considered these baffling statements for a time.

"Well," he said. "So long, Curry. I'll see you later."

With this ominous greeting, he departed, while Train got swiftly on with the work of saddling Whimsy. For Comstock, if he had common sense to befriend him, was sure to reconsider the matter and send out to arrest the progress of the messenger. Therefore, his hands flew as he saddled the good mare, and he was already mounted when Jack Rainier came upon him.

The valet, if his singular place in Comstock's household deserved that name, was puffing with excitement.

"Steve? Steve?" was all he could whisper, with a world of meaning in the word.

"I've got it!"

"Fifty thou—"

"Shut up! The air has ears!"

"I know—but why not make the split now?"

"No. At Curly's place, the way we fixed it up."

"It's too far. Why not now?"

"You fool—"

"Steve, if you try to double cross me—"

Rainier clutched at a pocket, in which there was plainly visible a large and threatening bulk of a gun.

"I'm not trying anything, Jack. But if we split here—you can't tell who's watching—Gresham—"

"I'll have my part now, by God, or else—"

"You fool, Jack! Well, here you are!"

He took out the brown-paper envelope. He counted out half the contents with speeding fingers. Then he folded half of them and returned them to his pocket. The other half he prepared to place in the thick envelope. And this, filled with a thick wad, he presently returned to the trembling, eager hands of Rainier.

"Good-by, Steve!"

"At Curly's, old-timer."

"What the devil could he mean by that?" said the valet to himself, but he had no chance to repeat the question to Train, for the latter had already started on, and the mare had soon carried him out of view down the first turn in the road.

Neither did Rainier have an immediate opportunity to count the money which had been given to him. He could only press his fat finger tips into the mass of paper and guess at his wealth. Before he could do anything to give himself a more exact idea, he saw the form of Gresham come sauntering around the corner of the barn, a short pipe between his teeth and his hand dropped jauntily into his coat pocket. Rainier, who would rather have seen the devil, cloven hoofs and all, at that moment, set his teeth and turned pale.

"Hello, there," said the detective. "Is this Curry—I mean Train—a friend of yours?"

"Friend? Why?"

"Well, you come out here to be the last man to say good-by to him, you see!"

He had seen something, or had he merely guessed? The wretched Rainier could not be sure.

"He borrowed a five spot off me," he explained carefully. "I came out to get it before he went. Kind of forgetful that way, he seems to be."

"Is he?" asked the detective. "D'you usually take five dollars in an envelope?"

The game was up, then! Rainier looked wildly about him. Thoughts were leaping into his brain in swift succession. If he shot Gresham, the noise of the gun would summon others to the barn before he could saddle a horse, and if he tried to escape on foot, his short legs and his fat sides would soon fail him.

He looked around him; he looked up in the pale sky to the place where a hawk swung low on effortless wings. Oh! to have such a power of escape—what blessed things were the birds!

The poetic thought was a small comfort to Jack Rainier.

"I dunno what you mean," was all he could mumble by way of dodging the issue.

"That inside coat pocket of yours would have a way of telling me, though," said the detective.

In spite of himself, Rainier could not help uttering a groan, but when he reached for his gun, he found that the broad muzzle of a forty-five caliber automatic pistol was already considering him steadily. His numbed hand fell away from his own weapon.

"Now, out with it!" snapped out Gresham. "I want it, friend. Just throw it on the ground here at my feet. No tricks, Rainier!"

And Rainier, sadly, with a breaking heart, took the envelope from his pocket and tossed it on the ground. When the detective stooped to raise it, he would—but alas, no such move was in the mind of Gresham. He merely applied a dexterous toe that ripped the envelope wide open. There the green, crisp contents were exposed to view, but when he saw them, Gresham uttered a cry of anger and of surprise.

"What the devil is this junk?" he cried. "You been playing a game with me, Rainier? Have you had the nerve to do that? You fat-faced pup!"

And he kicked the bunch of crisp green paper into the air. One of the slips fluttered down into the limp hand of Rainier. For the first time his dazed eyes were able to see and to understand. It was merely a long, green tobacco coupon. The wad of paper which the dexterity of the gambler had substituted for the greenbacks might be worth two or three dollars at a tobacco store—in trade!

8

Curly's had been selected as a rendezvous in the first place, by Rainier and Steve Train, because, though it lay thirty miles to the north and west of San Lorenzo, the little branch railroad could carry Rainier up to Curly's at the end of the day, and then a southbound train would bring him back again long before midnight. In this way, when his duties for the day were ended, he could slip off to the rendezvous, collect his share of the spoils, and get back again to the house on the hill of San

Lorenzo without being missed for any length of time. This was the more important because both Train and Rainier had decided that it would be best for the valet to remain at his post for some days after the division of the spoils had been made. Then Rainier could find some excuse for leaving the service of his master and could start East to begin the life of affluence for which he yearned.

It was at a nine-mile trot that Train proceeded on his course, only varying the pace to walk the mare down a steep slope or gallop her up a rising grade. In the thick of the dusk he was still ten miles from Curly's, but here he came most opportunely in sight of a shack with a white twist of smoke rising from the chimney, and when he came closer, the grateful fragrance of bacon simmering in the pan was wafted out to him.

His shout brought a white-haired old veteran to the door, who waved an iron fork at him and bade him dismount and "throw a feed into his hoss and then come inside and have a bite himself."

Train willingly obeyed. He carried with him some oats for Whimsy, so that he did not need to encroach upon the old fellow's supplies in that respect. He left the good mare eating and went inside where he found the cookery busily proceeding as the host dropped more thick slices of bacon into the pan and looked to the progress of his "pone." One end of the room was occupied by skins of wild cats and coyotes, drying upon stretchers. At the other end were the blankets of the veteran, his rifle standing near by.

To the "How's things?" of Train, the trapper replied that he had cleared up the "varmints" in those parts and that he was preparing to move on so soon as he should have sold his pelts at Curly's. Of Train he asked no questions, but he opened the conversation with a dicussion of the black mare.

"How'd you find her?" he asked Train.

"She'll do," said the latter.

"Well," said the trapper, going to the door for another look, "she's got a neck and four legs."

"She has," agreed Train.

"But you got to watch her feed, eh?"

"Every minute."

"Speaking personal, which you won't take no offense," said the kind old man, "I'd ruther have old Bumper, there. Come here, Bumper, darn your old eyes!"

40

Bumper, a Roman-nosed mustang whose roan hair had been turned half gray with age, tossed his head and shook it at his master with a malicious eye whose fires had not been dimmed by twenty years of labor.

"Hey, Bumper, ain't you got no company manners?" called the trapper.

Bumper switched his tail and kicked at the vacant air behind him as though he were destroying the master in effigy. The trapper was chuckling.

"That's the way with that old hoss," he said. "Never get on him in the morning without him trying to pitch his fool head off. Sort of warms me up and gets me ready for the day's work. Some folks when they get along in years take a nip of whisky in the morning. But I don't need no red eye while I got Bumper. Plumb stimulating, I call him! Twenty years him and me have been fighting it out, and there ain't no quitting in Bumper. Got to watch his teeth and his heels every minute. But then, he's got his points. He'll run all day and pitch your hind teeth out at the end of his run. That's Bumper. He'll do his fifty miles every day for a month, pretty near. I've held him on desert work with nothing but air to eat and drink for a couple of days. When he comes to the end of the trip, show him a muddy old tank where he can eat the wet mud in place of water, and give him sight of some dead tumbleweed for hay, and Bumper'll be ready to go on the next day. Can you say that for your mare, yonder?"

And he looked with pride and a challenge at Steve.

"No, I can't," admitted Steve Train.

"Well, sir," said the trapper, "every man to his likes, say I. But doggone me if a man don't need a desert hoss for desert work, and a desert man to ride him!"

And he glanced at Train with a good-humored doubt, as though he refused to admit the claims of Steve Train to the position of a "desert man." But Train merely smiled and nodded.

"They don't turn out many men like you, these days," he declared to the trapper. "Where can I lend a hand to get things ready?"

"Set down! Set down and rest your feet," cried the old man. "The devil, man, I ain't a cripple! I can do the fixings of this here party. Lemme fetch in some water, and then we'll be ready to eat while the water heats up for the dishes."

"I'll get the water," offered Train.

41

"Set down!" roared the trapper.

And Steve sat down, meekly.

However, the trapper was no sooner out of sight than Train was stealthily busy. It was not that he expected to gain any plunder from this humble old fellow, but when he was left alone in another man's house, he could not resist the temptation to look about him and find what he could find. In this case he went straight to the only place where things of value were apt to be kept—the blankets of the veteran.

He turned them back. All he found was a sewing kit and shaving set combined in one neat case, together with a roll of thin leather, rubbed and browned by time and much handling. He unstrapped it and unrolled it swiftly. On the inside, he found the sole treasure of the trapper. It was merely two sheets of a magazine. On one page there was a picture of a face which he instantly recognized as that of the trapper, though the photograph must have been taken some twenty years before. The article which accompanied the photograph told how Tom Alexander, whose picture appeared therewith, had ridden for seven years in the pony express, through districts infested with Indians and bandits, and had never lost a letter or a dollar entrusted to his keeping. He had left that arduous service with twenty dollars in his pocket and with eight scars upon his body, representing no less than five pitched battles against great odds.

There were only a few brief seconds during which Train could peruse this document, but when he had rolled the leather case again, and replaced the blankets in exactly their former condition, every wrinkle being represented in careful order, he sat down to wait for the return of the trapper, and to think his thoughts. They were such reflections as had often entered his mind before. He himself, Steven Train, an enemy of society, before his twenty-fifth year, was rich to the extent of twenty-five thousand dollars. He had lived an easy life, thrilled with all the dainties of danger and of excitement. Here, on the other hand, was a man who had worked long and hard as a servant of society. What was his reward? A wretched shack among the mountains, and even that was not his own. A few dollars in his pocket, a few pelts drying in the corner of the shack, an old horse, an older rifle—and, in his blankets a haphazard magazine article, scribbled by some careless news hunter to whom the figure of Alexander represented an hour's writing and a twenty-dollar check. This

42

article, this stern-featured photograph, already frayed and rubbed in spite of its sheltering case, was all that remained to Tom Alexander. This was his diploma of virtue. This was his reward from society—a scrap of paper, and no more.

Steve Train shook his head. It was a great mystery to him. And he said to himself: "Folks are like sheep. They do what the law says because the law barks at 'em. But there's some that see the law is a bluff. They're the wolves that slip down out of the mountains and live on fat mutton and don't do any work. Why should a man work if he can keep from it? Why should he? Doggone me, there ain't no reason!"

The trapper returned. They ate their bacon and pone and drank their coffee. Tom Alexander, in the meantime, told how he had been a teamster and on one occasion had driven a wagon in a provision train for a regiment of soldiers who had been attacked by an Apache war chief while they were marching in a long and straggling column through the hills.

"Them Apaches," said Tom Alexander, "busted loose with their yells at the end of the column where the sore foots was marching along wishing for possum and taters. Them Apaches come down out of the hills like just that many streaks of lightning', shakin' their guns in the air and hollering fit to kill.

"But they didn't kill a doggone one. No, sir, they wasn't drove back by the soldiers turning around and fighting. But every one of them boys tossed his gun away and started running to catch up with the column, and they run so fast that they left them Apaches behind like they was on hoss-back and the Indians was on foot. Them Apaches come yellin' and ravin' up behind them till they pretty near reached my wagon."

"How many Apaches did you get for yourself that day?" asked Train curiously.

"I didn't get me none of 'em," said the trapper, chuckling. "I was laughin' so hard that I couldn't hold my gun up. And when a couple of them redskin rascals come along and seen me laughing, they was too surprised to murder me. They give me a look, thought I was bad medicine or else plumb loco, and they turned around and rode off as hard as they could go."

And, at the memory, he burst into the heartiest laughter— the deep, strong laughter of a young man, holding his aching sides.

After that, Steve tried to stay to help clean up the tins, but again the old trapper refused all assistance.

"You're trying to make time," he said. "I ain't going to hold you up to do woman's work when maybe you got a man's job on hand."

"What makes you think I'm hurrying?"

"A gent don't ride a thousand-dollar hoss in these parts unless he wants to get there."

He was so satisfied with his own penetration and wisdom that he winked and nodded to Steve, as much as to say: "I know all about these things; ride along, son; I'll keep my tongue in my head."

"Do you ever get lonely, living out here?" asked Train when he was in the saddle again.

"Lonely?" said the trapper. "Look here, m' friend. When a gent gets along about eighty years old, he's got his thoughts to think. They're the best company he can have, I reckon."

"Thoughts of what?" asked Train.

"Of things he ain't done," said the trapper, with a shadow on his face. Then the shadow lifted, and he added quietly and proudly: "And of the things that he's done, son!"

With that, Steve Train turned the head of the mare, gave her an inch of leeway on the rein, and she swung off at the easy, rocking gallop which sweeps the miles away into nothingness. The mesquite shrubs darted past him near at hand. Farther away, the old hills rolled slowly across the dark of the night sky; and the stars traveled with him overhead.

Of these things he was only vaguely aware, for his gloomy mind was filled for the first time in his life with many doubts. If he reached the age of eighty, what would his thoughts be of the things he had done and of the things, alas, which he had left undone? He had dodged the fact many times before, but now it drove resistlessly home in his mind: there was a strength in honesty—there was a great strength in an honest man which did not need money for a comfort. With that thought in his mind, he came suddenly, for the hour's ride had seemed only a few moments, upon the edge of a hollow, and he saw in the thick of the night beneath him the lights of Curly's.

9

When Rainier's mind finally cleared and he understood the trick which Train had put upon him, his mind was equally divided between rage and relief: rage that he should have been so easily deceived, and relief that he was freed thereby from the danger of prison, represented by the person and the gun of the detective. There was no evidence upon which Gresham could hold him now. But also, instead of twenty-five thousand dollars, he had only a few tobacco coupons.

"Well," he said to Gresham, "I dunno what business this is of yours. What you mean by robbing me at the point of a gun?"

"Bah!" snapped out that disgusted officer of the law, and he turned upon his heel and strode hastily away toward the lower section of San Lorenzo, where the willows wept over the low roofs of the Mexican dobe houses.

But Rainier, in the meantime, had another thought. He remembered that the final greeting of his companion in crime had been: "At Curly's!" It had seemed a strange remark then, but perhaps it had a meaning now. Perhaps Train really intended to live up to his part of the contract. At least, he would have to take the chance that the gambler and gun fighter had that intention.

Therefore, since his day's work was ended, and he was free for the evening, he went to the railroad station in time to board the train for Curly's. He reached that place before dusk.

Curly's took its name from the founder of the town which, in the old days, had been at the crossing of several important cattle trails during the northward drives. The trails had disappeared in the course of time. Other and better routes had been found, and the southern cattle centers had greatly shifted. Most of the life had been drained from the little village by these shifts, but still it refused to utterly die away. It remained to eke out a mysterious existence upon the plains in a way which no one could quite understand.

When a town has once been born, it dies hard—at least, it dies hard in the West. When nothing is left but habit, habit alone is strong enough to lead many men back to places where they have gone before. So that a few still trooped to Curly's. Cowpunchers rode in from the neighboring ranches and did their best to consider Curly's a town big enough for a month-end celebration. Old Curly, himself, was still there, running the hotel which he had built in the beginning of the prosperity of the village, and old Curly's vein of conversation was a mine which was sufficiently rich for the lesser men of later days to come to work in the evenings, when the labors of the day were over on the range. For Curly could tell of the time when men were men, and guns spoke as often as tongues, and law was still a shy-faced stranger through the land.

So, at Curly's hotel, Rainier ate his supper. There were only three others at the table. The big dining room was filled with shadows. Only one lamp gave the light. It sufficed for the single table, and it showed the others in the distance—dull ghosts where, on a time, a hundred men had sat and feasted on ham and eggs. Those good old days were ended. Every month was a loss for Curly. Every month he had to encroach upon his savings, deeper and deeper. But still he would not give up his business. For, when the hotel closed, the town would die, and when the town died, his name, which was enshrined by its existence, would be blotted away from the face of the desert.

To Curly's stories, often repeated but never uninteresting, the valet listened with an inattentive ear until the name of Nair was mentioned. At that he lifted his head.

"Do you know Nair?" he asked sharply.

Curly spread his broad hands palm down upon the edge of the glistening oilcloth which covered the table.

46

"Everybody knows Nair," Curly said. "Everybody and nobody knows him."

"Ever see him?" asked the valet curiously.

"Sure. He came down here one time when he was on the hunt."

"Nair?" cried Rainier.

"Himself!"

The others turned curious eyes upon the little fat man. They had heard the story often; it seemed strange that every one did not know it.

"Kill anybody?" asked Rainier, his eyes big.

Curly chuckled. "He don't spend much time in these parts," said Curly. "I was counting the cash in the till one evening— that was before the dry days and the bar used to bring in quite a rakeoff when the boys rode into town. I was counting the cash, and I looks up and sees a big man standing in the door—shoulders wide enough to fill it, and arms twice as long as most folks have."

"Had his gun on you?" asked Rainier, keen with interest.

The hotel keeper chuckled again. "You dunno Nair," he said. "He don't pull no gun till he has to. Nope, he didn't have his gun out, but his hand was on his hip waiting for the need to make a draw. I didn't give him no need."

There was a general chuckle of enjoyment at this admission, not of weakness, but of common good sense.

" 'You got some coin there,' says he.

" 'I have,' says I.

" 'I'll take it,' says he.

" 'Your black face,' says I.

" 'Maybe you're a philanthropist—or a coward,' says he.

" 'Maybe I am,' says I, and I gives him a grin. 'Or maybe I've lived long enough to get used to it. Nobody but young men are willing to die, Nair.'

" 'You know me, then?' says he.

" 'Sure.'

" 'By what sign?'

" 'Your black face,' Says I.

" 'Black?' says he, giving me a frown that brought his fingers an inch closer to his gun.

" 'Black,' says I. And black it was in the look of him— black as murder is black.

"He tried to look me down, but I didn't bat an eye.

" 'Gimme the coin,' says he.

"I put it in his hand.

" 'There's five dollars and a half here,' says he. 'You've held something out on me.'

" 'I ain't a fool,' says I. 'That's all I took in.'

" 'In a whole day?' says he.

" 'Yep, in a whole day.'

"He drops the coin in his pocket and says: 'I'll eat, now.'

"I went into the kitchen with him and cooked him up a good feed. He sits there, never speaking.

" 'How's things coming with you?' says I after a while.

" 'Fair,' says he. 'How's things with you?'

" 'They'll be looking up from now on,' says I.

" 'How's that?' he asked me quick.

" 'The boys will ride in to have a drink and hear about the way Nair come in and the way he looked and the way he talked. It'll be worth five-fifty and then some, to me.'

" 'I may take a liking to some of the things in your store,' says he, scowling at me like a thunder sky.

" 'Sure,' says I. 'Help yourself.'

"He went on eating, finished his coffee and turned the cup upside down on the saucer.

" 'So long,' says he. 'You're a cool fellow, Curly. I'm glad that I've met you.'

"With that, he shakes hands with me, and comes almost close to a grin, the corners of his mouth jerking a little. Then he walks out."

"Did you try to get him after he left?" asked Rainier, eager with suspense. "Did you try to pot him when he went out?"

The hotel keeper regarded him with a silent glance of contempt for such an absurd suggestion, and he went on with his narrative without giving a more direct reply.

"When I lifted up that cup he'd turned over, there I seen the five dollars and fifty cents in silver that he'd took from me, and riding right on top of the heap there was a five-dollar gold piece!"

Rainier exclaimed. The others looked to one another with smiles. Plainly this stranger was not of their kind, if he could not understand such a bit of generosity on the part of a bandit, even.

So, when supper was ended, Rainier went out onto the veranda of the hotel to smoke his cigarette in loneliness, and the first person he saw, as he went through the door, was the form of Steven Train, sitting propped back against the wall at the farther end of the porch. He went hastily to Train, his heart beating wildly with joy.

"My God, Steve!" he cried, "I'm glad to see you. I thought for a minute back there—but I'll stop thinking where you're figuring in! You got the head, Steve. It'll make you rich, one of these days. You knew that the damned sneak, Gresham, would be soft-footing around and try a game with me after you left. He did, too, and he got hold of those coupons. Good old Steve—that was a wise play!"

"Thanks," said Train tersely, and said no more.

Rainier, waiting, grew a little uneasy.

"Well," he said finally, still humble, "I guess there ain't anything wrong with making our split now?"

"What split?" asked Train casually.

"What split! Why, Steve, are you kidding me?"

"You mean your part of the fifty thousand?"

"I mean just that."

"I'll tell you, Rainier. I been thinking things over. I'm going to split with you one half of what I got out of it."

He passed some bills to the other, who turned them hastily to the light. There was only a hundred dollars in his hand.

"One hundred!" he gasped out. "If you think that you can—"

"Wait a minute. I only got two hundred for expenses. There's your half of it. About the fifty thousand—I've changed my mind. I'm going to take every cent of it to Nair!"

"You—Train, you can't get away with it. You think I'm a fool, but I'll show you—"

His voice had risen.

"You flat-faced pup!" said Train softly. "Keep quiet. I got work to do. If you make a noise I'll step on you!"

He rose, backed from the porch, stepped down to the ground, then carefully mounted Whimsy, keeping his face to Rainier all the time. And Rainier was too paralyzed with fury and with fear to move a hand until he saw Train ride slowly away into the dark of the night.

10

There is nothing in the world so poisonous as the fury of a criminal who has been betrayed by another. And, considering that he had been deceived by Train, enraged more than all by the sense of his own importance and the feeling that the other had withdrawn among barren mountains where his own city-bred talents could never carry him, he collapsed into a chair and pondered for a time, weak with his excess of anger.

He would destroy Train; of that there was no doubt. He had only to find a means. He felt, indeed, that he could have borne the loss of his share of that magnificent loot rather than be insulted by such a lie as that which his companion had cast in his teeth before withdrawing. It was exquisitely tormenting that Train could have supposed that he would even lend an ear to such a ridiculous statement as that last; that he intended to deliver that fortune into the hands of the outlaw for whom the rancher had destined it.

What revenge was of mold so heroic that it would fit with such a crime, such a betrayal?

"Twenty years behind the bars for a bird like Train would be twenty times as bad as hanging once! That's his medicine, but how can I give it to him?"

So ran the theme of his thoughts as he sat there in the dark of Curly's veranda. Then the very engine which was fitted to this work came to his mind: The Law! His old enemy—the ghost which haunted his sleep every night—the demon whose fleshless hand must eventually crush him and seize him—this very law which was the poison of his own life, was the weapon which he would turn against Steve Train.

It was a conception so perfect that the breath of Rainier failed him, and tears of joy came stinging in his eyes. He would turn the law against Train. He would do even more. For the only thing of which he could conceive that was more dreadful than the roused might of justice was the anger of an honest man who has trusted another and who has been deceived. What was his own anger against Train? It was a passionate fury, indeed. It shook him to the ground more than avarice or fear had ever done.

But there were flaws in his armor. There was the case of his old pal, Lefty Sinclair, whom he had so basely abandoned in Chi. There were others. Indeed, if he told his tale he would be received rather with derision than with sympathy. But suppose that Comstock should find that the man in whom he had placed his faith so whole-heartedly had double crossed him? Then a hiding place a mile under ground would not save poor Train from the vengeance of the rancher.

Such was the elation of Rainier as he made his plans and rehearsed the possible effects that the trip back to San Lorenzo seemed the matter of a moment, and no more. Then he stood again in front of the house of Comstock, and hesitated for an instant.

His confession meant the severing of all relations between himself and Comstock, of course. Not only that, but the full rage of the rancher might hold many actual dangers for him. It was the end, also, of the quiet, happy life here on the hill. A horse neighed from the stable; a dog whined shrill in the kennel; and the cool, pungent scent of the eucalyptus trees blew to him. He had liked this life better than any he had known. But still, to give it up and to give up his claim upon Comstock was nothing compared with the satisfaction of wrecking Train.

And, rolling that thought upon his tongue, he entered the house and went straight to the rancher.

He found the latter, as always at that time of the day, in his library. The reading lamp and the white hair of his head, surrounded his face with a soft halo, and behind him appeared a few dim rows of books—rich levant in blues and red and deepest greens and browns. When Comstock laid down the book he was reading, Rainier blurted out the whole story as quickly as he could, for he wished to compress and make small his own villainy by comparing it with the greater crimes of Train.

"Mr. Comstock," he said, "I'm bringing you bad news!"

The rancher waited. He was never one to anticipate anything. He let news, he let the joys and troubles of life, he let the whole world come to him as it would.

"Very well," said he. "What's the bad news, Rainier?"

"Train!"

Comstock did not even sit straighter in his chair, and his hands, which were folded together, did not compress, so wonderful was his self-control!

"What of Train?"

"He's gone crooked on you—and on me!"

"How do you know that?"

"He's shoved the fifty thousand into his pocket and ridden off to salt it away where it'll do him the most good!" He nodded emphatically.

Now Comstock was indeed struck. Fifty thousand is not a small sum even to a millionaire. But it was not the thought of the money that made him pale with anger. Still he spoke calmly, feeling his way, making sure that he was right before he announced a decision.

"You know that Train carried fifty thousand dollars of my money or you think you know it?"

"I saw Train count it!"

"You did?"

"Mr. Comstock, it was all framed. God knows what you'll think of me—after all you've done for me, to turn on you. But—I knew there was big stuff in the air—and, well, sir, once crooked, always a crook! I guess that there's something in that!"

"There is not!" said the old man with emotion. "There is not, Rainier. I tell you that no matter what crimes you or other men may have committed, there is good in the worst of us—enough good to make us worthy citizens if it is used in the right way."

"Not in men like Train!"

"What do you know of him? You told me that he was the most honest man you ever knew—but lazy. I've proved his strength and courage. I've seen him with horses. But what is this you're telling me about him?"

"Mr. Comstock, he can do too much. That's what's wrong with him. I know all about him. When he was a kid, he could

52

tell lies so straight that they was never traced back and the truth found out. So why should he tell the truth when he can lie like that? And he could run faster, hit harder and faster, dodge easier, shoot quicker, aim straighter, last longer than other people. Why should he go honest when he could make so much more with himself by going crooked? That's the way with Train. I've known him for years. The slickest card sharp that ever trimmed a boob. He could palm a silver cup under your nose and pull a potted palm out of his sleeve. That's Train. He's got so many talents he doesn't know what to use them for. But why should a bird like that be honest? He's got too many good reasons for being a crook. If you ever saw Train turn straight, you'll see a white blackbird. That's where you're wrong when you say that every man can be honest!"

"Speak for yourself, Rainier," said the rancher sternly. "Don't dare to judge other men!"

His severity silenced the other. "Now to go on to the case of what Train has done," said Comstock coldly. "I'll hear what you have to say."

"Double crossed you."

"He has taken the money I sent with him and appropriated it to his own uses?"

"Yes, sir."

"You are sure?"

"It was all planned out. I brought him here. I knew that he was crooked. I knew, besides, that he was smart enough to seem honest—"

"You're wrong—you're wrong!" groaned Comstock. "I guessed at what he was, but I thought—" He beat his hands together in an agony of shame and disappointment.

Rainier was overawed. He hardly dared to whisper: "What, sir?"

"I thought that one big job—one great trust—one truly important mission would be enough to make him go straight. But perhaps I've been a fool. I thought he might steal ten thousand; but he would not dare to tamper with my fifty thousand dollars and my trust, above all!"

"Him?" cried Rainier. "He'd steal the gilding off a statue while it was being unveiled. He'd pick the pocket of a doctor that was attending him for nothing. He can't help being crooked. It's in his blood!"

The rancher favored the other with a dark look. "You brought him here to split with him whatever gains he—"

53

"Mr. Comstock—"

"Don't whine. I'd rather have you level a gun at my head than whine at me. Whatever you are—in your heart of hearts —speak out and let me know it. Be yourself!"

"I did that, Mr. Comstock. I brought him here. God knows I'm—"

The lips of Comstock worked. "It would have been better for him," he said finally, "to have robbed a bank than to have robbed me. If my last of life and my last of money goes to it, I'll have justice upon him."

A sigh of perfect peace broke from the lips of Rainier. "I knew you'd say that!" he whispered.

"As for you," said the rancher slowly, still picking his words with the greatest care, "you know that you are safe. I owe you too much to turn on you. And that you should have turned upon me is, I swear, an incredible thing. I owe you one thing more—a profound contempt. Leave me, Rainier!"

Even a face of brass cannot endure some things. Rainier, who felt that he could have confronted the rage and the hate of a hundred men, shrank before the scorn of one. He started sidling for the door as though the rancher covered him with a gun. He moved swiftly, but it seemed to him that there were burning miles between him and a hiding place.

At length he slipped into the hall, ran out into the patio, and drew a great breath.

"That's done!" sighed Rainier. "That's done, thank God. And Train is cooked now, or I don't know men."

He went off down the hill. He began to whistle, but midway to the lower town, he stopped in his stride and the whistle ceased. He shuddered violently, and then he went on. After all, there was a certain strength in an honest man.

In the meantime, Comstock had sent to the town, and his messenger returned at once with the detective, Gresham. The rancher was wonderfully blunt. No false pride kept him from admitting an error.

"You were right, Gresham," he said. "I was wrong."

The detective shrugged his shoulders.

"Not that I ever doubted your facts," said Comstock.

"You mean," gasped out the detective, "that you knew I was right when I told you what he was?"

"I knew it was all straight. I even knew that he was wearing two guns."

"Why did you stop me, then?"

"Because I had another hope. Suppose that I had been able to make Train into an honest man? Would any other person in the world be better fitted to go through great dangers and take to Nair what I wanted taken?"

"No," said the detective instantly. "No one in the world, *if* you could make him honest."

"I could not. I admit it now. I suppose that I have been a fool, but I don't intend to dwell on my folly. I have learned everything from Rainier. They were old chums. Rainier brought him here, sensing a big coup in the offing; they were to split the profits. Train refused to live up to his contract, I gather. So Rainier told me everything. Mind you, Rainier is not to be touched. But for Train—"

"Well?"

"Can you guarantee to catch him?"

The other hesitated. "No," he said finally.

"Why not?"

"Can't be sure of anything. Not in this work. I can do my best."

"I like that talk. Now, Gresham, I'm going to do my own best to help you while you help me. Tell me what I can do?"

"Give me money."

"Whatever you demand. No reward will be too high—nothing in any reason."

Gresham shook his head with a frown. "Not for myself. Reward? We can fix that later. My reward would be to catch that fox—in a trap!" He grinned savagely at the thought. "But I want money to help along the work. I'll need helpers. To stack up alone in this bunch of mountains against a man like Train, or whatever his name may be, would be like tying my hands and turning me loose against a tiger. I want money to hire men."

"Send your bills to me," said the rancher. "And the amounts will never stagger me."

Light flooded the pale eyes of Gresham. "Then," he said, "Train is my meat. Maybe tomorrow; maybe next year; but I'll get him in the end!"

The burro stood just within the circle of the firelight and the pricking of its ears was to the prospector the first warning that something living and dangerous was near. Then, looking down the starlit hollow, he saw the horseman sweep across it like the shadow of a low-swooping hawk. Up the hillside came the stranger, into the circle of the fire, and then dropped to the ground, lightly, as one who has not ridden a mile, though the salty incrustations on the hide of the black mare proved that the day had been a long and weary one for her. But though she was tired, her eyes were as bright and her head as high as that of her handsome young master. She followed close behind him as he advanced.

The prospector, in the meantime, had moved to a new position, so that the rifle which leaned against the rock would be under his hand with the muzzle ready to twitch quickly across and cover the newcomer. For one could never tell the nature of these midnight encounters beforehand, and there was something restless, eager, and terrible about this fellow who had come so suddenly up the hill.

He seemed entirely pacific, however. He dropped down cross-legged upon the ground, rolled a cigarette, and refused the proffer of food.

"I'm drifting north," he said calmly. "I eat when my belt is tight. It still has two notches to go."

And he smiled frankly at the prospector—the frankness,

the latter thought, which he had seen before in the eyes of a fighting bull terrier.

"What about the mare?" he asked.

"She's too hot to eat now," said the stranger, lifting his hand above his shoulder, where the shining black instantly nuzzled it with a sort of doglike affection.

He lifted a cigarette, and, in pulling out his matches from a vest pocket, two twenty-dollar bills—perhaps it was by chance—tumbled forth upon the ground. They fell conspicuously.

"Hey!" cried the jovial prospector. "Where'd you pick those leaves?"

"On the poker tree," said the other.

The prospector laughed. "Never found that darned tree in season," he said. "Got nothing but thorns for me."

"Well," said Train, "a gent has to have the right sort of fingers for the picking, sometimes."

At this faint hint of knavery, the prospector looked more keenly at his guest. But though the dark, bright eyes seemed open and frank enough, he found that they were impenetrable enough to any close scrutiny. The more he saw of this fellow the more he guessed that there might be in him to be seen. And he looked down to his own thick hands with a touch of regret. There were certainly some fields of work in this world which he could never explore. Those brawny hands might tear the secrets out of the rocks, but they could not cope with the nameless agility in the slim fingers of the stranger.

"Well," said the man of toil, "you don't want to be showing them pickings too free around these here parts. The big guy will be getting you."

"Who's that?"

"Him—you know?" said the other.

"Don't get your drift."

"That's queer. I mean—Nair!"

Even in that mountain night, in the emptiness of the surrounding spaces, he lowered his voice to speak of that name.

"Oh, I've heard of him!"

"I guess you have!"

"I'm from down south. We've heard 'em tell about Nair. I've always laid him down to some powerful big liar, speaking personal."

"Then," said the prospector, "you don't want to speak personal while you're up here."

"Got people scared?"

The prospector cast a glance over his shoulder and shivered a little.

"He's got *me* scared," he admitted frankly.

But he added, after a moment's thought: "Yet there ain't nothing for a gent like me to be afraid of, even if I made a strike!"

"How's that?"

"Nair knows that I've worked for it. Twenty-five years of darned long work. He'd help me along; he wouldn't knife me after I got it." And he added whimsically: "But them that pick the fruit off the poker tree—that's meat for Nair!"

"I see. Follows the games himself, eh?"

"Not that I know of."

"I'd like to meet up with him."

"You think that now!"

"I mean it."

"Whistle, some day, and he'll come running," said the big man, grinning.

"Well, I'll be ready for him."

"With a gun, eh?" asked the prospector sneeringly.

"Suppose that a gent was out of work—" began Train.

"Oh," said the other, frowning, "if you're that kind—"

"What kind?" asked Train sharply.

The prospector shrugged his heavy shoulders. "I don't argue," he said in blunt tones. "But if you're hunting Nair, most likely you'll find him."

He looked sharply at the other.

"How come?"

"It's tolerable close to the day."

"That's Greek to me."

"Go to Morriston and you'll find out what I mean."

"Where's Morriston?"

"Over the range, yonder."

"And when is the day?"

"Tomorrow, or the next day, I guess."

"What happens then?"

"Why, them that think they're good enough to ride with Nair mostly go to Morriston about this time of year. Them that haven't had luck at the poker tree, savvy?"

"Sure. What happens then?"

"Nair finds out the ones that he wants to use."

"How many does he take?"

58

"Last year, none."

"That so?"

"Year before, they say young Bill Matthews went with him. I dunno. That's the talk."

"How many come in?"

"About twenty come, last year."

"Sheriff sit still and watch?"

"The sheriff is a doggone good one, but Nair is a mite better."

"He sort of sounds interesting to me," said Train.

"Well," said the other frankly, "I hope you don't interest him that much."

"I'll go have a look and let him look, too! Hotel in Morriston?"

"Sure."

"So long, then."

"So long, partner. Luck!"

Train disappeared down the hill on the black mare. He had no sooner gone than a small, wide-made man rose from behind the rock against which the prospector was leaning.

"What you think of that, Chuck?" he asked of the prospector.

The prospector did not turn his head.

"One of the fresh kids," suggested the man behind the rock.

"Have a look at his face?" asked Chuck.

"Nope. I was lying too low for that."

"Well, he may be a kid, and he may be fresh—"

"Well?"

"He's something more. I wouldn't bother *him* none on a dark night! Fine hoss, too, Dan. Think the chief might want him just for the sake of his hoss. She's a jim dandy."

"He talks too much for the chief," said the other with much assurance. "Besides, Nair ain't taking in anybody this year."

"How d'you know?"

"He turned down my cousin, Slim Yates."

"That so?"

"It is. Slim met up with him and asked him face to face.

" 'I'm resting easy,' says the chief. 'Some other time I may call you.' "

"Sit down again by the fire."

"I'll slope. Maybe this here news would tickle Nair. Makes

him mad to have the kids trying to butt in with his men. Nothing under thirty for him."

"Why's that? I've seen a lot of good men live and die under thirty."

"Not for the chief. He says that he don't want nobody that ain't made up his mind for good and all, and he says that a gent under thirty ain't got no mind!"

They chuckled together over this bon mot.

In the meantime, Train was drifting north and west over the hills and climbing high and higher up the range. At midnight he halted with the valley beneath him and the lights of the town in sight, but instead of riding down to the place, he halted where he was. A trickle of water falling into a pool made an excellent watering place for Whimsy. There he gave her first a swallow of water and a mouthful of oats. Then, with a few handfuls of dead grass, he rubbed her down and led her back and forth. It was some minutes before, to his critical eye, she had been cooled enough. When that desirable moment came, he gave her the remainder of her grain, a hearty drink of water and then turned her loose.

There was no need of hobbles for Whimsy. She strayed in a short circle around her master and even stopped her own feeding to come and stand before him, begging for a piece of hard-tack. For hard-tack and water composed the simple meal of Train on this night. Then he rolled himself with a quick twist in his blanket, whistled a soft good night to Whimsy, and was presently sound asleep despite the stars which pried keenly at his closed eyes.

He wakened not with the sun, but with the first coming of the rosy hand of dawn. He rose, and breakfasted again on the hard-tack and the water, with much apparent gusto, saddled Whimsy when she had finished her morning frolic, and went down the slope of the mountain toward the town beneath. It had seemed large enough by the lights which glimmered in its far-off windows the night before. But now it was shrunk to a little crossroads town, dropped haphazard into the wedgelike bottom of a ravine. Every twisting of the trail among the trees cut off his view, but he went on with an eye keen with excitement. It had been a long trail, but he felt that, at last, he was coming close upon the traces of the great Nair.

12

Morriston hummed like a hive. When one puts into a flume more water than can easily run down, friction results, and from the friction the first effect is noise. When one pours into a town more people than can be easily accommodated, there is a resultant friction also, and many noises. So it was with Morriston. This was a warm day in the late August of the year, and the wind moved slowly among the great pines, laden with their resinous fragrance, and stirred into waves the white heads of the crowfoot grama grass. It was a lazy and a peaceful scene in the woods, where the blood-red sumac was buried in masses of black myrtle and the wild briers twined and clustered in dangerous thickets. But, coming out of this perfumed quiet into the foothills with their brakes of scrub cedar, Train could hear the beelike murmur of the town in the distance.

He waited, with his head raised and his eyes a little closed and a faint smile of indescribable pleasure upon his lips. That voice of a stirring crowd told him all that he wanted to know. It was the signal which gathered those who preyed upon pleasure hunters. He was one of the beasts of prey, and at the poker table he made his killings. He was glad he had come to Morriston. Quite apart from Jim Nair, this would be a festival place for him!

The moment he dipped out of the hills into the little town he saw that it was even better than his best expectations. To the original four hundred inhabitants of the village only

61

another hundred had been added, but the extra hundred consisted entirely of men—young men, wild men, gay men. They were equal to any thousand. Half a dozen of them looked like a thousand.

Perhaps there were twenty high spirits who had come into Morriston actually bent on trying to find a membership in the gang of the famous Jim Nair; the other fourscore had come to look on, they knew not at what. There might be brawls which they could take part in, or at least see. Perhaps, since there is little that is actually impossible, they might be able to see Jim Nair—they might pass him on the street—they might even be among the lucky ones who took part in his capture.

There was many an officer of the law here. In a hundred counties, in a dozen States, Jim Nair had offended, and persistent upholders of justice had come to Morriston this year. Every one knew that this was the muster of candidates for Nair's gang; and every one knew that Nair himself must be somewhere near to oversee the selection. They had known that every year for half a decade. But still no one had been able to corner the bandit. No one really expected to corner him on this occasion, but there was a ghost of a hope, and in the West men are willing to back long chances.

When Whimsy stepped daintily down the main street of Morriston, Steven Train, out of the first twenty men upon whose faces his eyes fell, marked a round dozen who would have done credit to any sheriff's posse of picked men. They were men of varying heights and varying weights, but all were burned lean by labors in the saddle or on foot under the hot suns of the mountains. They were grim-faced, quick-eyed fellows. There was a restlessness about their hands and their glances. The youngsters were boisterous and playful, with loud voices, the older men infinitely reserved.

There were all the signs of a surplus and idle population. Men were gathered in little knots at every point of interest. The owner of the hardware store, who was also the barber, was busily painting his red-and-white pole with bright, winding bands, and even this small amusement served to keep the eyes of half a score employed. There was a full score gathered in front of the butchery-grocery store, where a strong-made man with a gray beard and long gray hair was bargaining with the butcher for the sale of three fat steers which he had just driven into town. A girl, perhaps his daughter, sat her horse near by, and no doubt her brown, pretty face attracted the crowd even more than the bargaining.

But Train, with a sure instinct, passing by all of these little clusters, entered the hotel, and made his way at once to the rear room, where he found what he wanted. Half a dozen tables in that small chamber were crowded about with poker players. Others drifted here and there, picking their way. And the wind, beating feebly and ineffectually in at the window, only made dents in the cigarette smoke which grew hourly thicker.

At first, there was no room for Train in a single game, but room was soon made. When a man has much money to stake, gamesters will sense it. And he was invited to make a fifth at a corner table from which he could look through the window and out onto the street where the big man with the flowing hair was still trying to sell his steers to the butcher. To beat down the price, or because he did not need the meat, the latter remained reluctant.

After that glance, and a sweeping survey of the faces in the room, which assured him that no one he had ever seen before was there, Train bent all his attention on the game. He was in an ideal position. He had the wall at his back. He had a door in one direction before him and a window in another. In case of the need of a quick exit he could use either avenue of escape; and in games such as he played, such a need frequently arose.

This table was exactly to his liking. It consisted of two sharpers and two innocents who were being plucked to the skin of all their feathering of spare cash. The card sharps he spotted with a glance. Their method was also soon revealed to his studious eye, for, by the time he had lost his first bet, he had noted that the red backs of the cards were spotted with something besides red ink. At various places little red crayon smudges, so faint that the naked eye could barely make them out, and looking like blurs and variations in the pattern of the backs of the cards, indicated the value of each. That little, imperceptible smear of red told, by its position, the character of every card, and the game was in the hands of the sharpers. They could bet as securely as though they had the faces of the cards turned toward them.

Train called for a new deck. Before those deft workers could replace their spots, Train had stepped into the winnings with a daring stride. He won two pots in a row, secured the deal, stacked the deck, and won a third. In a trice he had placed two hundred dollars before him on the board, and the sharpers were beginning to regard him grimly. It was a joy to Train. Not the winning of money; cash was really dirt, in such small sums, but what he loved was the process of the game, the little shadows which appeared in the eyes and about the mouths of the gamesters, according as their hands were good or bad. The man off the street could not read that writing, but it was a legible character to Train. He only needed five minutes in order to form the alphabet of each man, at least in part.

When the redheaded man was raised and his hand was strong, he waited through a long and thoughtful pause; when his hand was poor and he was taking a long chance, his bet was placed quickly and cheerfully. When the fat sharper, who wore glasses, got his draw, he frowned a little—a reaction so long cultivated that it had become involuntary. These were only the first main details which were discovered by Train. There were many others. For every thought that flashes into the mind of man, for every emotion which stirs even a ripple of interest in his heart, there is some corresponding physical movement, be it no more than the quiver of an eyelid, or the stirring of a finger. It is a subtle language, but Train was a genius in deciphering it. Sometimes it is a language that goes by opposites. Some men frown in the strength of their desire to hide elation; some men smile to cover anger. He who sits back in his chair, relaxed, may be preparing a coup; he who sits eagerly forward in his chair may be masking an outrageous bluff. But this is true: What a man does once he will do again, and the memory of Train was as deep as the sea. He could not forget; so that the poker game was to him like the reading of a book. Once the alphabet was mastered, the incidents proceeded in a smoothly flowing narrative; while other players grew nerve racked by the long-sustained suspense, his mind was busy deciphering new links in the chain of the tale. He was a trickster and a consummate one, to be sure, but he played with men rather than with cards.

In the second five minutes he lost what he had won in the first five, but his gains were greater than his losses, and he had attained what he desired. The others in the game regarded him as a dashing, reckless adventurer with hard cash, honest as the day is long. From that moment they were in his hands. He was so completely their master that he could afford to pay attention to what went on in the room about him, and he now looked up just in time to receive an impression that a familiar face had appeared and disappeared in the doorway. It was so strong an impression that he was on the verge of going out to make sure, but finally he shrugged his shoulders and let the instinct die away.

Yet, as a matter of fact, if he had known who it was, he would have been out of the room in a flash, prepared for action, for it was none other than his acquaintance of long standing, Jack Rainier!

He scooped in a jack pot with the next hand and then glanced out the window. The little crowd had gone. The big man of the gray hair had sold his beeves and was taking the cash which the butcher was counting into his hand, while, in the meantime, a tall gallant had come to the head of the girl's horse and was addressing her, his hat in his hand. His smile, however, had grown stiff on his lips, for the girl seemed not to see or hear him, but, with a blank face, looked far off where the wind-fretted ridges of many-topped Music Mountain rose against the sky, with the bare limestone regions above timber line looking like soft gray clouds.

Another hand; he thought it wise to lose to bait the others, for the sharpers were growing just a trifle uneasy. Then he looked out the window again. Perhaps this handsome girl was deaf; perhaps she was simply profoundly indifferent to that fine fellow who with a red face was now stepping back from the head of her horse. In the second case, Steven Train felt that she was infinitely to his liking. For there are conquests and conquests, and the hardest are ever the most enthralling!

The gray-haired man was remounting, and now the rebuffed cavalier, smarting under the laughter of his companions, passed close by the big man with some remark which made the spectators lift their heads and which made the older man turn sharply in his saddle. The cow-puncher wheeled, dropped his hands on his hips, and spoke again. After that, a strange thing happened. For the big man leaned from his saddle with astonishing swiftness, when his bulk was considered, lifted his antagonist as though the latter had been a frail child, and twisted him in his hands. There was a wild yell of pain and fear; then the cowpuncher was dropped into the dust and lay there writhing, while his conqueror turned the head of his horse and the girl fell in at his side, still with the same calm, indifferent face.

All was not over, however. The fallen man, twisting to one side, snatched out a revolver and opened fire. Whereat the horseman, as though disdaining the use of a gun, or seeking for some more terrible vengeance, deliberately rode his horse across the body of the cow-puncher. There was a strangled cry of anguish, and the cowboy lay in a crumpled heap.

He was not without friends, however. Train saw the girl recover from her indifference at last. She caught the big man by the arm and tried to draw him away. But he shook her off and squared his horse at three or four men who were running out from the crowd. One came at the champion on the horse from the front. Two other circled behind him.

"Fair play!" cried Steven Train, and was out of his chair. The door was the easiest way, but the window was the quicker; he was through it in a flash and stopped the fray in its very beginning.

What had started him to his feet was the simple observance, as the horse of the gray-headed man turned, that there was no holster upon either side of the saddle. He was unarmed, facing three desperadoes with guns in their hands, whose fierce threats and brandished weapons were already scattering the crowd. A volley of curses were crashing through the air as Train slid through the window.

Then he heard the frightened cry of the girl: "Dad! Dad! Come away; they mean murder!"

He heard the deep roar of the old fellow, also: "A dozen rats like them can't worry a man!" And he would not budge.

"Get off, darn you!" shouted one assailant. "We'll see if you're limber enough to dance for us! Get off, or I'll—"

A gun exploded, and the hat leaped from the head of the big man. At that, with a cry of rage, he spurred his horse straight at the offender. The latter jerked up his revolver for a second shot. Then Train acted. So deft were his movements that it seemed to those who happened to catch sight of him that he snatched two heavy Colts out of the thin air. Three shots cracked in a cadence as close as the rattling hoofs of a galloping horse, and the three men went down, one in silence, two with yells of pain and surprise.

They were not dead. When the perspiring sheriff threw himself from his horse and leaned above the prostrate men, he discovered a singular and highly important fact. Each of the three had been shot through the fleshy part of the leg, between the knee and the hip; each might spend three weeks in bed, meditating upon the dangers which attend a gun play even when the odds are apparently three against one.

In the meantime, Train, on the back of Whimsy, was escorting the man and the girl he had rescued down the street. It was not that he wanted praise for what he had done, or to bask in the smiles of the girl, but he felt that there might still be danger. For it was plain that he of the gray hair was no favorite with the crowd.

Ordinarily, Westerners will not stand by while three men attack one. At least they would cheer one man who beat three. But there was no cheering now. With angry mutterings they looked to the fallen men, raised them, gathered up the battered form of him who lay groaning where the horse had trampled across his body, and shook their fists after the retreating horseman. To interpose between this gathering anger and its object, Train cantered up to join their company.

To his amazement, the pair galloped on without giving him so much as a look, but like two mutes, they rode face forward, out of the town and into the hills. On the verge of a thicket of pines, the older man drew rein, and Train prepared himself pleasantly to hear some profession of gratitude.

"Young man," said he of the gray hair, "did I ask you to ride with me?"

Train could only stare at him. He glanced at the girl, feeling certain that she must break out against this injustice, this brutal discourtesy on the part of her father. For, though the big man could not have seen the actual gun play which Train had made, since his back had been turned at the time, the girl had been directly facing him and could not have helped seeing it all. But now she was as oblivious of Train as though the place where he sat his horse had been empty air. It was not studied insolence; it was simply indifference. A squirrel chattered in a tree. She raised her head and watched the climbing of the little creature with a smile of pleasure.

This to Train whose most careless smile could bring a flush to the cheek of any girl! He was partly outraged, partly bewildered, and wholly crushed. Neither was it possible to make any reply to the father. He could only rein in his horse and let the others drift on and out of sight among the woods. But, when they were gone, curiosity and fury combined told him that he would never be contented unless he had traced these people to their home.

67

He only waited until the noise of their horses died out. Then he sent Whimsy swiftly in pursuit. She picked her way with most consummate deftness through the underbrush, shaking her dainty head at the thorns which pricked her. He pressed on for ten minutes, listening carefully, but he heard no sound. He came out from the forest onto open ground, where he could look upon all sides for the distance of a mile, but the two riders had vanished.

13

Impulse was something to which Jack Rainier rarely yielded, and having given way to it when he went to Comstock with his confession, he straightway repented. For he found himself at once stripped of a position which had never been work, in which he had been flattered by the important trusts which had been placed in his hands, and which was full of rich perquisites. If his salary was a mere twenty dollars a week, there was at least another thirty to be made in the service of one who handled so much money so carelessly as did the wealthy rancher. Besides fifty a week, then, in hard cash, he had a large and pleasant room to himself, a fine horse to ride, and the general respect and subservience of the other servants in the establishment.

He had given this up for the sake of denouncing Train, but he now began to see that it was most unlikely that the wrath of the rancher could endanger that elusive ghost of the desert and the mountains. Of the arrangement with Gresham, of course he knew nothing. He only felt that in order to strike at Train, he had dealt himself a crushing blow and accomplished nothing.

Such a reflection was enough to half madden him with spite and with the poison of ineffectual malice. He cast about him for another means of harming Train. He would go to the notorious outlaw, Nair. He would tell the whole story to that worthy, and when Nair learned that a man was wandering through the mountains with the vast sum of fifty thousand dollars which had been consigned to him as his real property, it would be strange if the brigand did not find a way of recovering his own, and the process of recovery would bring about the destruction of Train. More than this, it would be odd if he himself did not receive a subsantial portion of the coin as a reward, for it was well known that Nair did well by those who did well by him. He lived, in fact, by a stern construction of the Golden Rule.

The scheme of Rainier was so perfect, in his mind, that it kept him in a seventh heaven of happiness all during his journey toward Music Mountain. He admitted that, once there, it would be difficult to come in touch with the outlaw, but he trusted to his nimble wits to carry through that point. When he reached Morriston, however, he was astonished to find Train there, playing poker; and the sight made his brain whirl. It seemed to indicate that the gambler intended to live up to the letter of his promise to Comstock and attempt to reach the outlaw in order to put the money in his hands. Otherwise, why should Train have come to this particular section of the mountains where it was known that Nair would be near? For Train should have fled in the opposite direction as fast as the matchless speed of Whimsy could take him!

Yet something must be done. As for this indication of honesty, it did not make Train a whit more acceptable in the eyes of Jack Rainier, for Jack could only see that twenty-five thousand dollars, for which he had schemed, and which had been almost in his hands when the gambler had refused to give him his share of the loot. If he had hated Train before, because of his superior rascality, he hated him now trebly because there was an indication of superior honesty. In fact, the whole affair troubled and baffled Rainier, and such a shifty-minded fellow hates, above all things, to be confronted with an enigma that he cannot solve. A mystery gathered about Train. Rainier both hated him and stood in awe of him, now, and he was more determined than ever to crush out his life.

He had to arrange the tale which he was to tell to the outlaw, but he considered that the least of his troubles. He had simply to turn the truth inside out, and he would arrive at a story which would drive big Jim Nair wild with the hunger for blood. The story would have such a strange ring that it would never be doubted. Only the plausible stories are doubted; it is the superman, the fantastic, which takes in the multitude. A gold brick, if it is real, will not find a buyer, but a gilded bit of lead will tempt some of the foolish.

It only remained, therefore, for him to find Nair, and find

him at once before Train himself should reach the outlaw and turn over the money with which he was intrusted. Fifty thousand dollars surrendered without a struggle to the rightful possessor—it made the brain of Jack Rainier reel. And at last he cut short his confusion by deciding that Train had gone mad.

He was not in sight of Train when the brawl started in the street of Morriston. He was back on the outer edges of the crowd which gathered, but he saw all that happened, saw the opening of the quarrel, saw the triple shot of Train, and told himself that even Nair would find it difficult to corner such a man and beat him down. They must depend upon the strength of numbers against such a tigerish and deadly fighter. To be sure, in this brawl he had killed no one, but it needed only the face of real danger to have given Morriston three dead men instead of three wounded ones.

When the shooting ended, the entire crowd rushed to examine the stricken men, with only two exceptions: One was Jack Rainier; the other was a grizzled fellow who showed not the slightest emotion on account of this deadly display of skill which he must have witnessed. Instead, he turned upon his heel as though he had seen nothing more unusual and terrible than the snarling of a pair of strange dogs at one another. He sauntered off down the street, while Rainier went back to the hotel.

Rainier sought his room to think this matter over. Such a display of manslaughtering talent gave him pause, for it might be that the safety of his own skin would be involved. He had no sooner reached his bedroom than, glancing out the window, he saw the grizzled stranger, mounted on a pinto, trot across an open field behind the hotel and head straight for a trail which led into the foothills.

Rainier remembered the promptness with which this fellow had turned from the scene of the shooting. It was followed now by his quick leaving of the town, looking very much as though he were in haste to carry away a message concerning what he had just witnessed. There was another known fact: That Nair, during this season at Morriston, kept his agents to watch the crowds of would-be recruits to his gang. What if this man were one of these; had marked the notable exhibition of gun skill by Train, and had departed straightway to report to the outlaw? It was the only thing which could explain, to Rainier, the remarkable lack of curiosity on the part of the stranger; for nearly everyone else in Morriston would now convoke to talk over the details of that swift battle. History had just been made, and the witnesses would wish to consult and exchange viewpoints. He upon the pinto, therefore, might be the very torch bearer who could guide Rainier to the outlaw chieftain.

Upon that cue he acted. He rushed down to the stables, flung a saddle upon his horse, and galloped out in pursuit. He found the trail leading into the cedar brakes of the hills at once. In five minutes he had view of the paint horse and rider again, and his heart leaped.

He who journeyed under observation was at least in no apparent haste; he jogged on at the leisure of the horse, his reins knotted and dropped over the pommel of the saddle, while he rolled and smoked his cigarettes and looked about him, or tilted back his head and sang some droning tune of the range and the night herd. The pinto, in the meantime, picked its way steadily forward. It dipped uphill and down, crossed a pathless tract of sand, and then hit into a long and plainly marked cattle path.

All this time Rainier had grown more and more conscious of peril. It was quite apparent that the horse was taking the rider to some well-known rendezvous, and he felt that the chances were largely on the side of its being the resort of Jim Nair and some of his followers. This was what he wished, but in pursuing such an enemy, he could not be sure at what time the latter might become aware of the pursuit and turn back to hunt the hunter.

To keep up that trailing for any length of time he felt was impossible, for he was no trained rider of the mountains, and in the diplomacy of hunting across the mountain desert this man whom he trailed, if the latter were indeed one of those chosen followers of Nair, would have him at an infinite advantage. Had they been twisting and turning among the streets and the alleys of any great city from Frisco to New York, the tables would have been turned. It was mortally dangerous to continue on this open trail. Moreover, it was not necessary, if he could only secure the horse, for the horse seemed to know the way as well as the rider. Most of all, if the pinto were indeed headed for the rendezvous at which Nair himself might be found, there would surely be watchers who, if they saw the pinto followed by a second horseman, would be most apt to send a few rifle bullets his way.

All of these considerations made Rainier vary his scheme. From the hilltop on which his horse now stood he could see the trail before the pinto twist and dip out of view in the hollow, then zigzag up the steep farther slope.

A touch of the spurs sent Rainier's mount flying down the ridge until he could cross the valley, unobserved, behind the nearest of its bends. In ten minutes he was housed in a small grove of pines, thickened with a dense undergrowth of brush, and he had barely taken up this position when the pinto came in view, still dog-trotting with patient good nature along the trail, with no need of hand or voice to guide him, though now and again he cocked back an ear as though to listen to the foolish song which his master was singing. He was a beautiful horse, with a wise head that would have warmed the heart of an Arab sheik. Rainier considered these details with a grim eye, drawing his automatic at the same time. He waited until the pinto was fairly opposite, then a touch of the spurs drove his own horse out from the trees in a single bound.

The pinto's master whirled in the saddle and reached for a gun, which was half drawn from the holster before he saw the mouth of the automatic fixed steadily upon him. Still, for a long instant, he struggled against the knowledge that he was helplessly beaten before he had a chance to fight, but at length he took his hand from the butt of his Colt.

"Put 'em up," snapped out Rainier.

"Sure," said the other.

But his hands moved up only inch by inch, as though he were still hunting for a ghost of a fighting chance.

"Broke?" he asked, with an effort of good nature.

"Just can that talk," said Rainier, "I'll get on without it. Get those hands up higher. That's better."

He rode closer, shoved his gun into the ribs of the other, and then, cautiously, with his left hand, removed the rope from beside the saddle of the pinto's master. In another minute the latter was bound securely, as to his hands. He dismounted obediently and endured the continuation of the process by which his legs were confined also by the same swathing rope.

At length he sat on the ground, unable to move a muscle.

"All right," he said. "Now you can take what you want. I'm sorry you ain't going to get more'n two and a half out of this, partner."

"Would you sell the horse for that?" asked Rainier.

The face of the other grew black.

"If you take him—" he began. Then he shut his teeth together with a click, uttering not another word, while Rainier swung into the pinto's saddle.

"There's my outfit for the exchange," called Rainier, and galloped off down the trail with a rattle of oaths breaking the air behind him.

"It was a cinch—dead easy!" he told himself, letting the pinto come back to the jog trot again. But in spite of the ease with which he had executed that holdup, he was troubled, for he could not help remembering the set face and the glittering eyes of the man he had just robbed; and, even if he were stealing the horse of an honest man, it would go hard indeed with him. He began to feel that he had staked his chances upon a most tenuous adventure.

The steadiness with which the pinto continued to journey through the hills set his mind more at rest. They had climbed into the region of the tall pines whose heads trembled in the wind a hundred feet above the ground and now, breaking from a grove of these, the pinto left the beaten trail and cut straight across for a solid wall of white limestone. It seemed as though the journey must surely end at the foot of this great rock, until there appeared a narrow and ragged crevice in the side of the cliff which presently opened into a small pass with a roar of white water in its throat. Beside that stream the pinto passed and brought Rainier into a great box cañon. He turned to the right; the rock wall opened again; he climbed to a higher level into another flat-bottomed cañon, and so into another and another, a broken chain, each with a meager stream of water tumbling through its midst.

From an upper tableland he glanced down through a water gap upon a long series of these box cañons, beautiful with the walls of white limestone and the green laps through which the streams ran slender lines of silver. It was while he was enjoying this spectacle that he became aware of movement among the boulders behind him. He turned hastily and saw two riders coming into view around a rock as large as a small house. They were armed with long rifles balanced across the pommels of their saddles and revolvers in the saddle holsters. They were not masked, neither did they hasten to cover him with their guns, but he knew at once that his trail had been successful, and his guess had been correct, for these were certainly men who lived outside the law.

14

In the first place, they were mounted upon horses of the finest type. The people of Morriston, and in general those who ranged through Music Mountain, usually rode mustangs as agile as mountain sheep and not much larger—creatures as sure-footed as cats and inimitable for the rough cañons, but quite useless in long journeys across the level. But the two before Rainier were equipped with magnificent animals. Many hundred dollars had been sunk in the purchase of each, though cow-punchers are notably chary of money when they buy their horses.

Although their horses were such splendid mounts, their clothes showed the most abject poverty. The sombreros were rain-sagged of brim and sun-faded; their brown elbows pushed out through their sleeves; their leather chaps, so necessary for riding through the underbrush and tangling thorns among the forests of Music Mountain, had each been ripped in a hundred places and carefully patched again, or the edges rudely sewed together. Above all, their riding boots, the pride of every cow-puncher with self-respect, were far gone. They had been of the finest shop-made quality, but time and stress had worn them ragged.

The lowest drunkard among the cow-punchers who had come under his observation would have been ashamed of appearing in such outfits as these, but these men were neither beggared nor half starved, nor drunkards. They had the easy, confident manner of men in the best of circumstances, sure of themselves. They had, above all, the same keen eyes which Rainier had noticed before in the owner of the pinto.

He saw something stir. Looking high up the cliff, he watched a little black Mexican bear walking along a narrow ledge and staring down at them. With all his heart he wished that he could have changed places with the bear.

"Hello, stranger," one of the two had hailed him, amiably enough. "Where might you be heading for?"

"Yonder," said Rainier vaguely, waving in a general direction before him.

"Clean over the head of Music Mountain, eh? Well, friend, you got the sort of a horse that could take you there. Where'd you pick it up?"

Rainier hesitated. Yet by that question he saw that he was certainly in for trouble.

"I got it from a fellow who said that you'd know me," he answered.

They did not exchange glances or start, but their excess of indifference told against them.

"Who's the owner, then?" they asked.

"I haven't heard his name."

"But you've got his horse?" asked the taller and younger of the two with a sudden ring of a threat in his voice.

"Easy, Harry, easy!" cautioned his companion. "But this here sounds queer," he went on to Rainier. "You got the hoss of a friend of ours and you don't know his name. How come?"

"He's in trouble," said Rainier.

"What way?"

"That's what I can't tell except to one man."

"Who's that?"

"Jim Nair!"

Even then they showed neither surprise nor excitement, but regarded Rainier with steady eyes.

"What's he driving at?" asked Harry sullenly. "What's Nair to us?"

"Maybe nothing," suggested Rainier, "but if you can steer me to him, I guess he'll be a friend of yours afterward. This is fat news for Nair!"

The smaller man reined back his horse and beckoned his companion to follow. They consulted for a brief moment.

"Put it to him, Lefty," said the younger man.

"It don't sound reasonable," said Lefty, "that 'Chick' would

75

send you out to find a gent like Nair and not tell you the way."

"That's why he gave me his horse. He said that pinto would take me where I ought to go."

"That's right," admitted Harry. "Stay here, Lefty, and keep an eye on him. I'll be back in a minute."

He was as good as his word. He wheeled away at a rattling gallop among the rocks, and in a quarter of an hour he came back, riding at the side of a tall, wide-shouldered man, perhaps forty or forty-five years of age, sallow of skin, with gloomy black eyes out of which he studied Rainier as he came closer.

He rode straight up to Rainier before he drew rein. "You want me, young man?" he asked.

"I do, Mr. Nair."

"What's up with Chick?"

"I'll tell you, not the others."

Nair waved a hand. "Scatter back, boys," he said.

They drew away to a little distance.

"Now, tell me what's happened to Chick?" asked Nair, "and tell me what he means by sending a stranger to me?"

"Chick is an hour's ride back, sitting under a pine tree with his arms and his legs tied."

"Ah?" murmured Nair. "Is that the way of it? Who did it?"

"I did it."

The lips of Nair parted; but he closed them again without speaking a word. Yet Rainier shivered from head to foot.

He hastened to explain: "I started out to find you, Mr. Nair, and let you know that there's fifty thousand dollars coming to you that you been beat out of. I had to get at you; I didn't know how; but when I saw Chick drift out of Morriston today, I had an idea that he might be one of your men. I got his horse, because I could see that he was letting the pinto take him along without touching the reins. And here I am. There's no harm done to Chick."

"Talk it out," said Nair, making himself at ease in the saddle by twisting half to the side.

"It goes a ways back," answered Rainier. "It goes back to the time when your name was James Nair Cartwright."

He studied the effect of that shot, and saw it surely take effect. For Nair sat up straight, with a suddenness that jammed his feet hard into the stirrups. He glared at Rainier, for an instant, with a scowl that blackened his face.

"The name of the town—" began Rainier.

"Damn the town!" broke in Nair.

"Well, then," muttered Rainier, triumphant as he left the identification of his man established securely, "well, then, there was a friend of yours in that town named Patrick Comstock. You got his help to start with, and then through his advice you splurged in oil, lost your coin, and went West, leaving a lot of useless stock in his hands. One of these stocks came to life, and Comstock sold out your share for fifty thousand dollars. He gave that money to me to take north to James Nair, because he guessed by the names and by the descriptions of the two, that you and Cartwright was the same. I carried the coin north, got to Morriston, and there ran into an old friend of mine, fellow named Train. I told Train the hard job I had on hand and asked him to help me; instead of that, he waited for a chance, stuck me up, and gathered in the coin. There you are."

To this narrative Nair listened with the keenest interest. At length he said quietly: "Comstock trusted you with the fifty thousand in hard cash?"

"He did," said Rainier.

"Then Train double crossed you?"

"That's it. I woke up in the middle of the night with a gun barrel under my chin. That's how he got the loot. No use complaining to the sheriff. I couldn't explain. Last thing Comstock told me was that I mustn't let the law know about me and Nair."

"And you didn't?" asked Nair, hardly striving to conceal a sneer.

"I'm no fighting man," said Rainier, "unless I have my back against the wall. I'm not a fighter, and Train is a professional. This man Chick will tell you what Train did in Morriston today. He packs two guns, and he can use them both at once. He's as fast with his guns as he is with his cards, which is stepping some."

Nair regarded the other with a quiet little smile. "A card sharp, eh?"

"The slickest man in the world!"

Upon this information the outlaw pondered for some time. "He still hangs out in Morriston?"

"He's still there."

"Not worried about me finding him?"

"No one man worries Train."

"What's he look like?"

"Somewhere between twenty and twenty-five. If there was a hundred men, pick out the handsomest of the lot. That's Train."

"What do you get out of this, my friend?"

"Whatever you say. They tell me that Jim Nair is square."

"Where's Chick?"

"An hour back on the edge of some-pines. My roan horse ought to be near him still. There's an old cow trail that cuts across a hollow and then twists over the back of the hill and—"

"I know the place. Lefty!"

The smaller of the two riders came forward.

"What's your name?"

"Rainier."

"Lefty, this is Rainier. Take care of him till I come back. You boys can fix up your chuck out here. I'll be back—when I come. So long!"

He loosened his reins and his horse, a magnificent chestnut with bone and muscle sufficient to carry even the bulk of Nair with ease, shot away down the cañon at a swinging gallop. But there was no need of an hour's ride. In ten minutes he came upon Chick spurring a lathered roan up a slope. That worthy had sawed a rope through against the sharp edge of a rock, and he was riding with blood in his eye.

"What's wrong?" asked the leader, as they drew rein together.

"I'm on the trail of a coyote that's done me dirt," snarlingly replied Chick. "He grabbed the pinto. If I don't—" Chick's voice was ugly.

Nair raised his hand. "What did you see in Morriston this morning?" he asked.

Chick, swallowing his fury, saw that a tirade about his own misfortune would not be listened to.

"I saw the slickest gun play you ever heard of," he answered. "I saw a kid we need and need bad."

"Train?"

"How d'you know his name?"

"Never mind that, but go back to Morriston. Tie yourself to Train; stick to him like tar. Understand? Make yourself a bunkie of his."

"You want him, eh?"

"I want something that he has. Treat him like he was your

78

long-lost brother, but remember that he's a crook that has double crossed his oldest friend. He's a card sharp, and a cur. That's the inside. Now, go plant yourself on Train!"

15

Fame comes to all others slowly compared with that of the man conjurer with a six-shooter. So it was with Steven Train. Morriston had seen a treble-forked lightning flash strike down three practiced and well-reputed fighters, and it buzzed and stirred like a beehive in wonder and delight. There is no quality more appreciated in a brave man than modesty, and this new champion had no sooner distinguished himself than he had withdrawn from the town. Perhaps he was wiser to do so, for while he was away, rumor endowed him with the qualities of some ancient hero, some fabulous paladin.

He came back in the early afternoon and slipped unobserved into the hotel and up to his room. He was reasonably sure that no eye had seen him come, but he had not been five minutes inside the hotel before there was a tap on the door and he opened it upon a bow-legged little man nearly as broad as he was long, whose face was garnished with a pair of long, blond mustaches, and who looked at Train out of a pair of little, faded, wistful eyes.

"I'm Sheriff Methuen," said the little man. "I'd like to talk to you a bit."

Train invited him to a chair and closed the door slowly, wondering. He knew that Morris County was a marked district, and that only a distinguished man could hope to be sheriff there. When he turned again to the sheriff, it was to examine him with a swift and penetrating scrutiny. Then he discovered the one significant point; the body of Methuen was a knotted, deformed mass of muscle, but his hands were the long, slim hands of an artist—or a gun fighter!

"Have the makings?" proffered Train.

"Don't smoke nothing but cigars," said the sheriff.

"Here's something they call Havana," suggested Train, producing a small box.

"Don't smoke no cigars till after dinner," said the sheriff. "They don't agree with me. I ain't the man that I used to be.

79

All busted up and about ready for the junk heap." He sighed profoundly and shook his head in self-commiseration. "Which brings me around to you, Train. Me being a quiet old man that they've made sheriff agin' my will, I got considerable disturbed by a fight that give us three wounded men in one day."

"They was mobbing one old man," explained Train.

"One old man? The one old man was Tom Curtney. Maybe he'd of been able to take care of himself all by himself. He's done it before. Howsomever, I ain't blaming you. A gent always wants to keep in practice with his trigger fingers, eh?"

And he smiled benignantly upon Train. The latter shook his head and regarded the sheriff out of mildly protesting, half-dreamy eyes.

"I was drove to it," he said. "Me? I wouldn't hurt a dog."

"Me neither," agreed the sheriff. "Dogs has always been a weakness with me, a pile more'n men, you might say. I'm mighty glad you see things my way, Train. I was just going to say that three shootings in a day's work might get you into the habit. But Morriston is plumb fond of a peaceful life, Train. We hate noise around these parts. Noise of a gun going off is apt to keep me from sleeping the rest of the night. Just that nervous, d'you see? By the way, you was never over to Butte City, was you?"

Train yawned. "Never seen that town," he said. "It's considerable of a place, I've heard tell."

"Sort of," admitted the sheriff. "Well, Train, I won't keep you from taking a nap. Just thought that I'd drop in for a little chat."

He disappeared through the door and rolled down the hall with a stumbling and a heavy step.

Train had summed him up to his own perfect satisfaction. "Chain lightning on the draw; rather fight than eat; sort of hungry right now to get into a scrap with me. That's Methuen!"

Sleep was not in his mind, however. He had certain things which required much thought, and he pondered upon these with great deliberation. The slant sun of the midafternoon was now pouring into the room. It struck the legs of a chair and then its back. In that intense heat the varnish began to grow soft and then—for it was newly painted—to rise into small bubbles. The room was filled with a faint, sharp scent of the steaming varnish, but Train drew his chair into the full blast of that steaming sun. It burned through the leather of his boots, it pierced the stout cloth of his trousers like paper; it burned and seared him through his shirt; but still he did not move, but lay back in the chair with his eyes half closed, a faint smile of pleasure on his lips, his body relaxed.

But he was not thinking of his sun bath. Instead, his mind was filled with the image of the girl's face. At least, he had one more detail. The man's name was Tom Curtney. He would have given a great deal to have drawn out the sheriff on that subject, but it was hard for him to ask questions. Finally, he went downstairs and found the proprietor, who bellowed a greeting at him and drew a crowd at once by uttering his name.

"There's three men have all swore they'll get you, Train," he announced, "as soon as they're out of bed. Maybe you're plumb scared, eh?" And he roared at the ridiculous thought.

"I've just seen the sheriff," said the proprietor. "Old Baldy Methuen allows that you're a plumb peaceful man and would make a good voter in this here town." He laughed again. "Old Curtney might be thanking you still, if he'd got any manners."

"Who is this here Curtney?" asked Train.

The proprietor was still chuckling. "Only way of describing that old codger is to say that he's like himself. Don't do nothing like nobody else, just lives off yonder in the hills by himself."

"Where?"

"No fixed place. He keeps moving like a doggone Indian. Never has more'n a couple of pack mules and half a dozen horses and some canvas for throwin' up a tent. Him and the girl beat it around and live where the livin's good. In the summer they go clean up as high as timber line, sometimes, and in the winter they pick out a place down in the hollers among the hills, where it's tolerable warm. Mostly he has a few cows fattening."

"Live on that?"

"Never seems to be shy of coin. Does a little trapping. Sells a few cows every year."

"Hell on a girl, though, a life like that," suggested Train.

The proprietor winked at him. "Other gents have thought that," he said. "I aim to say that if she didn't like that way of living, she'd quit her dad and cut away for herself. She could make her own way!"

By this time the crowd was gathering rapidly, and Train

81

glided away. How he disappeared no one was quite sure. He seemed to make for the veranda, but he turned through a nearby door. When the proprietor followed with a question, Train was gone.

"Don't like to talk with his tongue," said the proprietor, returning, and Morriston voted its newcomer a man of parts indeed.

Train, however, was again on the back of Whimsy and off into the cedar brakes which encircled the town. Behind and above him the sun of the late afternoon was painting the bald rocks above timber line the softest yellows, and the pine forests on the sides of Music Mountain were black with shadow as he passed out of the foothills and into the upper region. He rode in great circles, starting from the place at which he had lost the trail of Curtney and the girl.

He jogged on, mile after mile, patiently, with his eyes alert, studying the ground, searching every thicket. But the afternoon reached sunset; a broad band of crimson edged with delicate pink rounded the sky, and Music Mountain, in the near distance, was black as jet against it, saving that the pale cliffs above timber line were now flushed with faintest rose; still he had no trace of the two strange riders, there was no living thing to see, there was no living sound except the rush and humming of the wind among the pine needles, and then, far away, the sudden yelling of a wolf.

It sounded, thought Train, like the deep voice of a lobo on the trail, though it was strange enough that a lofer wolf should hunt during the day. However, those wise and terrible beasts lived according to no rule and broke their oldest habits to mystify the hunters. The wail of the wolf died; it sounded again, nearer at hand, as though the course lay straight toward Train, and now he drew back into the edge of the copse behind him to watch for results. Even his own hunt grew dim in his mind compared with this rare chance of seeing a lofer in the midst of his work. He was upon the edge of a narrow little valley, the floor of which was covered with rich crowfoot grama, ghostly pale in the evening light, while a slow-running brook, bright with the red of sunset, swerved gracefully among the level meadows. There could not have been arranged a more perfect stage on which to witness a drama of the mountains and the forest.

The dénouement came at once. Out from the shadowy verge of the opposite woods came a white-tailed deer, racing like mad, with long bounds, its head thrust high into the wind of its running, its ears flagging back. It was already far spent. He could tell that not only because its speed was much sapped from what it should have been, but also because the poor creature staggered after every leap.

The cause of its dread followed swift behind. Out of the forest came a low-running gray shadow which melted at once into the white-tufted heads of the grama grass, and it was hardly distinguishable as it shot among them, like a pale ghost through a pale mist. That long grass was an advantage for the deer. For a time it gained, and the man who watched wished its deliverance with all his heart. For yonder was something of helpless beauty, gifted only with speed to preserve itself, and behind it came a destroyer, gifted with speed to overtake, with weapons and with cunning to slaughter. The grama thinned out and grew shorter. Now the creature in the rear began to gain again, and with astonishing quickness, for the lofer knows not what exhaustion means. It will kill every day, and at distances seventy miles apart, thinking nothing of such a journey, performed as if it were at its leisure.

Now the gray slayer closed on the poor fugitive. The deer dodged and doubled back, but alas, it lost its last hope of life by that maneuver, for the lofer cannot be deceived. It ran, now, at the very haunches of the terrified deer, and now Train caught his rifle out of its long sheath, which ran along the saddle, with its butt just beneath his hand. With a rifle his was not the consummate mastery which he possessed over the revolver, but with any weapon he was expert.

The deer, dying at every stride, had bounded across the brook now, and was swinging along straight toward him, but the dusk was thick, and it was half in daring that he took his aim and fired. Chance favored her devotee. There was a yell of fury and pain; the wolf leaped straight into the air, landed on its back, and then twisted to its feet and stood at bay, snarling terribly.

16

Train was in no hurry to finish the task of killing the wolf. His next shot would bring down the brute, which was probably too terribly wounded to flee, or else held there by sheer savagery, waiting for the unseen enemy to come forth before it flew at its throat. Train looked up the valley. There fled the deer, staggering and exhausted, but yet speeding on toward permanent safety.

Now a new actor came upon the scene. A figure on horseback broke from the forest opposite him, galloped furiously across the meadows, leaped the brook with a fine abandon, and rushed on. Two things now filled the mind of Train with awe. The first was that the rider was no other than the daughter of Curtney; he had recognized her in the first instant by the flush of the sunset light against her face. The second was that she headed straight at the wolf.

In vain he started out from his covert and shouted a warning. It did not keep back the girl. It merely converted the standing form of the beast of prey into a gray streak which shot through the grama straight toward him. He jerked up his rifle hastily, but before he could shoot he heard a shrill whistle and then:

"Here, boy! Here, Jerry!"

Behold! the wolfish animal hesitated, slowed, and then turned and skulked back toward the girl, all the while snarling ominously over his shoulder at Train.

The latter was dumfounded. It was a lofer wolf, surely.

There were the same high and bulky shoulders, the rather dwindling rear quarters, the great, wise head, wrinkled between the brows, the eyes of human intelligence. He made surer of these things as he sent Whimsy forward.

The girl flung herself from her horse and dropped to her knees beside the lobo, which had turned its head toward Train and greeted his coming with furious deep growls. Coming closer, he began to see differences between the brute and the lofer kind. The gray was only on the sides, belly and tail, and this was much darker than usual. The back was a rich brown, and so was much of the face of the brute, which was bleeding freely from a bullet slash across the right shoulder.

"Keep back!" said the girl, as he dismounted. "Keep back, or I won't answer for Jerry."

"I will, though," answered Train, and he stepped boldly to the head of the monster.

His heart was in his teeth as he did so, but he had never yet failed with dog or horse, and if there were enough canine blood in this great brute, he felt that he would be safe enough. Jerry shrank toward the ground, crouching for a spring, but there he hung, rumbling his anger in the hollow of his belly, his loose hide twitching, his hair standing up in bristles in his rage. But Train stretched out his hand, let that savage killer sniff it, and at once the growling died away. As for the girl, she looked up from her examination of the wound with wonder.

"How did you do that?" she asked. "I thought he would fly at you."

"Maybe you almost wished it?" suggested Train.

She flushed a little, saw with a final glance that it was only a surface cut, after all, which had stopped her dog, and then stood up.

"What harm had he done you?" she answered angrily.

"I thought that it was a wolf," he answered with all humility.

"A wolf hunting by day?" she cried, full of scorn at such ignorance. "Besides, did you ever see a wolf run as Jerry runs, or has he a wolf's tail?"

He could see, now, that it was not the heavy brush of a wolf, but a long feathering, and he stood before her abashed.

"Lady," he said, "I'm mighty sorry. Lemme take him down to the creek and wash it clean of—"

"The blood has washed it clean enough," she replied. "The

only thing to do is to get him home before the wound stiffens or he catches cold in it. Here, boy!"

She leaped into her saddle with the agility of a boy. And there was much of the boy rather than the girl in her supple body, in the steadiness of her eyes. There was no more of the shrinking woman in her, no more of the feminine charm, than there was gentleness in the fire-eyed mustang which she bestrode. She ruled that Roman-nosed, unconquerable brute by the force of stinging spurs and strong wrist, and when he resented the sudden impact of her body on his back by leaping into a tangle of convulsive bucking, she sat the saddle with exquisite ease and balance. Train cantered on at her side, but as soon as she noticed this, she brought her mustang to a sharp halt and faced him.

"Jerry doesn't need your help to get home," she said. "Neither do I!"

The blood stung his face at this blunt insolence. He raised his hat to her and bowed over the pommel of his saddle.

"Lady," he said, "it's the second time that you've sent me away. Nobody will ever send me three times. Good night!"

"The second time?" she cried. "Why, I've never seen you before."

A hundred conquered women's hearts were rich in the memory of Steven Train, and at this calm effrontery his mind reeled.

"She ain't a woman," he told himself. "She's made out of stone!" But here she reined her mustang close behind his and stared at him with her face not a foot from his own.

"Why," she cried suddenly, "you're the man who saved father today!"

And she laid a hand upon his arm and smiled straight into his eyes. She might be boyish enough at all other times, but there was no doubt that when she chose to smile the very sweetness and fragrance of womanhood breathed from her. It seemed as though Jerry, even, understood the change in the attitude of his mistress, for now he reared and planted his great forepaws on the knee of the man, sniffing eagerly at him with sharply pricked ears.

"That's why Jerry would let you come close without biting. Jerry knew—he knows everything."

"You'll have to hurry on," said Train, still hurt and stiff. "The cold of the night'll get into Jerry's shoulder." And he reined back Whimsy.

"Don't be grouchy," said this strange girl, frowning. "I'm sorry I was rude. I'm sorrier still that dad was like that to-day. But he was worked up so high that even I was afraid of him. He's like that, you know—like a dry prairie. Anything is apt to start a fire running in dad, and when he breaks loose, he wrecks things."

"I saw him start in Morriston," replied Train.

"That wasn't a start," she insisted. "He was holding himself hard all the time. But if he'd started, he'd have smashed through that crowd of—of fools!" she went on, with a fine ring of sternness in her throat. "They daren't stand up to him man to man. They have to fight three to one against my dad!"

What an enthusiasm of pride was hers! Her head went back! Her eyes filled with a bright moisture.

"But I keep him from it!" she said. "Only, I was so full of the thought of him that I hardly saw you. I'm sorry for that. Because I remember how you handled your guns. Will you teach me to draw 'em like that? Will you teach me how to handle two at once?"

In the joy of that prospect, she could hardly sit still in the saddle.

"You handle guns, do you?" asked Train.

"Enough to live by," she said, without pride. "Look at that chipmunk sassing us. I'll talk back to him—one word!"

The chipmunk, barking angrily at the foot of a tree, had reared upon his hind legs to view them the better, and the girl whipped out her revolver from the saddle holster and tried a snapshot. A puff of dust arose. When it disappeared, the chipmunk had gone likewise.

"You see?" said the girl. "I come close enough to scare things, anyway!"

"If that had been a man," said Train, "he'd be dead, now."

"You can't live by selling the skins of men," said she, and then they chuckled together. "Come on. Dad will be waiting for me to get supper ready."

She broke away and sent her horse off at a rapid gallop. Down the valley they went, with the dusk settling every instant, but he needed no brighter light to see her. She had settled in his mind at the first half dozen glances, and the picture would never grow dim thereafter; but he could dwell now on pleasant details as he let Whimsy loiter half a length to the rear. He could watch the delicate turn of the nape of her neck, and the sway of her body to the hard gallop of the mustang.

They talked as they galloped.

"Where did you get such a dog?"

"When it was a puppy. I found it in a trap."

"Who trained it?"

"I did."

"Hard work?"

"No. The whip did the work. It was easy!"

To show how well that work had been done, she called a word to Jerry, and the great wolf-dog slunk to the rear and followed at the very heels of the mustang. Then she smiled at Train, but he had no smile in reply. She had trained with the whip. What a mysterious mixture she was of man and woman, gentleness and cold cruelty.

Suddenly, in the midst of their galloping, she raised a sudden hand and reined back the mustang to a halt. With her head half turned, she listened. There was a tense silence.

"I thought I heard—"

The ears of Train were quick enough, but he had not marked a sound.

"There!" cried the girl. "Do you hear?"

Perhaps something lived in the wind. He could not be sure.

"I don't hear nothing," admitted Train.

"There it is again! It's he!"

He heard it now, a thin, far-off whistle, blowing down the wind.

"Who is it?" he asked. "Your father?"

"No, no, no! Good-by. Some day come out and we'll hunt together."

"Where?" he asked.

But she was already off at full speed, waving back to him over her shoulder. He had not realized, until that instant, that the coming of the night had advanced so far. But in a trice she was gone from view and had plunged among the trees on the farthest side of the little valley. He followed at once, for he had grown sick at heart at the thought that she was so wildly devoted to another man. Fast flew the mustang through the forest, but faster far was Whimsy behind it. Up hill and down they went, through thicket and wood until she was met by a tall rider on a great horse. He could see no more than the shadowy bigness of the man and his horse, and how the unknown took the girl in his arms.

The heartsickness of Steve Train turned to a passion of unreasoning anger. He did not know why he was so moved. But the revolver came into his hand almost before he knew it. Then he told himself, bitterly, that he had no business here, not even as a spectator. He reined Whimsy away. From behind him floated a musical burst of girl's laughter, and as though this maddened Train, he touched Whimsy with the spurs and sent her flying through the night.

17

There was one room left in the hotel; Chick Logan took it for the night. That was the first step he could think of in approaching Train, and afterward he lingered downstairs, listening to the talk. Most of it turned on that day's fight, and the only notable thing that had happened was the display made by Train. As for big Tim Curtney, the people of Morriston seemed to know him and expect just such a display of savage strength. They passed him over and told and retold how Steve Train had leaped through the window and ended the battle at a blow.

All of this was carefully digested by Chick. He had formed his own opinions as an eyewitness of the combat, but finding them confirmed, he decided that the task to which he had been assigned by his chief was a most difficult one. He was himself a grimly efficient fighter, but he recognized his master in the uncanny speed, the strange accuracy of the younger man.

As for the hypocrisy which was needed to win the friendship of Train and afterward betray him for the advantage of the gang of Nair, this did not trouble the outlaw. So he sat on the veranda through the dusk and into the night, and listened to the talk and waited for the coming of Train and some incident which would give him his chance.

The deep rumble of voices went slowly up and down the porch. Cigarettes pulsed like fireflies through the shadows. From the street there blew thin, stinging drifts of dust now and again, and the rattle of children playing, laughing, came to them. The heat of the day had not yet lifted, for the chill of the night winds was only beginning to pry at the town from time to time. His neighbor, a stocky fellow with blond hair and pale eyes, asked for a match; Chick gave it without using that opportunity to open a conversation. He was too busy listening to others.

"We'll never see Train again," said some one.

"Why not?"

"Nair'll get him. He's too fast with his guns for Nair to let him go."

"Maybe he won't go crooked?"

"Nair can persuade a gent to anything, they tell me."

Chick smiled and said nothing. It was not the first time he had heard random gossip about his chief, and everything he had heard had been wrong. Yet, after all, it occurred to him that he himself did not know the big fellow. The mind of Nair was a sealed book. Perhaps that was the secret of his power.

Then a whisper went the rounds that Train had returned to the hotel, entered by the back door, and gone to his room.

"Don't want to be talked about, maybe," said the righthand neighbor of Chick Logan. "I guess Train's modest!"

With this he rose, stretched himself with a great yawn, and disappeared into the hotel. Chick, however, was not yet sleepy, and he went for a stroll through the large vacant stretch of land next to the hotel, weaving back and forth among the underbrush and the saplings. The night was thick now, but presently the eastern horizon began to lighten, and he stood still to watch the rising of the moon. He had not been there five minutes when two men approached, turned about and studied the hotel.

"He's doused his light," said one. "Looks like he's an early sleeper."

"He's apt to have queer dreams tonight, though," said the other, and they laughed with suppressed mirth.

One can feel evil as well as hear or see it. Chick Logan felt it, now, until the blood ran tingling in his veins. These two had designs upon someone in that hotel. He could have sworn it. In the meantime, he studied the lights along the side of the hotel. All of them in the second story where the bedrooms were, were burning, except the second from the front of the building. Through the gloom he could see the two sit down and make themselves comfortable for a long watch, and since the moon had now risen and was slowly climbing through the branches of the trees before him, Chick Logan only waited until it had floated into the empty heavens above; then he stole away.

It was no affair of his. He walked on in leisurely fashion for an hour. Then he reëntered the hotel and went upstairs. In the upper hall he encountered the little man who had departed for bed so long before, but he was still dressed, and, it seemed to Chick, he had been loitering in front of number nineteen.

"Too hot to sleep," said the pale-eyed man good naturedly.

"Sure," said Chick, and went on to his own room. He was about to draw off his boots when it occurred to him that nineteen was the second room from the front of the hotel; it was the door corresponding with the window which the two men on the outside of the hotel had been watching.

He went downstairs at once and inquired of the night clerk who had number nineteen.

"Somebody we've all heard about," said the clerk, grinning. "That's Train, in that there room."

"That's right," returned Logan. "I thought that I seen him go in there. I wasn't quite sure."

He went back to his room and pondered this newest information. There was no doubt in his mind, now, that both the blond stranger and the two men among the trees on the outside of the room were spying upon Train. They could not be written down as friends of any of the three who had been injured earlier in that day. Chick knew the inhabitants of Morriston well enough, and all of these were strangers to him. There were other powers interested in Train, it seemed, and vitally interested at that.

In the meantime, there was the strong injunction of Nair laid upon him; he must become a bunkie and familiar of Train. Therefore, at the last, he went to the door of Train's room and knocked. Instantly there was an answer, and in the voice of one wide awake. Then a match scratched and the yellow lamplight framed the door with a broken line. Finally the door was opened, but not rashly exposing Train. The latter had stepped far to the side, so that he was as apt to take by surprise his visitor as to be surprised himself.

"He's a fox!" said Logan to himself. "The chief has given me a handful."

He said aloud: "Name's Logan, Train. Glad to know you."

"H'ware you? Come in and rest your feet, Logan. How's things?"

Logan, thus welcomed, took a chair in the corner of the little chamber.

"Things are middling fair for me," he said. "It ain't about my business that I've dropped in."

"I'm listening, partner."

He reclined on his bed, yawning, watching Chick out of the slumberous brown eyes. The latter looked anxiously around him. No guns were in sight, yet he knew that Train was armed.

"You've got friends around here that don't give you no peace, day or night, I see," began Logan.

"How come?"

"I seen two squatting under a tree outside and watching where the light was turned out in your room."

"You knowed the room, eh?"

"Not then. I come upstairs and seen a gent hanging around your door."

"I heard him," said Train, and showed his teeth in a mirthless smile. "I was waiting and listening for him."

Chick Logan regarded the youth with awe and wonder. He had himself been in many a peril, but to lie prone in quiet enjoyment while an unknown peril stood working at the door, was a degree of cold daring which he could not comprehend. Danger seemed to be the breath of life in the nostrils of this strange adventurer.

"How did he look?" asked Train.

"Sort of sawed-off. No color in his eyes."

"Ah?" said Train, sitting up. "Look like a fighter, eh?"

"That's it. Looked like a bulldog."

"Gresham?" murmured Train to himself.

He began to ponder the question quietly. Then he stood up and slipped into leather chaps which he had bought that day and which were so essential for riding through the brush of that district. He donned his coat next, Chick noting that in all of these maneuvers he so managed that his face was ever toward his visitor.

"I might say that I'm glad to know all of this," he told Logan, at last. "How'd you happen to come to tell me about it?"

"I seen you work today," answered Logan. "Besides, I been leading a dull life so long that I was looking for excitement. Been breaking diorite and my heart. Worst ground to break that was ever invented!"

Train nodded. From beneath his pillow he drew forth something which had the glitter of steel and bestowed it in his coat with so swift a movement that his visitor could not be sure of its shape, but he knew well enough that it was a gun. Last of all, Train put a hat on his head.

"So long," he said, "and much obliged."

"Look here," said Logan, standing about on one foot and then on the other. "Look here, Train, you ain't after a game that two could play, are you?"

Train, pausing at the door, darted a sharp glance at the other.

"Like what?" he said.

"A single trail is a lonesome trail," suggested Logan.

The younger man half closed his eyes in thought. Mentally, he was flipping a coin to make his next choice of a course of action.

"Why not?" he said aloud. "But look here, Logan, d'you know that you might be in for some wild stuff?"

"I've lived tame long enough."

"Logan, if you want my game, you're welcome to it."

"It means riding?" asked Chick.

"Sure."

"Stay here, then. I'll saddle my hoss and yours. You wait up here. When I got your mare saddled, I—"

"You know her?"

"Can a man forget a hoss like her? I'll snake 'em both out among the trees. You go out and meet me there. West of the stable of the hotel. If they're watching you to nab you before a getaway they'll never suspect nothing unless they see you head for the stable. Savvy?"

"Logan, you got a head. Blaze away. Lemme hear a whistle when you're ready. I'll have my window open."

18

At the door of the stable, as he sauntered out to the work, Chick Logan found young Brewer leaning against one side of the door.

"H'ware you, Chick?" asked the young worthy. "What's the noise tonight?"

Logan stepped to the side. "D'you come in from the chief?" he asked.

"Yep. I'm to take back the news."

"All good. Somebody else has spotted Train. A dick, I think. At any rate, he's cutting and running, and I'm going along with him. I'm a hard-working prospector that's tired of work and wants some excitement. I warned him, and then I asked him if I could go along."

"Hard-working? You?" And Sid Brewer grinned. "If he's got half an eye, he'll tumble to you, pal."

"Let him tumble. But I guess not. I'm his benefactor, old son. I'll have him tied to me before the night's over."

"You may have a call before the morning."

"Some of the boys going to ride along behind?"

"Me and Harry Tice."

"That all?"

"Ain't it enough?"

"Not by my way of thinking. This Train is a fox. You can lay to that! And if he gets suspicious, we'll wish we was thirty instead of three."

"He's good, eh?"

"He's lightning, son. I seen him work."

"Keep an ear open. That's all I'm told to tell you. And don't ride your hoss to death. We may want some time on your trail."

"I'll fix that. Be easy on that, Sid."

Brewer strolled away toward the hotel; Logan went on to the saddling of the horses which he led, as agreed, into the thickly grouped trees west of the stable. Then he whistled. A moment later Train was with him.

They rode by broad moonlight to the rear of Morriston, then circled around it and struck away to the north and east. There was no particular goal in the mind's eye of Train. He only wished to put a few comfortable miles between him and Gresham. And, on the way, he told his companion something of the little detective.

"He takes hold of a trail like a bulldog on the end of a rope," he said to Chick. "He's the gent that run down Lew Hendricks two years ago. He stuck eight months on Lew's trail. Dodged him from New York to Montreal, to Vancouver, to Sydney, to Shanghai to Frisco, and then to Havana. Got him when he landed in New Orleans on the return trip. Kept that scent for eight months. That's the way with Gresham.

I'd rather have a hundred after me than that one Gresham. And if he finds you're with me, he'll rake over your past until he ties something on you, if he can. Better be sure of yourself if you ride with me tonight, old-timer!"

And with this, he turned a little in the saddle and searched the face of Logan; but he was met by a cheerful blank.

They camped beside a small spring, among the mountains, ten miles from the town. There they boiled a cup of coffee and afterward turned in.

But Chick Logan only waited until he heard the deep and regular breathing of his companion. Then he slipped from his blanket and stood up. For the last half hour, at regular intervals, he had been hearing the note of a hoot owl, softened by the distance. Toward the point from which this noise had blown up to their camp, he now made his way, and within a few hundred steps he was stopped by Brewer and Harry Tice. They were shivering with the cold of the night and cursing their work.

"What's up with Train?" they asked him.

"He don't suspect a thing."

"Tice has brought orders straight down from the chief. There's big coin on Train. We're to take no chances. Bump him off and take the loot we can get on him."

Logan whistled. "That doesn't sound like the chief."

"He's sore at this Train. Says he's a snake."

Chick considered for a moment. "It goes hard to pull off a game like this," he said sullenly. "But if the chief give them orders, we got to do it. He must have his reasons."

"Go back and take a look at the lay of the land. We'll sneak up and lay low a few steps from the rocks where you got your fire. If you want us to start a rush to finish things, stand up and stay standing. If you want us to vamose, stand up and then sit down again. But I guess you won't do that. If things should go wrong, and you should find that Train smells a rat and there ain't anything to be made of him on this deal tonight, the next orders from the chief is for you to lead Train up into the Culver Draw tomorrow. Enough of the boys will be there to finish his business."

With these directions, Logan shrugged his shoulders and turned back toward his sleeping bunkie. It was bitterly against the grain, this work for which he was commissioned. But he reflected, as he had sometimes reflected in the past, that dead men cannot speak reproaches, and therefore he was determined to go ahead with his instructions and carry them out to the letter.

When he reached the dying embers of the camp fire again, he found all as it had been before. Train lay in the same position, flat on his back, his face sheltered from the moonshine by the black shadow of a rock, his arms within the blanket. These things were observed by Chick Logan as he sat down on his own bunk and turned the blankets back. They were observed with careful side glances, lest the other apparent sleeper should be feigning a part and should, in reality, be watching every motion from the shelter of the long black eyelashes. However, the breathing of Train was faintly audible, his breast rose and fell in slow pulsations. Then came a sharp little gust of wind that knocked up some of the ashes into a white whirlpool and gave Chick Logan a sight that stopped the beating of his heart.

For the wind, pressing against the blankets of Train, outlined his body closely, and along his right thigh showed some object clearly defined. It was not the hand of the sleeper; it was placed much too low and too long for that. It was not a fold of the blanket; it was far too firm for that supposition. Then the truth came to Logan in a flash; it was a six-shooter, gripped steadily in the hand of Train. He lay there, in very fact, feigning his unconsciousness, and courting the beginning of trouble.

And the whirling brain of Chick Logan went back to another thing he had learned that day—Train lying on his bed in the hotel listening to the stealthy maneuvers of some unknown man trying to open his door—waiting without giving an alarm, eager to trap the danger when it strove to strike at him!

He stood up, barely showed his shoulders above the rocks, and sat hastily down again. Let that serve as a signal to the other two, waiting and shivering there in the dark! For, though the odds of three to one might destroy Train in a quick battle, yet at least one or two would be sure to fall before the lightning precision of his guns, as he lay there like a cat, feigning indifference, while the foolish mice stole within reach of his paws.

When he lay within shelter of his blanket again, the heart of Logan was thundering in his throat. He felt as though he had dangled from the edge of a precipice by one hand; for he had been near to a destruction no less swift and certain. It was a long hour before, at length, he fell asleep. When he wakened, the rose of the morning was in the sky, and the fire was blazing. It was the scent of the coffee which roused him.

He sat up, rubbing the sleep out of his eyes, and yawning prodigiously, but back of that yawn, his mind was busily working. For he was a light sleeper, and he would have sworn that no man in the world could have kindled a fire within five paces of him in the stillness of the mountain air without rousing him. That miracle, however, had been accomplished. And as he looked at the bland young face of Train on the farther side of the smoke which rose from the fire, he decided that the youthful worthy was in truth more ancient than the hills, and he himself was an infant in swaddling clothes, so far as real dexterity was concerned. He had respected Train before, but he was ready to treat the latter now as the wary old miner treats his box of dynamite or the yegg handles his bottle of soup.

Their breakfast consisted of hard crackers and coffee, and when they were finished, Logan asked what the plans were.

"Looks like a quiet party to me," he suggested. "Maybe this here Gresham ain't quite at home out in the mountains. He needs pavements under his feet and electric lights to work by!"

"A change of scenery ain't going to bother Gresham very long," answered Train. "He'll figure things out in a new way, if he has to. I know that bird, and the way he flies. He can head up agin' a strong wind, and don't make no mistake!"

"Where do we head for, then, today?"

"You know this map around here. Where d'you think?"

The heart of Chick Logan beat more steadily, for this request showed that, if Train had wakened the night before and grown suspicious during the absence of his companion, he had cherished no more than a momentary suspicion. Today, he felt that he could trust to his new-found bunkie.

"Culver Draw would be playing it safe," said Chick. "It has a lie pretty near to the town, and it seems like you want to hang around that place."

"That's it."

"And it feeds up into the mountains. After you get a ways into it, there are twenty cañons you can ride up in case we got to run for it."

The suggestion suited Train perfectly, to all appearances.

He agreed at once that they should ride on toward the Culver, and accordingly in that direction they shaped their course.

They rode back, therefore, toward the beetling crests of Music Mountain, stretching high in the west and the south, following a broad semicircle so as to keep as much distance as possible between them and the town, from which Gresham and his men could be supposed to be radiating in their search for the missing man.

In the midmorning they reached a narrow little river which raced down the heart of a cañon. It was extremely compacted in many places, but what it lacked in breadth it made up in extreme velocity and in depth. So great was the force of the stream that, when the brown waters cleared a little in places, they could see the heavy stones moved by the current; and before their eyes the stripped trunk of a sapling was hurled over the edge of a rapids like a javelin from a strong hand. The stream was small, to be sure, but it had a voice like a giant's, and the cliff faces along the valley cast back the echoes in a thousand trumpetings.

They could cross the river, as Chick explained, by riding down the valley some distance to a point where the water spread wide and thin over a bottom of hard sand, but so doing, their detour would bring them perilously close to Morriston.

"Can your hoss jump?" he asked Train.

"Like a bird!"

"I'll try this roan." He put his mount at a low-lying boulder near the bank, and the roan cleared it with a long, flying leap. "That'll do," said Chick. "This cayuse will clear the water if yours can."

The words were hardly out of his mouth before Whimsy, light as a feather, rose to the jump and sailed across, landing gently upon the level beyond the steep bank.

"Now!" called Train, turning in the saddle.

Chick, with a whoop, put the roan at the stream, and the horse jumped gallantly. A stone rolled under its hoofs as it took off, however. As they rose in the air with a lurch, Chick saw that the spring would fall short, for they were driving far too low to clear the gap between bank and bank. His horse struck the farther bank with his forefeet above the edge, however. There he scrambled like a cat to gain a firmer footing. The ledge crumbled under the strain, and horse and rider toppled back toward the arrow-like stream.

19

What Chick saw, as he fell, was, first of all, the sun-whitened sky; then, beneath him, he faced the muddy, racing waters.

Horse and man whirled under. Savage as the stream had seemed, he had not dreamed that there could be such force in it, but speed had made the water like iron hands. It fixed upon him and tore him. The currents pressed upon his legs and arms like heavy weights; jets of water were forced down his nostrils. Swift as he was shot under, he whirled up again. He caught a blind glimpse of sun, rocks, trembling hot sky, and then he was wrenched under the surface again, and the noise made death more terrible. It bellowed and rolled upon his ears; it took on a voice and a meaning.

"I'm done," thought Chick, "and I'm finished doing the crookedest and lowest-down thing that I ever tackled in my life. This is all for trying to double cross Train. Even in hell they'll hate me!"

He shot to the surface again. There was the frightened head of the roan appearing above water at the same instant, with wild eyes and nostrils distended. And the poor brute, recognizing its rider near by and hoping for help from that infinite wisdom of mankind which seems to mock at and defy all difficulties, pricked its ears.

At the same instant Chick gripped the projecting horn of the saddle. They were caught in a whirl of water, and spun round and round. Along the shore Chick saw a horse galloping, saw the rider swing from the saddle and land at one reckless leap at the edge of the water like a circus performer. Through the mist of thunder which quivered and roared between the banks of the stream, Chick had time to wonder dimly what Train could even attempt in the way of a rescue. For his own part, he thought back to the sapling which he had seen whipped out of the water by the sheer driving force of the currents. Had he seen a comrade fall into that maelstrom, even a blood brother, he would simply have folded his hands, shaken his head, and waited helplessly for the tragedy to be consummated.

Then a black-headed rock, with a cream of foam about its lips, reached at him. It caught the shoulder of his shirt as he whirled, and ripped the cloth away like a knife edge. The next time would be the last! And the next time was hardly a second away. He saw white water just before him; the roar of the stream rose to a terrible crescendo, and then a miracle happened.

He felt the roan straighten out and cease to whirl around in those dazing circles. Above a smother of foam, he raised his head, still clinging fast to the pommel of the saddle, and there he saw Train gripping the ends of the bridle reins which had floated out from the head of the roan. Train, himself, was lost in water to the hips. He was leaning far back, his head thrown high, his face contorted with an agony of effort.

And still it seemed impossible, for the water wrapped a thousand strong hands around the body of horse and man and pulled viciously. Its pressure crowded the breath from Chick Logan when he strove to kick out and swim; the very velocity of the stream forced him to the surface. For a second—or an age—the battle hung in suspense, and Chick found that he was swinging in toward the shore.

The power of Train could not suffice to draw them in against the force of the river, but the current itself was crowding them toward the bank while Train held them fast. Another moment, and the stout roan scrambled, found a footing, and dragged itself from the muddy waters with Chick still clinging to the saddle.

He released himself with firm land once more underfoot. There was no fear that the roan would try to flee, for the poor beast was quivering and shaking with the terror of the death which had been so narrowly escaped. It even crowded after Chick as he turned toward Train, as though it felt how surely the agency of man had saved it from destruction.

Train lay on the bank, with his arms thrown out wide, his face purple, his mouth gasping to regain his wind. He had not held those reins for five seconds, perhaps, but the five seconds had been ones of mortal effort. When Chick lifted him, the body of the rescuer was limp as though he had fainted. For a time not a word was spoken, until the color of Train grew more natural and his gasping ceased. Then he got to his feet staggering. They climbed, together, to the edge of the bank, and there they sat smoking their cigarettes with numbed, trembling fingers, and looking foolishly down to the tumult of the waters. How faint and far that uproar sounded now in the ear of Chick Logan!

He began to hunt in his brain for something to say. But his brain refused to respond. He had owed things to people before. He had owed money, entertainment, good fellowship, but there his debts had ceased. In his forty years of harsh experience, if he had aided some comrade in trouble, it was because both were members of the same gang and mutual service was the only manner in which all could be sure of safety. He had helped others just as they had helped him, but this was quite a different matter. Having joined this stranger under an idle pretext, he had striven with all his power to betray the man only to be snatched from death by his victim's strength and courage.

He stole a glance at Train. That youth had propped his back against a rock, half closed his eyes, and was apparently intent upon nothing more than the enjoyment of a sun bath, but the dim marks of his recent great effort had not yet left him. The veins of his wrists were black and swollen; there was another network of veins cording his forehead; and his breathing was still deep. It puzzled Chick Logan to the bottom of his heart. He would have selected this man as an agile and clever athlete, but never as one of great strength, yet he had found in his being the strength of a giant, hoarded and ready for use.

The longer he was with Train, the more that stranger seemed to him a mystery. First, there was the revelation of fighting prowess in that brief battle in the street of Morriston. Then followed the interview in the hotel room, the strange might of the river. Train grew to a colossus. The lazier and more youthfully good-natured his conduct and appearance, the more tremendous seemed the hidden qualities which made him formidable.

101

But to express gratitude was impossible.

"We still got a ride to Culver Draw," said Train, rising, as he finished his smoke. "Let's start along, Chick. I reckon the hosses have rested themselves."

Chick mounted as one in a dream, but when his wet boots were fitted into the stirrups again and he realized that life, having been almost withdrawn from him, had suddenly been given to him again, words came. "We ain't heading for the Culver Draw," he said gloomily.

"What's up? More rivers in the way, Chick?"

"Darn the rivers! Nope. But I don't like the lay of the land over in these parts. The air is plumb uncongenial today; we'll hit another trail."

He spoke very positively, at the same time studiously avoiding the eye of his companion, which he felt upon him.

"Well," said Train, "I never cottoned to that name. Culver Draw sounded like a gun fight to me."

And he chuckled with the greatest good nature at his rather feeble pun. Chick, however, dared not look at his riding mate. Nothing could be plainer, after his last speech, than that Train had been suspecting him from the first. He grew crimson, partly with shame, and partly with mortification, and partly because he was completely mystified, because he could not discover in what fashion he had betrayed his hand.

Suddenly he turned in the saddle, squarely upon Train.

"How did I spill the beans, Steve?" he asked point-blank.

"You never done nothing," said Steve, with equal frankness. "But when you wanted to go riding with me, when you didn't know where I was heading or who was after me, or how many there was, or what I'd done to get chased, it sounded a little wild to me. I've got plumb restless and tired of sitting still myself, sometimes, but I've always tried to get action out of hunting more'n being hunted!"

After this sage remark, he chuckled again.

Emotion swelled in the throat of Chick. "You knew I was aiming to double cross you, Steve? But still you made a try to yank me out of the water?"

"Lay off of that," said Train quietly.

"But tell me this: Why'd you keep on with me when you knowed that I was agin' you?"

"Did you ever bet on a bad hand—a regular bust—just for the sake of calling another gent to see what he was holding?"

That strange answer stopped all conversation. It amazed

102

Chick so thoroughly that he could not speak, for though he had spent the greater part of his life among hardy men to whom danger was a playmate and constant companion, yet it seemed impossible that a sane man would deliberately seek out a terrible and unknown peril and live with it, as Train had done for the space of a full day with Chick. He was so baffled that, when they entered the cool gloom of a pine forest, he drew rein. Whimsy stopped in the same instant to touch noses with the roan, and for a moment they let the quiet of the wood settle around them.

It was with a hushed voice that Chick finally murmured: "Train, you got me beat. I don't figure you. Where do you stand? Where do I stand? I dunno. Why are you still riding on with me?"

"Well," answered Train, "after I've paid good money to *see* your hand, d'you think I'll quit the game?" Then he added, more frankly: "Chick, you belong to Nair?"

Chick Logan swore with surprise. "What makes you think that?"

"The butt of that gun of yours is considerable wore and polished—hand polished, you might say!"

"Is this the only old gun that's packed in Morriston and around Music Mountain?"

"Turn your hand up, Chick?"

Logan raised the right hand, palm up.

"Prospecting is tolerable hard work," said Train. "Mostly a prospector wanders along with a hammer, ready to chip rock and have a look at the insides of things. Well, there ain't many calluses on your hand, Chick."

"You seen that?"

"Sure. Right away."

"Did I open my hand for you?"

"Nope. But work like that gives a gent crooked fingers. Yours are straight. Besides, you got it in your eye, Chick."

The bandit sighed. "I'm getting old and stupid, maybe," he said. "Didn't know that I went around with the door unlocked and a light burning inside so's gents could see the inside of the house this easy. Well, Train, you're too fast for me. I'll say that! What's your game, then?"

"Nair is my game."

"Good God, man, are you after *him?*"

"I want to join up, Chick."

Chick Logan clapped a hand against his forehead. Then he

burst into the heartiest laugher. "And here we been—" he began, but he broke off short, for he remembered that it was usually foolish and dangerous to reveal anything of the mind of his chief until he was ordered to do so.

"Look here," Chick said finally, "you stay here and take it easy. I've got a little ride ahead of me. Might take me three hours. Might take me less. Will you wait here for me?"

"What's in it?"

"I'm going to try to fix things up for you."

"With Nair?"

"I'm naming no names."

Train yawned. "There's a tolerable thick bed of pine needles over yonder," he remarked. "I'll have a snooze while you're gone, Chick. Didn't rest much last night; had bad dreams!" And he winked broadly at Chick.

20

The shack stood above the region of the great white pines and where the lodge poles alone, with a scattering of those other hardy trees which clamber on up toward timber line and there front the sweeping winds in a shuddering line, swarmed up the steep slope of the mountain. But they did not serve to screen the little building. It stood in a clearing, fully open to the view for miles and miles. Nothing shielded it except that the logs had been dried and weathered to a pale color which fitted in well with the tone of the rocky mountainside.

Here the mountain put forth a wide and ample shoulder, covered with richest grama grass, and on the grass a dozen horses were pasturing. Below that fine meadow the trees began again, and a vast rubble of broken rock of all dimensions, tumbling down to a little lake in the hollow foot of the valley.

A wisp of smoke was twisting up idly from the top of the rickety chimney, which looked forth above the roof of the hut; there was an air of careless peace over the place. In front of the house half a dozen men loitered, variously occupied. One, with needle and thread selected from a neat little sewing kit which rested on the ground beside him, was replacing vanishing buttons on an old flannel shirt. Another, with the care of a barber honing a razor, put a keen edge upon his hunting knife, and one man was plaiting a horse-hair throat-latch for his bridle. Only two of the six were idle, and idleness, as usual, was breeding mischief.

"I says to Chuck," says one of the idlers, continuing a narration, "I says: 'I'll roll that can from the path to the gate without touching it with my hand or my foot, or with a stick or with nothing.'"

"Chuck says: 'It can't be done.'"

" 'Money talks,' says I.

" 'Here's ten,' says Chuck, 'that says you can't do it.'

" 'Seein' is believin',' says I.

"I puts up an old tomato can on the gravel, and I pulls out my guns and begins to blaze away. I slogged them chunks of lead right into the gravel behind the can. Every time they landed they spat gravel at the can and made her jump. Doggone me if it took more'n eight shots to land that can agin' the gate! Well, old Chuck paid me, and that there ten bucks was the stake that I started on. I went back to town and seen the gent in the barber shop and says—"

The other idler broke in slowly: "You must of lost some of your shooting eye since them days, Nick."

"Are you aiming to disbelieve what I been sayin'?" asked the other. "Don't seem no ways possible, Tod, to you?"

Tod Witt, long and lean and melancholy of face, covered a yawn.

"Maybe you was just talkin'," he said. "I'm a son of a gun if I mind talk. Blaze away. What did you say to the gent in the barber shop?"

But Nick Hunter was an aggressive little chunk of a man, full of an opulent belief in himself and his deeds, real and imaginary. He was more full of words than a chestnut bur is full of stickers.

"I remember that as well as if it was yesterday," he said. "That tomato can was Parker brand. I remember the name on it. I remember the blue-paper label that was half wore away, and it loosened and come off before the can got to the gate."

He announced these minute details with convincing assurance.

"I remember a white blackbird that I seen once," said Nick Hunter thoughtfully. "It had a red bill, and one foot was blue and the other one was green. I seen it standing on a stump, stretching out its wings, feather by feather, you might say, and cawin' at the moon. It was by night, d'you see? I remember it, because that was the day that I run away from home because ma gave two pieces of pie to my brother Bill, and only one piece to me."

There was a subdued muttering of laughter. The others looked up from their work and eyed Tod Witt, waiting for his retort, but Tod was not a humorist. He stirred in the place where he sat, crosslegged, and glared at Nick's solemn, unsmiling face.

"Are you guying me?" he asked coldly.

"Me? I'm narreratin' a strange thing that I seen, once," said Nick. "That's all. Tell you another queer thing. I looked at the moon over my left shoulder once, and two months later, doggone me if my hoss didn't stumble while it was workin' up a rocky trail. That was on a Black Friday. I remember it because the next day was Saturday."

There was more laughter, less controlled, but Witt grew black of brow. He looked down at his hands, his teeth set hard, considering whether or not this was a sufficient offense to make him resent these mockeries in hot language.

He said carefully, at last: "You're considerable of a crack shot yourself, Nick, ain't you?"

"Not enough to talk about," said Nick dryly.

There was a third laugh, and Tod crimsoned to the hair.

"There's a pair of tin cans lyin' over yonder," he declared. "Yonder is a sandy bit of ground that's pretty level. I got twenty bucks, right here, that says you can't roll a can across that ground quicker'n I can."

"I'll tell you what," said Nick. "That's interestin' but it ain't important. When you get along in life, like me, you won't be willin' to work for small pay like that, son."

"I got fifty dollars that says the same thing then!" snapped out Tod.

"Well, well, well!" murmured Nick in amazement. "Who give you all that money, me'boy?"

At this, there was a roar of amusement, and Tod jumped to his feet.

"A hundred dollars!" he said a little hoarsely. "I'll bet you a hundred dollars that I can do it. Or I'll bet you two hundred —or five hundred—or a thousand—and what's more, here's the coin."

He unbuckled a money belt and slammed it heavily upon the ground.

"They's about fifteen hundred berries in that belt," he declared, his jaw thrusting out as he spoke, and his eyes glittering. "Now, put up or shut up, Nick!"

The tall, lean man stretched forth his arms and unkinked the muscles in them.

"Always hated these get-rich-quick schemes," he announced without enthusiasm. "I ain't no promoter, as you boys can set and say. But when a gent comes around and wants to *drop* the coin in my pocket, well, I guess I'm human. Speakin' personal, old son, I got to say that I loves to be tempted and loves to fall!"

He rose, unlimbered his great length by stretching himself again, and then considered the subject of the money.

"I'm kind of short of change," he said. "I ain't sportin' no more'n two thousand in this kit, but I guess that it's enough to cover what you got in your belt."

He took out a well-stuffed wallet and tossed it to the man in front of whom Tod had slammed down his money belt. A fifteen-hundred-dollar bet had lifted this affair out of the realms of jest. The matter of the cans was next considered. One was large, and the other was a shade smaller. The smaller one was apt to roll more slowly, because it would be a poorer target for the bullet-raised showers of dirt.

They tossed a coin. To the lot of Tod fell the large can—a tomato can—which bore a magnificent label. The other was a more modest tin can which had once been occupied, said the title upon it, by pork and beans. This done, the two cans were placed at one end of a sandy open space which was perhaps ten strides in length. Behind them the contestants took their positions, each with a gun in either hand—the second merely to replace the first when the latter should be emptied, for neither of the two were really two-gun men.

"Gents," said the stakeholder, "get ready! You start when I drop my hat. The tin that hits the grass at the far end first, and ain't been hit by a slug but nothin' but dirt, wins and takes the coin. Get set, boys. Yo-o-o-w!"

With a wild yell, enough to have unsettled the nerves of a regiment standing shoulder to shoulder, he dropped his hat, and the two guns began to chatter at once. Each was a practiced marksman. Each drove his bullets home just behind his selected can, and the little spitting showers of sand and pebbles rattled against the cans and rolled them swiftly forward.

But the advantage was all with Tod. His larger can was one handicap in his favor. Another feature was the rapidity of his fire. It was a celebrated fact that the marksmanship of long Nick Hunter was mortally certain to hit his target; but he had not the speed of finger which distinguished the gun play of his shorter rival. The big can tumbled merrily ahead. It was a full yard in front of the spinning can of the other when it lodged in front of a tiny hill of soft sand and stuck there. There was a roar of indignation and rage from Tod. Twice he fired. The empty bean can rolled smoothly and surely past his own. It neared the mark. Again Tod blazed away, and—behold, the tomato can fairly leaped from its place and rolled across the edge of the grass, a scant inch or two in the lead of the bean can. This was carefully marked and agreed upon by the four spectators, who leaned over close to the finish, utterly reckless of the danger of a wild-driven bullet.

They announced the result with whoops of excitement.

"Just count out fifteen hundred bucks out of his wallet, Sim," requested Tod of the stakeholder. "That'll fix things about right, maybe."

So saying, he kicked his victorious can into the tall grass and the stakeholder opened the wallet.

"Wait a minute!" called Nick, and, stepping into the grama, he came back bearing the tomato can. He lifted it to the light and exposed to their interested view a little niche bitten cleanly out of one side. He added, in his drawling voice: "Looks like as how you must of give your can the spur when you seen it coming into the stretch, old son!"

There was a hasty consultation; it was plainly to be seen and plainly agreed by the four non-combatants that the last shot of Tod's which had produced such fine results, must have actually nicked the can itself and produced this hole at the same time, but Tod had other views upon this important matter.

"Who knows that this here can is the one that I kicked into the grass?"

The remark was received in such disapproving silence that he struck out on a different tack at once.

"What one of the gents picked that can up and looked her over before the shootin' started? What one of you'd swear to a judge that you knowed this here hole was made by my gun?"

They scratched their heads at this, but Nick Hunter seemed fully convinced that he was in the right.

He said: "Are you backing down, Tod?"

"What d'you mean?" snapped out Tod Witt. "I back down for no long-legged, wall-eyed—"

"Why, you little runt!" murmured Nick judicially.

"Hunter, I've took enough of your lip to-day, and by the heavens—"

They had their hands upon their guns, their bodies were tensed, and the four who had witnessed the shooting at the cans now hastily drew back. Not one among them attempted to interfere, but with savage and silent smiles of enjoyment they looked on, like gladiators of the Roman theater, relishing a deadly battle between comrades, banishing all pity for the love of the mortal combat. Each glanced swiftly from one of the pair to the other, judging chances. Had there been time, the cold-blooded ruffians would have placed bets upon the result of the fight.

But, at this moment, just before the double lightning flashed, a tall form appeared in the door of the shack, a man of perhaps forty years, tall, thick shouldered, with a gloomy and a commanding eye.

"What in the devil is this foolishness?" he roared.

The two straightened; their hands left their guns. They approached him sheepishly, with muttered exclamations. But when he knew the gist of the argument, he made short work of the whole affair.

"Tod," he said, "you're wrong. You pay Nick ten dollars. That's enough to square up an idiotic game like this. You'll shake hands, too, and do it pronto, or the two of you can saddle your horses and ride. I'll have no murder in my camp."

Slowly their hands met; then the eye of Nick kindled. "Tod," he said, "I'm sorry. I pestered you till you was plumb riled. Keep the ten bucks. I need you more'n I need the coin."

"Nick," said the younger man, breathing what was perhaps a great sigh of relief, "maybe I acted like a short sport. But I'll make it up to you when the time comes."

Two minutes later, they were cleaning their guns, sitting side by side, and chatting like brothers.

Then a whistle sounded from among the rocks down the mountainside—a whistle twice repeated, that brought every man to his feet.

21

"Somebody's paying us a call," said Nick. "Let's hit the timber, boys, before the gent lays eyes on us. If he's come to talk, he can do his talking to Nair. But every gent that sees us together is just one more that may be the hanging of us all, one of these days."

There was enough shrewd wisdom in this remark to make them hurry into the cover of the lodge-pole pines which hemmed in the clearing in which the shack stood.

They were hardly under cover when the man whose coming the watcher down the hill had just announced, rode into view on a fine black horse, covered with perspiration from the haste of the master and the difficulties of the trail. The rider looked hastily and somewhat timidly around him. Then, spying the shack, he advanced halfway to it, halted his horse, seemed for a time in a state of indecision, and finally dismounted and continued his way on foot, leading his black behind him. At the door of the shack he paused again, looked about him in a troubled fashion, as though he expected danger to be sneaking upon him from the rear, and at length tapped gingerly at the door, then started back as though he feared the consequences of his act.

He was perhaps fifty years old, bowed with labor, with a seamed and troubled face of worry, and he watched the empty doorway with the wistful eyes of an honest and overburdened man. Presently, from the interior of the house, a deep and musical bass voice called:

"Who's there?"

"Joe More," answered the other in a voice of uncertain strength.

A heavy step approached the doorway; the big man with the gloomy eyes stood there.

"Mr. Nair," said More, "I took the liberty of comin' up here—"

"A large liberty it is!" said Nair, with no further greeting. "If you trail around after me, from place to place, you'll soon be blazing the trail for the sheriffs and the fools who ride in their posses. Hark to this, More: Because you had a son who joined me, it gives you no claim on me. If he died, he died for his own service—not for mine. If the young blockhead had followed my orders, he'd still be alive, but he was young enough to think that he knew more than his elders."

"Poor Tommy," said the other sadly. "I ain't blamin' his death on you, Mr. Nair. He was always a wild one. God knows he give us nothin' but sorrow from the day that he was born!"

"Well," said Nair, without kindliness in his tone, "since you're here, come inside."

He turned away, and More stepped gingerly through the doorway. He found himself in the larger of the two compartments into which the log cabin had been divided by the builder. Nothing could have been more desolate, more utterly barren. There were saddles and bridles and other gear of the riders hanging along the wall. From the smaller room adjoining, a few circles of thinnest smoke twisted into the main apartment; in that place, then, Nair had apparently been sitting when the voice of More called him. There was still someone in the other division of the house, for a chair was at this moment moved in it.

In the meantime, More cast a curious glance at the walls. Upon them were the only decorations of any kind in the place, and the decorations were, to say the least, curiously in character with the present uses of the building.

They were placards of varying sizes, in varying states of wear and raggedness. But they all told the same story. It was announced by one in huge letters and with many staring exclamation points scattered here and there through its length, that the State of Nevada would pay ten thousand dollars in hard cash to the person or persons who apprehended or who directly or indirectly aided in the apprehension of the mur-

111

derer, robber, and thief, Jim Nair. The State of Nevada had changed its mind later on. Ten thousand dollars was not enough. The amount had been raised by the generous subscription of sundry banks and wealthy ranchers and miners to the tidy sum of fifteen thousand dollars. This was not all. Montana offered five thousand dollars for the head of the outlaw. And Montana's offer was the smallest of all. There was Utah, which declared that the body of Jim Nair would be legal tender to the State treasury to the extent of eight thousand dollars. Then there were other great placards and handbills representing the persuasive efforts of Oregon State, of Wyoming, of Colorado, of Arizona, of New Mexico, Texas, Idaho, and Washington. Practically every State in the great West was clamoring for the destruction of this celebrated destroyer of men and waster of property.

Yet he still survived, though, as More well knew, the same proclamations and the same offers had been in existence for the past half dozen years, at the least. But here was Jim Nair as big, as formidable, as secure as ever. More secure, indeed, for he had gathered around him such a reputation of invincibility that it was like an impenetrable suit of armor. The law had done its best; he had foiled all its agents; and great though the rewards for his destruction were, men said that the day was far off before he would be taken.

"Now," said Nair, "what's the story? What's brought you up here to me, More?"

"It's Pete. My boy Pete."

"What's happened to him?"

More pointed guardedly to the next room, and Nair at once crossed to it and closed the door.

"Well?" he said, turning back to his visitor.

"It's Hal Griffith again," said More, the keenness of anger entering his mild eyes. "He wasn't satisfied with what he done to my Tom. He turned Tom crooked. When Tom died, he started right in on Pete. Pete wouldn't see him, for a while. Everybody knowed that Pete was honest. Then he got that job in the Creighton Bank. And when—"

He paused, for Nair had started and looked upon him with a new interest.

"Didn't you know that?" asked More.

"No."

"That's where Pete is. He was doing fine. He got to be assistant cashier, they trusted him so much in the bank. Being honest and having a high-school education—that's what put Pete ahead. But last year he got married—had a baby this spring—his wife got sick—he had to have doctors—big bills —everything started going wrong. And then Hal Griffith started in on him again, and, Mr. Nair, that's why I've come up here to you. I know that Griffith sets up jobs for you."

"Who told you that?"

"I've guessed it; I've guessed a pile more than guessed it—I know!"

"Tell the police, then!"

"It ain't evidence for a judge. But I know, and I've come up here to ask you to tell Griffith to leave my boy alone!"

"What hold has he on your son?"

"Pete's in debt; I know that he owes his doctor three hundred dollars. And being in debt is killing Pete. He can't sleep for thinking of it. So Griffith comes and talks to him. I keep track, and I know that they're together a lot. I think that Pete is holding off. I think that he's playing straight, but pretty soon he may crack—he may go in for a crooked game —Mr. Nair, you've done enough to my family. Let my other boy go straight. You can call off Griffith."

He twisted his sun-blackened hands together in the fierceness of his entreaty, and the eye of Nair grew dark with thought.

"Three hundred?" he asked finally, his face clearing a little. "Why don't you help your boy out?"

"I've tried to, but the old ranch is so plastered up to the eyes with mortgages already, that I couldn't raise another cent on it. Not a cent! I tried three banks. It wouldn't work."

There was another significant pause. Then Nair pulled a wallet from his coat and counted from a sheaf of bills six fifty-dollar notes.

"Take these," he said to More, handing the money to him. "Go with these and pay that doctor bill that's such a weight on Pete's conscience. If he really *wants* to go straight, I'll never pull him down or let Griffith touch him."

The old rancher took the money with the expression of face of one who has glimpsed heaven at midday. He put it in his own frayed wallet and then looked at the robber out of rounded eyes.

"Mr. Nair," he stammered. "Mr. Nair—what I mean to say—"

"Say nothing," said Nair. "Take that money and hurry down to Creighton."

"When Pete knows what—"

"Never mind that. Run along, More. And remember this: I don't corrupt virtuous young men; I only use the crookedness of people who won't go straight. Good-by, More!"

The rancher backed through the door, hat crushed against his breast with both hands. It seemed that this one good action made Nair more formidable than a dozen bad ones. At least More, who choked in vain upon half a dozen expressions of gratitude, now mounted his black horse, on which the mountain wind had already dried the sweat and left the sleek hide streaked with white salt, and rode away from the clearing and down toward the valley as fast as he could go.

Those who had watched his going from the edge of the wood now trooped out again with various comments and suggestions. Some one decided that it would be best to go to Nair and ask what had happened, but Nick Hunter put a decisive veto upon this.

"It don't do no good ever to ask questions of Nair," he declared. "Besides, the chief ain't feeling like talk—not since he started that game with the little skunk—Rainier!"

To the gentleman who had been referred to in this vigorous fashion, Nair had now returned and took his former seat at a table upon which the money was stacked, the cards dealt, and a flask of liquor standing by a pair of glasses. Opposite him sat Rainier, much at his ease, and smoking a long and fragrant cigar. He had been smoking rapidly; from being repeatedly dusted off, there was no sign of an ash at the end of the cigar, and the coal was of great size and glowing red.

"You've been listening, Rainier," said Nair, more in contempt than in anger.

A denial formed itself upon the lips of Rainier, but upon second thought he swallowed the words and nodded. "I couldn't help it," he said. "I could hear you through the wall —kind of a thin wall, you know."

For an answer, Nair pointed to a spot near the door where there was a small quantity of gray cigar ashes. In the face of this mute evidence, Rainier did not persist in his denial. He merely shrugged his shoulders and grinned up to the big outlaw.

"I ain't arguing," he confessed. "I ain't a lawyer, Nair."

There was only a shadow on the face of Nair; he did not allow his anger to come to a head, but hastily swept up the cards and started dealing. It was the longest and most disastrous game at which he had ever sat. All through the night it had endured. In the morning, they had slept for a few hours, and then they had started again. For though Nair played seldom, when he did take to the cards he gambled as he did everything else—with his whole heart and soul. He was now several thousand dollars in hard cash behind the game, and he was desperately bent on winning back what he had lost. It was not that he valued the money; but it maddened him to be beaten by a man whose intelligence he despised.

He knew Rainier for a rascal and a sneak, and he was waiting for the time when the luck should turn his way. He did not know that it was sleight of hand rather than luck which had been overcoming him. As for Rainier, he would have been glad to end this game at any time, for he felt that he was tampering with death. One careless move, and his trickery being exposed, he knew that a gun would leap from the holster of the outlaw.

Yet he could not stop cheating. A golden tide was flowing through his hands. Already he had reaped a harvest of thirty-five hundred dollars, and still the winnings grew. Lust for the coin drove him on the one hand; terror restrained him on the other, and he felt himself disintegrating under the double strain.

He strove to turn the subject by taking up the subject of More. "Did you mean that, Nair?" he asked. "Did you mean that you never work except on them that are crooks already?"

A smile appeared upon the stern lips of Nair. "Did you ever know a man that wasn't a crook—at heart?" he asked.

It was a sudden light upon his own hardened villainy. Even Rainier was appalled, for in his darkest moments he had never conceived of humanity in strains so low, but to Nair, all were in secret as scoundrelly as he was in the open. The difference existed in this alone; he dared confess himself to be what he was—others were not only rascals, but they were also cowards.

They had discarded and were drawing when another summons came for Nair. It was now big Tom Curtney who stood in the doorway, but how changed from the day before! It was big Tom Curtney, with his face pale and drawn, his eyes sunk in purple shadows, and all his huge form quivering with weakness. He did not speak to answer the alarmed query of

Nair, but sank silently onto a box which served as a chair. Nair waited only to request Rainier to walk outside for a moment. Then he returned to Curtney.

22

It was strange to see Nair show so much feeling for any cause whatever, but now he grew almost as pale with alarm as Curtney.

"Tom," he said, "what's wrong? What's happened? Has Alice—"

"Not Alice," said Curtney, "though she's what bothers me. What happens to me is nothing. But when I'm finished off, what will come of Alice?"

"She'll never lack, Tom. I've sworn that to you. But what's happened?"

"My heart," said Curtney briefly. "I was riding up the trail and fainted out of the saddle. I lay for two hours before I came to myself again."

There was an exclamation of horror from Nair.

"What caused it?" he asked.

"Too long a story to tell, and I won't trouble you about it. I've known it for years. It's that devilish temper of mine, Jim. The trouble in Morriston was the start of this. I would have smashed some heads yesterday, but after I'd picked up that hound and broken him in two, I felt my heart begin to go. That's why I got out of town. Today, I got the reaction."

Nair looked upon him in bewilderment. It seemed, indeed, miraculous that so stanch a body, framed for great efforts, designed for crushing power, could ever have failed. Even in this time of sickness and weakness, Curtney looked powerful enough to have handled even the athletic bulk of Nair as Nair might have handled a child.

"How long have you known that you were going down hill?" asked Nair.

"For years."

"Without telling me?"

"Why should I talk about it?"

"If you needed a quiet life, with no work, I could have

provided for that. It would have been nothing for me to have provided that, Tom."

"Nothing to you, but a great deal to me. I can't take charity, Jim. Now, however, I see that matters are drawing to an end for me."

"Nonsense, Tom. You'll live to eighty and bury all of us."

Curtney raised one huge hand as though he would not deign to argue against such polite protestations, while at the same time he understood their perfect futility.

"I'm about to die, my friend. I know it very well, and I am not alarmed. At least, I am not alarmed on my own account. But I have some one else to think of. There's Alice, Jim. What the devil I'm to do with her, I can't make out!"

A flush passed over the face of Nair. "Will you take advice?" he asked.

"You mean that you'll offer to support her?"

"I'll take care of her as if she were my sister!"

"Or daughter, Jim, eh? You're about old enough to play that part better than the older brother." He smiled a little sardonically, while the color deepened over the face of Nair.

"But that's not the important point, Jim," went on Curtney more kindly. "I know that you'd do for Alice what you would do for me, and more, but I can't leave my daughter for charity to take care of her. I can't do that!"

His voice was firm and clear; he looked at Nair unfalteringly.

At this Nair seemed covered with consternation and dismay. He began to walk up and down through the room. He took out a pipe, packed it with tobacco, and then lighted two matches and let them burn out without kindling his tobacco. Finally he put away the pipe again and turned sharply upon Curtney, having apparently made up his mind.

"Where's Alice?" he asked.

"Out yonder, talking to the lads."

"I want to talk to her—alone. Will you let me have five minutes with her?"

"About what, Jim?"

"I can't tell you now. And yet—why not? Tom, I want to ask her to let me take care of her—not as a brother would, but as a husband!"

It brought Curtney from his chair. "What—" he began.

But Nair broke in smoothly. "I'll say everything that you have in mind: I'm about twenty years older than she is; I'm an

117

outlaw, hunted through the mountains. I can never die in the States except with my boots on, and I'm not good enough for her. Let me answer some of those things one after another. If I'm twenty years older than she is, it means that I'll be true to her so long as I live. It means that after I've seen the world and the women in it, I'm willing to stake everything I have to be happy with Alice.

"I'm forty-one. She's twenty. That sounds like a big gap. But remember that when I'm sixty, she'll be forty. When I'm seventy, she'll be fifty. The difference is not so important then. It's only at the start. Marry her to some callow youngster of her own age, and when she's forty, he'll be tired of her wrinkles and ready to hunt about for better company. Look over the stories of married people you've known. They mostly read that way.

"Take up the next point. I'm an outlaw, and I admit it. But I can put together a quarter of a million in money, Tom. I can put that money together by tomorrow and let you have a look at it—count it, if you wish to make sure. What good will my money do her, when she has to flee up and down the mountains with her husband, you say? But I tell you, Tom, that if ever there was a hope of making Alice my wife, I'd go to the ends of the world for her sake; I'd go to Australia, or to New Zealand, and we could even settle down in South Africa, for that matter. I have ways of getting out of the country with perfect safety and taking my coin with me. I could drop south across the border. In Mexico, I can do as I please. I can ship from a Mexican port with a new name. Or I can go on farther south to Peru. Perhaps Alice would like it there, among the mountains. A thousand places in this world where I can go, Tom, and live a safe life and live on the interest of the money that I've made."

Many different expressions had appeared upon the face of the other during his harangue. There had been, at the first, only outraged pride, then wonder, then wild anger, but this in turn having grown subdued, had been replaced by a sort of sardonic mirth.

"Why haven't you made off with your money before this, then?" he asked calmly.

"For two very good reasons," answered Nair. "In the first place I couldn't bear to be separated from you and Alice. In the second place, I couldn't leave the life, and the excitement. I've followed it too long!"

"But you'd leave it now, Jim, to marry my girl?"

Curtney asked this sharply.

"I'd leave a kingdom for her, Tom!"

Curtney shook his massive head slowly. "It won't do, Jim. It won't do! You've stuck fast to me, Jim, and I'm fond of you as a friend. But still you—"

"I'm a lawbreaker!"

"You are," said Curtney slowly. "Not taking their purses only, but you've taken lives as well!"

"In the old days, Tom, when men wore armor, a life taken now and then, in fair fight, was considered an honor, not a disgrace."

"But these aren't the days of armor. These aren't the Middle Ages. As for fair fight—what's fair when a practiced fighter like you, Jim, meets an ordinary man? You roll over him and leave him smashed behind you. He has had no chance. There couldn't be a fight. He's like a child before you."

"You insist on looking at this in the worst way for me," said Nair blankly.

"I insist on facing the facts, and I insist that you shall not blind me, nor think for a moment that you are succeeding. When you first came West, you were simply—well, restless! But you've turned into a destroyer. I know it. You yourself ought to know it. Marry you to Alice? In the name of God, Jim, what's taken possession of you? She looks on you as a sort of a second father! She'd be horrified!"

Curtney's voice rang with revulsion.

Even the resolution and the fiery hope of Nair might have been daunted by the strong expressions of the father, had not, at that instant, the light and thrilling laughter of the girl blown faintly on the wind through the door of the shack and filling the interior of the old building with music.

Nair sighed, and then muttered: "Let me talk alone with Alice for five minutes. Then we'll both stick by her answer!"

"Not alone with her, Jim. You're too persuasive."

"Five minutes, only!" urged Nair. "You can't deny me that. Good heavens, Tom, do you think that I'm a conjurer, and that I can bewitch her?"

At this, big Tom Curtney slowly heaved himself from his place and advanced from the house into the clearing beyond. There he saw his daughter in the very act of mounting to the back of a small-eyed, long-eared mustang. She whipped into the saddle like a circus performer. A wild duel began between her and the mustang, which pitched for thirty seconds like a small demon, twisting into small knots in the air—dropping out of the sky and crashing down heavily upon one hoof. For thirty seconds, Alice Curtney rode as fairly and bravely as any man, grasping the reins with one hand and with the other swinging her hat to challenge and encourage the antics of the horse. Her hair was tossed to wildness; her face grew flushed; her eyes rolled with the constant shocks of the bucking; then the mustang suddenly began to pivot, swinging round and round with amazing speed. He had caught the girl off balance, and though she struggled desperately to regain her equilibrium while the stalwart ruffians of Nair's gang yelled and laughed and cheered in their enthusiasm, fate was against her.

She swayed farther and farther out toward the horizontal. Finally, a whipsnap jerk of the mustang threw her from the saddle and she flew out into the thin air. Had she struck the hard ground she must almost certainly have been badly injured, but her flying body landed against tall Nick Hunter, who broke the violence of her impetus as they both crashed to the earth amid the cheers and the yells of the others.

Here was a girl, and an amazingly pretty one, and yet the cow-punchers and long riders of the mountains, so celebrated for chivalry, stirred not a hand to assist her to her feet in spite of her fall. They merely smote one another upon the back as though in the greatest enjoyment, and with much laughter declared to her that she had lost her bet to them. Their actions seemed incredible.

She was fairly stunned by her fall. Yet she leaped to her feet at once, and though she was a trifle unsteady, though her eyes still rolled and her face was crimson, she laughed while she staggered, and, nodding her head in perfect good humor to signify that she well understood that she had lost her game. She drew out a wallet, picked from one of its pockets half a dozen fifty-cent pieces, and threw them to the various men. The coin which came to the share of Tod, that worthy kissed with much ceremony and then put into his vest pocket, declaring he would never be without luck from that moment forward!

"You pay me double," insisted tall Nick Hunter, scrambling to his feet with a groan, and still gasping. "I won the bet and then I caught you when you fell, Al."

"Sure," said Alice. "Here's the bet, and here's for catching me!"

With this, she tossed him the fifty-cent piece which was apparently the amount of the bet in each case, and then, stooping with amazing quickness, caught up a handful of fine sand and cast it at him.

What a yell of approbation rose from their throats at that. For Nick was feared as much as he was respected for his wisdom and his valor, in equal parts. Now they saw him gasping and choking and spitting, and wiping the sand out of his hair and his mouth and his eyes, only to have it trickle down inside his shirt in a steady stream. He wriggled and groaned with his discomfort; then he made a lurch toward Alice.

She fled, however, like a deer. Behind her the long legs of Nick Hunter plied with a furious energy. He had caught up, as he ran, a tough switch, broken from a neighboring tree, and he promised her, as he pursued, such a dressing down that her manners would be improved for the rest of her life. No girl encumbered with skirts could have escaped from the headlong rush of Nick. But Alice was dressed in plain riding breeches with supple, soft-leather riding boots. If she made any concession to womanly modesty, it was a knee-length linen duster which she wore. But indeed, no such concessions were necessary, for a boy's clothes seemed more fitted to her needs than a woman's. They suited her perfectly.

So dressed, then, she showed the most amazing activity. She could not match the speed of long Nick, but she doubled back and forth out of the grip of his reaching hands with the activity of a rabbit. Once he tripped and fell in his rush. Once he stumbled against a tree. These accidents roused him to the highest pitch of excitement, and now he put forth his greatest efforts. The danger which Alice had escaped before, she now felt growing to a certain doom behind her. Accordingly, running straight at a young tree, she caught one of the lower branches and, in a trice, swung herself up among the upper limbs. Long Nick had only time to grasp vainly at the fluttering coat tail of the linen duster. And then, giving up his chase, he leaned, panting, against the trunk of the tree and vowed that women were designed by the Creator to punish the sins of man. Across this rioting of voices, struck the heavy note of Tom Curtney. "Alice, come here!"

She was out of sight in the upper part of the tree, but

almost instantly she dropped into view, hanging for an instant from a lower branch by one hand. Then she flashed across the clearing and stood beside her father.

"Go inside," he commanded. "Nair wants to talk with you."

"Have you had trouble with him, dad?" she asked, quick to see that there was a change in the manner of her father.

"I'm not talking about trouble," rumbled Tom Curtney. "I'm telling you that Jim wants to see you. Hurry along. And then come back out here."

She regarded him for another instant, nodding shrewdly to herself as she saw that something had indeed happened between them, and then she went on toward the door of the shack, singing from the full happiness of her heart.

23

She found Nair in the middle of the larger room, standing like a soldier facing the muskets of a firing squad. His arms were folded across his breast. He was drawn to the full of his imposing height. She had never before so keenly felt two things in his presence—the noble height and dimensions of his forehead, or the darkness and the danger in his eye.

When he saw her, he unfolded his arms and strove to bring a more cheerful expression to his face, but his brow was still gloomy with concern when she stood before him.

"Dad says that you want to talk with me about something," she said. Then she put up a hasty hand and gathered her wildly shaken hair into better order, for she had felt his glance go slowly, carefully over her, resting on her hair, on her eyes, on her smile. There was a meaning in that look of his which made her tremble; she could not tell why.

"I wanted to talk to you about things your father wouldn't let me say, Alice," he answered her. "The first thing is this. He has been very sick."

"How did you guess that?"

"By his face when I saw him."

"Yes. He was pale. Did he tell you what was wrong with him? He wouldn't tell me, Jim!"

"He wouldn't tell you because it's too serious."

"Jim! It's not—"

"Exactly! What you and I have both guessed before. His heart. Steady, Al!"

She nerved herself bravely, and then: "Is it something that may come—I mean—"

"It may come at any moment," said the outlaw. "That's why I have to talk frankly to you. Alice, you must take your father away from the mountains, away from this strenuous life, and down to a pleasanter climate. He must spend the rest of his life resting easily."

Her eyes opened. "D'you think we have a stake cached away, Jim? Why, we haven't a cent, hardly! I've patched these breeches until there isn't any cloth to sew the patches on!"

"That's it, Al. That's what I wanted to talk to you about. I wish to go along and take care of Tom."

"Jim, you old dear! But he'd never let you."

"He couldn't help himself if I were—if I were—in short, if you and I were to marry, Al!"

He brought out the final words in a sort of agony of shame and fear and embarrassment, while the girl watched him with dull, uncomprehending eyes for a moment. Then, as the understanding came to her, he saw in her face first of all what seemed to him the wildest horror. It passed a little, but still she was shrinking from him.

"Mind you," groaned Nair, "I'm not forcing myself on you, Al. I'm not trying to buy you. Whether you marry me or not, I'll take care of your father if Tom will let me!"

The girl pushed this thought away, as though she insisted on dealing only with the main essentials of this strange situation.

"Did you tell dad what you were going to say to me?" she asked at length, still looking down on the floor as though she were unable to bear the weight of his gaze.

"I did," he said.

"And he told you that he approved?"

"Not a bit. He said that he wouldn't martyr you by letting you marry a man who was old enough to be your father."

He forced out these damning words one by one, driven by a sort of perverse imp of self-torture. The result was quite the opposite of what he might have suspected. For suddenly she had run to him and was patting him on the shoulder in a strange sort of motherly way.

"Dear old Jim!" she said.

"You see, Alice," he explained desperately, "it was a different matter a few years ago. When you were fifteen and I was thirty-five, it was one thing; but now you're older, and as I pointed out to your father, when you're forty, I'll be sixty. Sixty isn't so very old for a man whose wife is forty, Al. Is it?"

He spoke with a profound seriousness, his fists doubled tightly, his brows gathered in a frown, and his face covered with perspiration. All of these things were noted by Alice Curtney with sorrow rather than horror now; and with a sigh she answered.

"I'm a little sick, Jim. It doesn't seem right, somehow, but what else can be done? Dad has to be cared for. I'm not able to do it. There's nothing we can use to pay for that care except—me!"

She looked hopelessly at Nair, and he, with all his might, strove to meet the gaze, but his eyes fell to the floor. He had hoped, after all, that he could tell her of his love, and sweep her from her feet with his passion. But of love, now that he faced her, he could not say a word, for her youth and her beauty had a power which silenced him.

He had hoped to win her with persuasion, but in the end he found that all he could do was to hold her up, as it were, at the point of a gun and let her sell herself for the sake of her father. He knew, too, that she was beginning to despise him, and yet he could not speak, for he realized now that he wanted her more than he had ever wanted power or money.

He heard her say: "When you want me, Jim, I'll marry you. There's no other way. We'll go back to our camp. So long!"

She was backing to the door. He made a great effort to look up again, but he could not. Then he found that she was gone, and he heard, at the same time, an outbreak of voices from the clearing beyond the house; he distinguished the name of Chick Logan. In another moment, Logan himself was before his chief.

"Chief," said that stanch henchman, "I played the game the best I could, and I was beat. We tried to trap Train, but he was like a cat and outguessed us. Then I tried to get him here into the Culver Draw. But on the way I had a tumble into the river and came within a inch of kicking out, but Train pulled me clear. After that, I couldn't double cross him. Besides, he'd guessed at the job we were trying to put up on him. We had a talk, and he told me that the thing he was aiming at was to throw in with the rest of us and work with you. That's why he came to Morriston. And I rode on to fix things up with you."

"You told him," growled out Nair, "that you were one of my men?"

"Told him nothing. Didn't have to. He guessed it all before."

"The devil!"

"He's worse than that. He's a fox, right enough, chief. And take it from me, he'll go straight with the rest of us. You'll never be sorry for it if you take him in. I'll swear to that, chief! If you don't believe it, take a chance and try him out!"

There had been black anger in the face of Nair at first, but the anger gradually was controlled and disappeared.

"What could he do, Chick?" he asked.

"Anything!"

"From crooked cards to a stick-up?"

"That's it. I dunno about the cards, but I know that wherever a game gent with a pair of handy guns could be useful, Train is the man for you. He's as cool as steel and as steady as a rock and as quick as a cat. He never sleeps. That's Train!"

The leader of the gang now lighted his pipe, and his eyes grew veiled with thought. Even the problem of Alice and the nature of that dubious victory which he had gained over her a short time before became a second interest to him.

He said suddenly: "Do you know Creighton?"

"Sure. Used to work for old Henshaw, five miles out from Creighton; saw the old town every Saturday night for a couple of years!"

"Where's Train?"

"Down in the hills."

"Get Train; tell him that he's to be tried out. Go straight for Creighton. No matter how fast you ride, I'll be there before you. You understand?"

"Where'll we meet you?"

"How long has it been since you were in the town?"

"Five years, pretty near."

"Nobody will remember you after that length of time. Go to the hotel and put up there."

"And wait for you?"

"Yes."

"Nothing to do?"

"Yes, get a room in the front of the hotel, overlooking the bank, you understand?"

"Ah, is that the dodge? The old Creighton Bank. There's a mule load of stuff in that dump!"

"I haven't told you what I'm after. Take some powder along with you. Before you hit Creighton, make a stop and cook up the stuff and strain out the soup."

"I understand. Have you got a flask?"

"Here's one. Don't let it get too cold at night."

"I'm not a tenderfoot in this game, chief. I've carried soup before, and run it in the mold, for that matter. You know that!"

"I know it. If I had five more like you, Chick, we'd all get rich and run no risks about it. Start now. Do you need any money?"

"Not a cent. I'm fixed for a month."

"About Train—"

"I'll vouch for him."

"I've never seen you sure of any man before—not even Nick Hunter, and you and Hunter have been pals for years."

"I never had the chance to know anybody the way that I've got to know Train."

"He's square, eh?"

"There's only one man in the world that I'd rather have with me in a pinch."

"Who's that?"

"Yourself, chief!"

"Would he play big for a big stake?"

"He'd play for a million without batting an eye."

"You're sure, Chick?"

"Surer than I am of myself. He wants to get into the gang, and he's the sort that gets what he wants. He's lucky!"

A faint smile, which Chick could not understand, came over the lips of Jim Nair. Then the big man nodded. "When you meet Train, you can tell him that he's on trial with me and that I'm watching eveything he does. Take a fresh horse, Chick. Take that bay with the white stocking on the near foreleg. He's made of iron. I rode him through the Big Bend last year, and I know him."

Chick Logan hastened off to execute this order, and on the way he passed Rainier. The latter sheered hastily to one side and gave the other plenty of elbow room. Then he came on to Nair.

"The game with Train is almost up," said the outlaw. "You can stop worrying about that, Rainier. I have my hand ready to close on him."

24

"How," said Train, "will Nair get in touch with us?"

He lay on the bed in the hotel at Creighton with his shoulders propped by a pillow and his heels perched upon the top of the foot of the bed.

"Nobody knows how Nair does things," said Chick Logan. "I've seen gents plumb bust their hearts trying to foller the way Nair was going, but—"

Here he was interrupted by the soft rustle of paper, and turning his head hastily, he saw an envelope being pushed under the door of the room. He leaped from his chair and jerked the door open, but although he had reached it in a single second, and far too quickly to have enabled the bearer of the letter to disappear, the hall was empty. Not a soul was in sight, and Chick Logan, as he closed the door again and picked up the letter, said: "That was shoved under here by somebody that went into one of the rooms next to ours as soon as he's turned the trick. Hello! This is for you, Train. Your name is all wrote out on it!"

At this, Train for the first time lifted his head a little. The effort seemed too great for him. He sank into the pillow once more and yawned prodigiously.

"Read it aloud, partner," he requested. "Doggone me if my eyes ain't going back on me so's I can't hardly use 'em none!"

Logan chuckled, but then he opened the letter and read as follows:

DEAR TRAIN: Logan has told you the main purpose for the trip to Creighton. At least, he's hinted as much as he could guess to you. The fact is that we must make a try on the Creighton Bank. There are other ways which might be attempted, but the easiest is simply to get the combinations. There is only one bank official who knows them and who may be approached. That is Peter More, the assistant cashier. More has just accepted a few hundred dollars from me to pay bills; he'll at least listen to you when you come in my name. More has gone straight until this time, but his brother was crooked before him, and I think that Peter will be crooked also. At least, we'll make a try with him. I am inclosing with this letter ten fifty-dollar bills. If you run out of words, you may try the money and see if it will persuade him. He is to write out the combinations and give them to you. If you can manage this affair, I will come to see you in your room at the hotel.

More's house is the second one east of the blacksmith shop and on the north side of the street. You will find him at home to-night. If you are successful after talking with More, raise the shade of your window and put the lamp on the table beside it.

Yours very truly,

N.

The letter thus finished, there was an exclamation of wonder from Logan, who passed the missive, together with the crisp new bills which it contained, to his companion.

"I dunno," he said. "It beats me, Train. I've told the chief that you're a hundred per cent worth trustin'. But this is putting his cards on the table with a bang. Doggone me if it ain't! D'you start now?"

Train reared himself slowly from the bed, examined the money and the letter with a glance, and then looked out the window, where the slant yellow light of the afternoon was waning rapidly toward the dusk.

"I start now," he answered, and instantly left the room.

In the street, he paused in front of the hotel to permit a drove of cattle to be herded past, the shrill yells and yipping of two cow-punchers crowding the frightened beasts down the way. He saw the long, crooked horns flashing in the sunset light, the gleaming of reddened eyes through the cloud of dust, and after the herd had passed he still waited for a time until the dust should have settled.

While he waited, he saw a horseman coming from the west, in which direction the cattle had just passed. He was powdered with white from head to foot and was still coughing and sneezing; behind him three more horsemen followed. They advanced straight down the street and past the hotel, while Train slunk back from view.

He had recognized the leader of the little troop as Gresham, fearfully ill at ease in the saddle and stirring from time to time as though riding were a painful task to him. Yet it was Gresham, unmistakable even in the pseudo-cow-puncher attire which he wore, and a strange thrill of fear passed through the heart of Train. He became aware of a crushing weight near his heart where lay the little packet wrapped in oiled paper and cloth which contained the fifty thousand dollars which Comstock had given to him for delivery to James Nair Cartwright. That packet, if it were not delivered soon, would be his damnation, for if it were found upon him, he could not hesitate long in guessing at what his fate would be.

But why was Gresham so like a bulldog on his trail? And where had he found the money to hire, for his work, three such fellows as those who were following in his rear? Train knew well enough that they were hardened veterans of the range, though they were young as well. But by the stoop of their shoulders, the sway of their bodies to the movement of the horse, and something indescribable about the carriage of their heads and the squinting of their eyes, he recognized mountain warriors. Three men like these would, for pay, board and room, cost a pretty penny every day. Gresham was not rich. How, then, could he afford such allies?

These problems began to trouble the mind of Train as he made his way down the street after the little troop had disappeared around the next turning of the streets. But he had made it a rule to never worry today about what was to be met tomorrow. So he shrugged his shoulders, when he reached the second house east of the blacksmith shop, and swung the gate open, determined to think of nothing but the problem before him.

In the meantime, as he passed slowly toward the front porch, he studied the yard. A front yard is like a man's face; it reveals character. What Train saw was enough to puzzle him. The other yards, up and down the street, were barren, sunburned plots, but this was kept with a meticulous care. There was a little square patch of lawn on either side of a clean walk of red bricks. Beyond the lawn was a wide border planted, according to a bewildering pattern, with twenty different flower patches through which tiny paths meandered. Twice a day that little garden must be watered, and once a day it must need the rake or the hoe. To one side a sprinkler was spinning and clicking and filling the air with the deliciously cool whisper of falling spray upon the grass while Train breathed the fresh scent of newly turned sod still drinking this artificial rainfall.

If the master of the house had anything to do with the care of this garden, he was a precision, a man of almost feminine neatness.

The door of the house was open; the entrance was closed by a screen only, and when he knocked he saw a dapper little man in glasses come out of the kitchen door, followed by a little smoke of cookery. He was arrayed in clean shirt sleeves, with a white apron gathered snugly about him.

"Hello!" he said, as he opened the door. Then, as his nearsighted eyes took in the details of Train's rough garb; "Who sent you to me, my friend?"

It was a sharp, querulous voice, as of one whose nerves were frayed thin by struggling all of every day with the intricacies of figures.

"I'm busted," said Train. "I smelled chuck when I come by here, and I thought that you might give me a hand-out, partner."

"A hand-out. A hand-out?" snapped out the other. "This town is full of work. Nobody that's honest enough to work need go hungry!"

"I ain't had a chance to get a job. I just blew in!"

"Blow out again, then!" responded Peter More. "You're not wanted in Creighton. We have no use for wastrels in this town."

"That's kind of hard talk, partner," said Train. "It's a long stretch to the next town and a lot of doggone hungry mountains in between!"

"Don't talk to me about hunger!" cried More. "Hunger is what men of your class need. It'll teach you to save your money—run up a bank account. Just the sort of a lesson for you. I've worked for what I have. You go do the same." He drew back.

"Wait a minute—"

"I haven't any minutes to waste. My time is valuable." And he slammed the door in Train's face.

"A skunk!" moralized Train to himself, perspiring with anger. "A plain, low-down one!"

He went around to the rear of the house. The back yard

was a strange contrast with the front. It was littered with piles of junk and tin cans and surrounded by a tall board fence which would serve to shut away his family disgrace from the eyes of curious neighbors. This spectacle Train, remembering the scrupulous neatness of the front garden, viewed with a sardonic smile. Then he tapped at the rear door.

It was opened by the bank clerk, who had no sooner adjusted his spectacles to view the intruder than he roared out: "You again! Why, you vagrant—"

The boot of Train barred the door as it was about to crash shut in his face.

"Easy, partner," he said slowly. "I come here to have a little chat!"

Peter More recoiled a little, as though he sensed a threat in this. He even glanced hastily around him as if in a search for weapons, and finding none, he said in an altered voice: "I'm doing my own cooking while my wife's away, my friend. That's why I have no food to offer you."

"Talk will serve me just as good as food," said Train.

"Talk? What d'you mean?"

"I was sent to you by a friend."

"You? By a friend of mine?"

The eyes of More fairly popped with indignation at the idea that such a person could claim a mutual acquaintance.

"What friend?" he snapped out.

"Jim Nair!"

It was as though the clerk had received a stunning blow. He gave back a sudden pace and then glanced timidly over his shoulder as though the hiss of the bacon frying in the pan on the kitchen stove were the voice of one giving him warning of danger. At length he gasped out: "Nair! Did he send you here?"

Train had no time to answer, for, thrusting the door wide open, More took his visitor by the arm and drew him hastily inside.

"Come in quick!" he commanded. "And talk low—for heaven's sake! Nair! I might have known—something told me — Well, well? What does he want with me?"

25

Train was in no hurry to answer. He suggested that they talk in a front room, away from the kitchen smells, and More hustled him instantly into the parlor. There he sat Train down under the enlarged photograph of a gentleman with wide, bushy whiskers and a frowning brow. He looked as if he were running for judge and posing for a political picture, so ponderous was his expression. But More himself could not keep in a chair. He was continually up and down, fidgeting about the room, straightening a rumpled edge of the rug, adjusting the books upon the center table.

"What is it?" he kept asking.

"Nothing," said Train, "except that Nair thought that you was in trouble, and he wanted to help you."

"Him? He told you, then?"

"Sure. Everything."

"He was kind—very kind," stammered More, "but I didn't send my father to him to ask for aid. The last thing that ever came into my mind. The money he sent me was very welcome. If he wants it back—I'll pay it to him—all in good time—all in good time!"

"A welsher, too!" murmured Train to himself.

"He ain't sending me for the money," he hastened to say.

The assistant cashier sighed with heartfelt relief.

"Well," he said more kindly, "what *does* he want?"

"Only thing he felt was that if you was in trouble, a little more hard cash might be a help to you."

"Ah?" said Peter More with a beaming face. "I have no doubt that Nair feels that he owes something to my family because of what he did with my poor brother. Well, perhaps he is right. And, now that you speak of it, it's true that I can use a little money. Times have been bad with me—mighty bad!"

"I have it in my pocket," said Train.

He picked out the folded bills and watched the eyes of More bulge when they distinguished the denomination of the bill which lay on top.

"Very well," said the clerk. "Hand it over, and you can go back and tell Nair that I'm a grateful friend of his!"

"I'm going to do that, I hope," commented Train. "But my chief figures things just the same way that you do. This here town of Creighton is full of work. Nobody don't need to go without money if he's willing to work!"

"Work?" cried the little man in a fury of self-pity. "I'm the hardest-worked man in the West. I work all day every day. There are no Sundays in my life!"

"It's as bad to work at a thing that doesn't pay," said Train, "as it is not to work at all. That's me. I had been hunting around for the right sort of work, and ain't been able to find it all these years."

He grinned broadly at his host, but the latter saw nothing amusing in such a remark.

"Look here," said Train more frankly, "ain't there any job in that bank that would pay better than yours? What do you do?"

"Pay out money to people, very largely. Sometimes many thousands in a single day!" And his breast swelled with pride.

"Suppose you was to be paying some of that into your own pocket. Just a little here and there? Wouldn't that pay you better?"

The clerk jumped up and struck his hands together in a passion. "I see!" he cried. "I might have known this. But you can go to Nair and tell him that nobody in the world has even been able to question my integrity. When I die, no matter what else I may be, I shall be an honest man!"

"Partner," said Train, "you talk pretty near as good as a book, but I ain't voting in this town. Save this here talk for the next election."

With this shot, he folded the bills, stowed them in his coat pocket, rose, settled his hat firmly on his head, and turned to the front door.

"Wait!" breathed Peter More faintly.

Train turned and saw that the other had collapsed in a chair, trembling with terror and with greed.

"What—what does Nair want?"

"He wants you to help yourself to a little prosperity, old son. That's all."

"How?" gasped out the clerk.

"How much coin is there in the Creighton Bank vaults right this minute?"

"Near a million, I guess. Or half a million, anyway!"

"Ah!" murmured Train, drawing a long breath.

"Does Nair dare to suggest that I put my hands into the pockets of employers who have trusted me with their uttermost—"

"Hush up that chatter," said Train. "Look here, young man; you're goin' to go through with this here deal, and you're goin' to do it inside of five minutes. I can see it comin'. Doggone me if I can't!"

He jerked the bills from his pocket and tossed them on the table. "There's five hundred," he said. "How many weeks would you have to work for that? But that five hundred Nair'll give to you for a couple of scratches with your pencil. And he'll pay more. If the job goes through, he'll split the profits with you on a good basis. Nair will take care of you—"

"D'you think I don't understand that I'd go to prison?"

"Why?"

"Such things are always found out!"

"Are they? The robberies that are traced up are the ones that are talked about. The gents that ain't tried, old sons, are a pile thicker than the ones that *are* tried!"

"They finish in jail!" persisted More stubbornly.

"Is Nair in jail?"

More was silenced for the moment, at least. Meantime, his eyes could not leave the money on the table. He touched it. The heap sifted into a scattering of bills—fifty dollars each and ten of them. He would work nearly twenty weeks to earn as much money as this. Nearly twenty weeks—which meant nearly five months. And all of this his for a gesture.

"What am I to do?"

"Write down the combinations."

"No, no, no!"

"Have I stuck a knife in you? Nope! I ain't forcing you to do nothin'. If you don't want the coin, you don't have to take it. You get this five hundred for a sweetener, to hold you over. Then if the deal goes through, you'd get ten per cent, anyways. What's ten per cent of half a million? That's fifty thousand berries, partner. At six per cent, there's your three thousand a year. By the way, More, how much are you making now?"

The last question seemed to be a heavy blow, and More shrank in his chair. He remained silent for so long that Train presently stepped to the table and made as though to scoop up the bribe money. "Well," he said, "I'll take this along. Sorry you can't see things our way!"

But the thin hand of More made a sudden grab for the bills and clutched it with a noisy rustling.

"No!" he said huskily. "I think—I think—the trail could be covered!"

"Sure!"

"If they suspect me?"

"Are you the only one that knows the combinations?"

"No, no!" cried More with a voice suddenly edged with malice. "There's that new man they brought in from New York and slammed in right over my head. What about him? I'm a proved man, but what about the newcomer?"

He rubbed his hands together in great glee at this thought. "They'll knife Smithson for this," he said snarlingly. "That's what'll happen. Here—wait till I get a piece of paper—" He took one from a drawer and began to write feverishly upon it.

Suddenly he looked up with a query: "How'll I be sure that Nair will split everything with me—ten per cent to me? Why should I get only ten per cent? He couldn't do a thing without my help!"

"Couldn't he? You don't know him, More. If you don't take the bait, Smithson will swallow it quick!"

"Right!" gasped out More. "That crooked dog. I could see it in his eye the first day he came into the bank. I'll do it—just to keep the money out of Smithson's hands!"

He wrote on in the most feverish haste, and when he had concluded, he thrust the paper into Train's hand.

"There you are. But now," he added, suddenly stricken

with a new fear, "how many have seen you come into this house?"

"About as many as will see me go out!" Train exclaimed sneeringly, and he walked out through the garden to the gate.

The sprinkler had run too long; the brick walk was covered with a standing pool of water, black in the dull light of the dusk, and as Train sauntered down the street he saw More rush out from the house, run halfway toward the gate as though of a mind to call back his visitor, then change again and go back toward his cottage with a fallen head.

Whatever else that day had done, it had taken from one man all the possibilities of honest happiness thereafter. Though Train had seen men tempted and had seen them fall long before this, many of them more attractive in characrer than Peter More with his arrogance, his self-sufficiency, his whining consciousness of virtue, nevertheless the heart of Train grew strangely cold and small in him when he recalled what he had done to the soul of this wretched fellow. Fire could not do to a house what he had done to the self-respect of the smug little cashier.

When he reached the hotel again, he paused on the stairs. What had happened to the bacon which was frying on the stove when he first entered? It must have been consumed to a smudge of soft charcoal before he left the house of More.

He went on again, and, when he came to the room, he found Chick Logan there, pale with impatient anxiety.

"You missed!" he exclaimed, seeing the sick look on the face of Train.

For answer, the latter raised the shade and placed the lamp on the little table before it.

"I've been fishing in a sewer," he said, shuddering with disgust. "This is a rotten game, Logan!"

"Are you too good for it?" snapped out Logan. "Are you too good to take a share in a hundred thousand or so?"

Train answered not a word. His thoughts were all the deeper, and those thoughts were so strange that he could hardly recognize them as coming from his own brain, for he was wondering if money he took by stealth could ever be anything more than a weight on his thoughts. What was wrong with him?

Suddenly he spoke a thought aloud: "Chick, d'you think that going straight could be made a habit, just like going crooked?"

Chick could only stare at him.

"What in the devil are you talkin' about, Steve?"

"Nothin'," answered Train. "Let it drop."

26

"Will Nair call us out, or come in?" asked Train after a time.

"Nobody can ever tell what he'll do. Might drop through the ceiling or come up through the floor, for all that I know. Figure out just what Nair is going to do, and he's sure to do just the opposite!"

And, in fact, the entrance of Nair was a surprise to Train. He felt the floor of the room quiver a little as a heavy step passed up the hallway; some one with a deep bass voice was humming a song; then a hand rapped loudly at the door.

"There's that darned Griffith again," said Chick Logan snarlingly, and opened the door straightway on Nair!

Train felt a thoughtful, gloomy eye fixed steadily upon him. He had never before met a man who impressed him in this fashion, for he felt half hypnotized. It was impossible for him, during some minutes, to note any of the details of the man's presence, but in sheer force of mind and the drive of nervous energy, he felt himself overmatched, for the first time in his life. A fighting man learns to judge an opponent with a glance which plumbs another to the heart, but the searching scrutiny of Train, well veiled as it was, failed to sum up all the powers of the outlaw.

His second emotion was one of immense relief that he was to be able to take the fifty thousand dollars from his pocket, in a few moments, and take from Nair, in return, a receipt for payment which could be shown in due time to Patrick Comstock. The matter would be ended; his dangerous and difficult mission would be triumphantly concluded. These were the thoughts of Train as he confronted Jim Nair.

The latter, in the meantime, advanced slowly across the room and spoke in his soft, deep voice. "You're Train, I suppose. I'm glad to know you, and I'm glad to have you with us. There was a time when I thought that you were out gunning for a little reputation—and me!"

His smile was rather more sinister than mirthful. "But," he

added, "Logan tells me that you're as straight as they make 'em and I trust Logan."

A cool, strong hand swallowed that of Train's, and the latter said to himself: "But I don't trust Nair; not for half a second!"

He said aloud: "More swallowed the coin and gave me the combinations. Here they are."

Nair took the paper, but did not open it at once.

"Was More easy?" he said.

"Nothing to it," said Train.

Nair chuckled. "It's in the blood. His brother was a crook. Pete More is a crook, too. I've always known it, but he was too much of a coward to go wrong until something big—and safe—came his way."

"I told him ten per cent," said Train.

"You did? He has his pay already," said the outlaw sneeringly.

"You don't split with him, eh?"

"A fool like More? Of course not. He's worthless to me now. I've squeezed that orange dry. He'll never have another job that'll be worth while working!" And, still chuckling, he opened the paper.

"He'll yell like a whipped dog when he finds out that he's been working for nothing," said Chick Logan.

But Train was much troubled. In the first place, he had given his word to the man, feeling that ten per cent was surely small enough to satisfy Nair. In the second place, there was something about the attitude of Nair which puzzled him.

James Nair Cartwright, in the old days, had been an eminently honest man—a man so honest that he had refused to let a friend give him a new start in business after speculations had taken all of his coin. Cartwright, in fact, was a man who had absolutely won the confidence of one who was no fool, and who was himself as honest as the day was long. But it was hard to believe that the Jim Nair who now stood before him had ever had such a character. Cruelty and cunning combined were the traits which were stamped upon the face of this man, and no matter what physical description and the matter of the strikingly similar names pointed out, Train felt that he must receive a better proof of the identity of Nair with Cartwright before he could freely hand over to him the fifty thousand.

These disturbing conclusions passed through his mind while

he heard Nair reading aloud the combinations of the outer door of the vault and the left-hand and right-hand inside doors.

He folded the paper and stuffed it into his pocket.

"You have the soup ready, Chick?"

That worthy produced the flask. There was enough nitro-glycerine in it to have rent the hotel in twain.

"Have you seen Griffith?" went on Nair.

"He spotted me when we came into town. He looked me up and begun talking about a big job that he'd been framing. Didn't say anything particular, but seems like he was working on somebody in the bank here."

"He works, but he works too slowly to suit me. We won't need him after tonight, if we have any luck!"

Nair cleared his throat and looked steadily upon them. "Boys," he said solemnly, "I'm about to tackle a job tonight that I usually would have spent a week or a year planning on. But tonight I'm taking a chance. I ought to have six men, but I'm only using three, counting myself. There'll be all the more credit for us and all the more cash if we work this game. We split it this way: ten per cent to each of you—thirty per cent to me, and one half to the rest of the gang. We work for them when they're not with us, just as they work for us when we're not along. Is that satisfactory?"

It seemed rather a top-heavy division of the spoils, to Train, but he saw that Chick Logan nodded with satisfaction, and he himself agreed that all would be well. That done, they left the room at once, proceeded in various directions, and reassembled at the side door of the bank. A jimmy, in the expert hands of Chick Logan, opened the door, and they slid inside the building at the very moment that the watchman, walking his beat, turned the corner and strolled down in their direction.

They waited in hushed silence until he had gone by.

Then said Nair: "That's awkward, that watchman. If I'd taken time with this job, I should have fixed him. It's too late to worry about that. Did you notice, boys, that while they have a mighty strong front door, their side door isn't any stronger than the door to any kitchen in the town? The difference is that a kitchen door guards bacon and eggs while this door guards greenbacks. Come along; we'll see if Pete More gave us the right numbers."

It was a tall, ponderous, old-fashioned vault before which

139

they came in the interior of the bank, Logan guiding the way with an electric lantern. There was a real need for such a formidable receptacle of wealth, Nair told them, for ever since its beginning, the town of Creighton had been a depository for the rich cow and lumber districts which surrounded the town. He declared that he had had his eye on that little bank for years, well knowing that its interior was far better furnished with coin than that of many a more imposing structure.

Now the talk stopped as they came to the vault itself. Nair held the light, and Logan worked the combination as Train read off the numbers. It handled smoothly enough; a final click announced that the combination had been solved. They threw back the bolts and opened the doors. Inside, two more small doors of steel confronted them, but again the numbers which the assistant cashier had given worked perfectly, the doors opened, and they had before them the drawers which held all the securities and the wealth of the bank.

That same moment, there came a heavy tapping on the front door of the bank.

That sound made Nair flash out the lantern. They stood swallowed by the pulsing darkness.

"What now, chief?" whispered Logan in an uncertain voice.

"Darn these impromptu jobs!" groaned Nair. "Is that the watchman or a clerk coming down to work who has forgotten his key and hopes that there may be some one inside."

A faint and far voice called.

"The devil!" muttered Nair. "We'll have to stop that. Come on to the front door. We'll let him in; perhaps he won't walk far!"

And again, as on the instant when his eyes first encountered the tall form of the bandit, the blood of Train turned cold. For there was that in the big man which he could only think of as perfect evil. There were tales of generosity and open-handedness to the poor and suffering which circulated through the countryside concerning Nair, but as Train followed the looming form of the bandit through the dark of the bank, he could not help thinking that even these acts of apparent goodness were all the result of a cold calculation.

Even an outlaw must have friends, and Nair had deliberately built up a sort of Robin Hood legendary air to surround him. If he took from the rich and gave something of his plunder to the poor, it was because he needed to reinforce himself with supporters.

Now they glided softly through the gloom and came to the front door of the bank, where Nair gave them swiftly whispered instructions. Then he stepped forward and opened the door. Instantly he who had been waiting so impatiently outside, stepped in, saying angrily: "What's the trick, Jenkins? want to keep me standing out there all night waiting? Have you started on the books? Or—"

He said this as he came in; then, as the silence and the blackness fell with a greater weight upon him, he stopped in midstride and caught his breath with a curious little hissing sound of terror. It was too late for him to spring back, however. The long arm of Nair shot forward with a glimmer of the smoothly polished leather cuffs about his wrists and forearms. In his hand there winked the barrel of a descending revolver. The heavy steel struck with a thud into the side of the man's head, and the clerk dropped without a sound.

"He's dead!" said Train, shuddering.

"Maybe," said Nair coolly, "but we can't be sure of that. We'll have to gag the dog. Fix him, Chick. Come back with me, Train."

They hurried back to the vault, Nair saying as they went along:

"We have more interruptions ahead of us. This poor fool whom I've just now tapped on the head apparently thought that another clerk named Jenkins had already come to the bank to do some night work and had a key to open the door of the bank. Jenkins will probably be along at any moment, and we must finish our job before Jenkins shows up. Finish up, and then get to the side door and through it; in the meantime, what if the horses should be taken?"

For they had left the three horses around the corner, tethered to a hitching rack in front of a hardware store. At the necessity of leaving the horses without a guard, Nair cursed roundly again, beneath his breath, and vowed that he would never again undertake such a work short-handed.

In the meantime, the drawers of the vault were hastily opened and with a dexterous hand the chief of the gang went through the contents. He dumped what he took into a large canvas bag, and then secured the top with a leather string at the same time that Chick Logan returned from the door to announce that the victim was securely gagged and trussed.

"We're done, thank heavens!" said Nair, "and we can leave now. I think that we have enough stuff here to retire on, if we feel like stopping work. In the meantime, let's get out to the horses before Jenkins comes down."

They started hurriedly for the side door, and as they took their first steps, they heard the grating of metal on metal; then the front door swung wide and a gust of the cool night air entered the building and set the papers rustling. It was Jenkins, beyond all doubt.

They were close to the side door, however, before the clerk turned on a light, and as he did so, they heard his scream of terror and surprise. He had sighted the prostrate body of his fellow clerk lying upon the floor!

"Quick!" said Nair, and, jerking open the door before them, all three pressed out into the open air. Jenkins, in the meantime, had run out through the front door and was filling the air with his shouts for help and cries of "Murder!"

"We should have stayed and cracked his head for him," said Nair. "He'll have the town up in a trice."

Windows and doors were indeed slamming open. Voices that promised help were heard shouting an answer, and through a doorway just before them, as they turned the corner, half a dozen armed men poured out from a rooming house.

"What's up?" they asked Nair.

"Somebody's delirious," answered that worthy calmly, and walked on, while the half dozen streamed around the corner to make sure. When they had dissappeared, the fugitives looked to one another in silent horror. They had come within full view of the hitching rack in front of the hardware store, and the three horses were nowhere to be seen.

27

"We've been double crossed," said Nair with wonderful quiet. "But now, lads, no quitting. Stand fast and all together. Follow me!"

With this, he doubled down through a little alley and struck away through an open field beyond. Behind them, before they had fairly started into the open, there came an uproar of shouting men and the clattering hoofs of horses.

"This way!" shouted the ringing voice of the leader. "They went this way. Ride like the devil, boys, and we'll have them!"

The heart of Train swelled in him, for he had recognized the peculiar nasal voice of Gresham, the detective, and he thought, bitterly, that the end had come at last to his long and adventurous career, for Gresham was like fate behind him. To be caught now, indeed, would be a delightful stroke of irony, for it was the first time in his life that he had attempted a good action of such magnitude. As for the robbery of the bank, it was as nothing; a mere detail into which he had allowed himself to be dragged because he must be close to Nair until he had satisfactorily established the identity of James Nair. All was subservient to the honest delivery of the fifty thousand dollars which was still in his pocket. But if he were captured with the others, the bank loot would tell against him as much as against any of the others; it was ruin for them all. He thought of this and ground his teeth together.

In the meantime, Nair suddenly stopped running, and threw down the heavy canvas bag.

"Stand with me, lads," he cried, "and we'll pepper these fools behind us. Drive them back this once, and we'll be inside the forest before they can get at us. After that, with any luck, we can give them the slip!"

They turned at his command, their guns in their hands, and they saw before them a fine picture of some ten or a dozen riders rushing toward them, already opening a scattering fire. And, in the lead, Train recognized the squat figure of Gresham, seated upon the magnificent body of Whimsy herself! It was Gresham, then, who had blocked their way to escape.

Raising his gun with the others, Train told himself that Gresham should fall by his fire, no matter what happened to the others among the assailants. He leveled the gun, he drew his bead, and then, to his horror, he found that he could not fire. Something was wrong with him—something was far, far wrong! For, with his finger trembling about the trigger, he summoned a picture of Gresham stretched in cold death, silent forever.

He fired, at last, but only after he had switched up the muzzle of his gun, and the bullet sped high above the heads of the pursuers. Not so with the shots of his companions, however. No newborn scruples disturbed their aim; they fought for life and a treasure in hard cash and securities. In answer to the explosion of their guns, two yells of pain rose from among the leaders of the charge, and two men pitched from their saddles. The others, shrinking before such murderous efficiency, turned their horses, so that the charge split into two sections and rolled away harmlessly on either side, while the horsemen poured in a heavy but ineffectual fire. For it takes a genius with weapons to strike even a daylight target from the back of a moving horse, and these men had only a dull moon to show them their enemies.

There was no time for the three to make good their stand, however. The mouth of the alley which yawned upon the open field was emitting armed riders every instant, now, and, catching up the fallen sack of treasure, big Jim Nair set the example of flight for the nearest trees. They reached them with the horsemen thundering just behind their backs, and a rain of lead spattering among the trees before and around them.

A hedge of brier rose before them. They leaped it, made agile with terror.

"Down!" cried Nair, and flattened himself accordingly along the ground, with his face in the dirt.

Past them, almost over them, rode fifty horses, and ever the ringing voice of Gresham was in the distance, leading, exhorting. Those behind him, following the lightning speed of Whimsy as well as they might, were firing at shadows, crying out now and again to one another that they saw their men just before, charging every new covert, riding on again with yells of disappointment to ride down some new shadow which had showed itself before another section of the hunters.

Then Nair gave the signal again, and they rose from the ground. How well he had commanded, Train was willing to admit. The wood was full of searchers—new men were constantly coming from the town, but now they had a ghost of a hope to escape. Running when they could, or walking through tearing tangles of the underbrush, they skirted the edge of the wood. Now they crouched to avoid the coming of some belated recruit to the hunt, which was rolling deeper and deeper into the heart of the wood; now they rose and made on at the best speed they might. In half an hour they had put two miles behind them. Still they were within hearing of the workers from Creighton. Guns barked in the distance, shouts rang through the woodland, but none of these were immediate terrors, and they felt that they might safely push ahead in whatever direction they chose from this point. Nair picked the angle of their march, promising to lead them to friends and horses within the hour, if they walked on smartly.

They had journeyed on for perhaps half this distance, with Nair setting a tremendous pace in spite of the burden of the canvas sack upon his back, when Chick Logan made a halt and urgently advised that the contents of the sack be divided into three portions, partly to ease Nair of the load, and partly because, if they were hunted more closely by the pursuers, they could divide and go each man his way. In such a case, even though one or two might be taken, at least one of them was reasonably sure to make good his escape, and the third of the loot would be sufficient to make a stake for the gang as well as provide the thews of war for the legal battle of delivering the pair who were captured, or buying them off from the officers of the law, if that were possible.

"That is *not* possible," put in Train at this point.

"What do you mean by that?" asked the outlaw leader sharply.

"What I say. I saw Gresham, the detective, at the head of those fellows. And Gresham has been hunting me through the length and the breadth of the mountains. He must have recognized Whimsy and taken her. If it hadn't been for Gresham, we never would have had this scare."

"It's on your account, then?" said Nair savagely. "You've brought that much more luck with you to my men?"

"D'you want to load all the blame on me?" asked Train, sneering, but feeling that he was stepping into deep and deeper water.

"Train," said Nair suddenly, "I think I know. You've joined me in order that you may lead the flatties up to me. That's your game, I'll swear!"

"Chief," put in Chick Logan, loyal to his new friend, "I got to say that you're mighty hard on Train. Maybe he's brought us bad luck, but that's not out of any wish of his. He sure has run as much risk and chance tonight as any of us!"

But Nair raised a broad hand and waved Logan back to silence and a distance. It was as though he were brushing away a small obstacle, in order the better to get at the work which lay just before him. That work was Train, and the longer Nair fixed his attention upon the former, the blacker his rage seemed to grow.

"You're one of these lads who'll never learn," he declared to Chick Logan. "You've had chances enough and you're old enough. But still you can't learn that a man who talks straight may nevertheless be as crooked as a bent stick!"

There was no doubt about the root-and-branch hostility of Nair by this time. It meant trouble for Train. It meant, in fact, battle. The only question was: Would Nair fight alone with him, or would Chick Logan rally to the support of his chief? Handle them both, Train could not. But if he were left to fight it out with Nair alone, he felt that he might have at least an even chance of victory.

It was the first time in his life that the slightest doubt had ever come to him. The very existence of that doubt puzzled and baffled him. It was not that he had up to this point seen any signs of great agility of hand in Nair, but nevertheless he felt that it would be a great, almost an impossible, task to beat down the other. For Nair carried in his face the sign of invincibility as plainly marked as it is in the front of the lion. Here was a king of beasts, and though Train might be a veritable black panther among men, he could not but shrink instinctively, as from before an overwhelming power, when this man was his opponent.

"You've nothing against me, Nair," he said calmly, keying himself up to the struggle which he saw must come. "You've nothing that you can really bring up against me."

"I haven't?" Nair laughed in his growing fury. "Listen to me, Train. Listen to me, Logan, while I tell you a story about this honest man you believe in so much. A few days ago in Morriston, Train met an old pal of his, Rainier. You saw Rainier at camp."

"And liked him darned little," admitted Logan. "He had the look of a cheat, the skunk!"

"No matter about his looks, I say that he was an old friend of Train. Is that right?"

"He once was a friend of mine before I ever reached Morriston. But if he was there, I didn't meet him!"

Then he uttered a faint exclamation, for he was recalling the face which had appeared and disappeared at the door of the gaming room in which he had been sitting—the face which had so vaguely alarmed him that he had been on the point of rising from his chair and going out to make inquiry.

"You remember now, eh?" queried Nair sneeringly. "You met Rainier, and you heard a queer story from him of how a strange old fellow in the south had given him fifty thousand dollars and told him to ride north to find Nair and give James Nair that whole big sum of money, because it was coming to him legally."

"That money was coming to James Nair Cartwright," answered Train, "not to James Nair."

"Why?" roared Nair, falling back a stride.

"I tell you it was coming to Cartwright."

"Who the devil are you?" thundered Nair. "Have you been spying into my past?"

His rage was so sudden and so real that it seemed to Train, for the moment, that all his doubts must be foolish—this was Cartwright himself. How else might his passion of resentment be explained other than that, having lived a double life, he hoped that the first part of his existence might be remembered as that of a good and law-abiding citizen, while the second half had a new existence as a destroyer. But now he found that the chain of his history had been found and the missing links were told over. At least, this was one interpretation which could be placed upon his sudden fury.

"This much more, Logan," exclaimed Jim Nair. "When Train found out what his friend was doing, he stuck him up, took the coin away from him, and said he would tend to the delivering of it to himself. There was nothing for Rainier to do, because he was not a fighting man, but at least he had the courage to take a long chance and ride out to find me—at your expense, Chick!"

"Oh, I remember that well enough," growled out Chick Logan. "He got my pinto, but I'll have the heart out between his ribs, one of these days!"

"Now, then," said Nair, "having stolen fifty thousand dollars in cash which should have belonged to me and sat in my pocket the instant that Rainier found me, as he did find me, Train turns around and lays a pot to make more money still. He's not contented with the wrong that he's done me, but he decides that he'll collect still more coin at my expense. He decides, Logan, and mark you this, he decides that he'll try to worm his way into my gang and then use his position to betray me to the law. He talks of a detective. You can lay your wagers here and now that this Gresham, the detective, is working hand in glove with Train himself. Why? Because there is enough blood money in my murder to line both of their pockets!"

There was something at once diabolical and plausible in this explanation; it was founded, no doubt, upon a lie so black and treasonable on the part of Rainier, that even Train was taken back for the moment.

"That sounds bad!" admitted Chick Logan, scowling fiercely at Train, as though he would pluck the truth out of his heart. "But still I think that there must be some sort of an explanation. Steve, let's hear you talk."

"It ain't talk that Nair wants," replied Train slowly. "He wants action. There's too much money from the bank in that sack, and he doesn't want to split it with too many people. If he can get rid of me, that's one thing gained. If he can get rid of you afterward, that's a pile more gained, Chick. After that, he can bury part of the coin and show the gang only half of what he took. Can't you see that? Mighty easy to explain, too. He'll say that you and me had a fight—we dropped one another!"

A brutal snarl broke from the lips of Nair. For an instant he faced Train, trembling with concentrated fury. Then his hand whipped out his gun. Train had moved almost at the same instant; there was no excuse for him. He had been watching Nair as the cat watches the dog. But even so, he felt before his fingers touched the butt of his gun that he was lost. Still, he managed to get his Colt out; he heard his weapon explode, and at the same instant, or a fraction of a split part of a second before, the weapon roared from the hand of Nair. Red lightning darted across the eyes of Train—lightning flashed through a cloud of black which then closed across his brain. There was a hot, searing pain in his head, and he fell forward upon his face.

28

He wakened slowly. He seemed to be climbing a stairway infinitely long. Somewhere at the top there was consciousness, and gradually he dragged himself into it. The light grew upon his brain. And at length he was breathing, living once more.

He found that he was lying as he had fallen, flat upon his

face, which was buried in the damp pine needles. His head was one consuming, throbbing ache, and in his mind was the strange new knowledge that he had been faced by equal odds in battle, and that he had been beaten.

At length he pushed himself to his hands and knees. He was trembling with fatigue, and with the weakness of shattered nerves. When he finally had managed to shove himself into a sitting posture, he sat with his back against a sapling, grateful for that support and waiting for the sickness and the confusion to leave his mind. It was some minutes before he was enough himself to start examining the extent of his injury. Then, gingerly, with the tips of his fingers, he explored the wound. It began at the right-hand corner of his forehead, just beneath the line of the hair. There, at the place of impact, was a broad and deep cut, where the bullet had driven through to the bone, but, glancing luckily from the skull, the slug of lead had whipped a furrow along the side of his head.

Why had Nair left him living? He could only grasp at one possible explanation. That warrior and destroyer thought his man was dead. Indeed, such a wound, masked by the still flowing blood and accompanied by his complete insensibility, might well have seemed a mortal one. Next, with a start of terror, he fumbled for the packet which had contained the fifty thousand dollars which Comstock had committed to his care. It was gone!

But still, when he found the first pocket empty, he continued to search through every part of his clothes, hoping against hope, sick with the sense of his failure. There was no sign of the packet, however. Yet such was his sorrow for the loss, that he could not even then rest content with the certainty of it, but continued to hunt through the dense masses of the pine needles for the treasure which, he assured himself, might have slipped from his pocket. But no, it was not to be found, and he told himself, at last, that he was a fool of the first water to have imagined for an instant that the bandit chief could have failed to secure so huge a prize instantly upon the fall of his victim.

In the meantime, that search for the packet had fully roused him. The wound ceased aching, very nearly, so far greater was his mental distress. He was alert, alive, and on his feet, with his brain completely cleared, and a savage anger growing momently in him. He had dared so many dangers, he told himself, and endured so much in order to come to Nair, and now he had been struck down and the money taken from him by force. What a tale would this be to tell honest Patrick Comstock! And could Comstock be expected to believe such romancing?

He shook his head with a groan, and as he did so, a warm trickle coursed down his cheek. He must bind up the wound, he knew, if he expected that it would not be chilled and perhaps turn into a mortal hurt in spite of its surface nature. So he took off his undershirt and from the torn strips of it he made a bandage. It was slow work to make it and then to wind it around his head.

The bandaging was completed at last, and now he looked at his watch. Allowing about half an hour from the moment they fled from the town to the moment he was shot down by Nair, still the whole time since they left the looted bank had not been more than one hour or a few minutes more. He felt as though he had lain there among the needles unconscious for half the length of the night. In reality, his eyes must have been closed for only a few moments.

The resolution which he took then would have seemed foolish to any other. It was that, wounded as he was, and weak and trembling, he would attempt to follow on foot the course in which Nair had been walking and so come up with the two again. Or perhaps there would only be one by the time he arrived.

He could only hope for success, in such a course, if the outlaw leader had been walking straight toward his goal. He remembered that they had passed by a great, lightning-blasted stump of a burned tree. It was still visible in the mottling moonshine, and he placed himself in line between it and the spot where he had fallen. From this place he could sight forward through a gap in the tress before him to a great peak lying close to the eminence of Music Mountain. That must be his guiding mark. He considered it carefully; then he marched ahead with resolution.

There was this consolation, if no other, that the walking immensely recruited his spirits, stirred his blood, and took his attention from the ache of his wound. So he went on steadily, not daring to think whether he would succeed or fail in finding the outlaw chief, or what the outcome of a second battle with him could be, or, if the battle were successful if the packet of money could still be found on his person. Could he even be sure that Nair was not Cartwright? If he were, the goal was attained and his task had been accomplished involuntarily, so it would be folly for him to continue the pursuit. For, no matter what his personal feelings of humiliation might be because of the lost fight with Nair, he had no desire to renew the struggle. Nair, he felt, was his master, and nothing could make him risk a renewal of the fight except the doubt as to whether or not Nair were the true Cartwright. Yet, so long as that question were unsettled, he must strike ahead on the trail.

He came first on a small ranch house among the hills, and approaching it more closely, he found half a dozen perspiring horses standing in front of it. No doubt they were some of the searchers from the town of Creighton, who had paused here to refresh themselves and talk over the ardors of the pursuit. He smiled grimly to himself, at this, and, cutting a detour around the place, he went on.

In three quarters of an hour from the beginning of his journey, he dipped down from the crest of a small hollow, and in a central clearing, where a brook danced and chattered musically in the moonlight, he found a small house. It was a place which, at the first glance, he would have put down at once as uninhabited. Two or three sheds, which he could see to the rear of the building, had fallen completely in to disrepair, and one had broken down its supports with the weight of its roof.

As for the house itself, it had been too solidly constructed to collapse in a similar fashion, but he could see that the panes had been smashed from the windows and the door was merely propped in place to shut out some of the cold night air. He stole closer to the house, and venturing cautiously up on the rotten veranda, he came to an open window from which a light flickered blindly and feebly, not with the steady and soft radiance of a lamp.

Through that window he peered into the ruined living room of the old house. It was far gone. The plaster, falling from the ceiling, revealed the slats everywhere. Great cracks and seams had opened in the wall. The furniture which had been left when the house was abandoned consisted of a table staggering upon three bending legs and a few broken chairs. Lighting all of this sad destruction, on the hearth of the open fireplace some dead logs were burning, and by their illumination he saw that the room was occupied by four people. One was Nair himself, another was Chick Logan, and the other two were big Tom Curtney and his daughter Alice. She was busy serving coffee to the two wearied travelers. Last of all, he noticed the canvas sack, lying close in front of the feet of Nair.

The latter was untouched by any wound. The bullet which Train had fired must have flown wild, and yet he could have sworn that it was well centered upon the target when he pulled the trigger of his gun. He had simply been struck down by Nair's fire a shade of a second before he discharged his weapon, and so his aim had been spoiled. That was the explanation.

So he crouched at the window, and his heart swelled with satisfaction. For, although the game was still to be played to its conclusion, he felt that strong cards were in his hand. Curtney and his daughter now left the room to get something which they had left in another part of the house, and during the interval, Nair spoke swiftly to Chick Logan.

"Have you had enough chance to think things over now, Logan?"

"I been thinking," said Chick sullenly.

"What's your conclusion?"

"That Train helped frame the deal and played square with us, far as I can see. He ought to be here right now. Instead of that, you've left him back there for the buzzards to get or the coyotes!"

Nair frowned black upon his companion.

"You heard what I said to Train?"

"Where'd you learn them things about Train? From Rainier! And ain't Rainier proved himself to be a skunk? If he had something agin' Train, why didn't he fight it out with him instead of running to you for help?"

"He's not a fighting man. I've told you that!"

"I heard you say it. He's a sneak, I say."

"You hate him because he stuck you up, Chick. That's the main reason."

Chick shrugged his shoulders and glowered into the fire. But in the instant that his face was turned to the fire, Train saw a look of unspeakable cruelty and malice flash across the face of the outlaw. It was gone before Chick looked up again.

"Well," said Nair, "I suppose that you'll tell the boys what you think?"

"I dunno," said Chick. "Never seen you play a game like the one you've played tonight."

"Didn't I give Train a fair chance in the fight?"

"You grabbed your gun without no warning. You got the first move on him. I ain't no match for him, but even I might of had luck with a handicap like that on my side!"

There was a snarl of anger from Nair.

But Chick continued: "Tell what you've done to big Tom and Alice. See how they figure it!"

Nair exclaimed: "Leave them out of it. If you mention a word of what has happened to Alice—"

"Ah," murmured Chick, "you're turnin' on me, now?"

"You've talked like a fool, Chick!"

But at that moment, Curtney and his daughter returned; the debate between the two ended at once.

29

Two points in this debate offered the keenest satisfaction to Train. The one was that in the opinion of an eyewitness of the combat, he had been tricked rather than fairly beaten. The other was that Chick Logan had remained true to him. Even if the faith of the outlaw in his new-found friend had not made him attack Nair—and indeed such an action was hardly to be expected even from the most devoted friend—yet he was holding his head against the persuasion of Nair in the most indomitable fashion.

Curtney came back and threw down a rope in the corner of the room. Alice had brought in some sliced bacon and bread, and above the open fire, with dexterous hands, she now prepared to fry the bacon, which was soon hissing and smoking; its fragrance sent a stab of hunger through Train.

"You'd better take that gray gelding and the old brown mare, Jim," Curtney said to Nair. "They're in good shape. I haven't ridden either of them for a week. They're fresh, and they have the foot—plenty of it! If the Creighton people get on your trail, they'll have their work cut out trying to catch you."

"Will they?" asked Chick, challenging the last statement. "I tell you that they's one hoss in that outfit that'll run over anything else in the mountains. It's the mare that—"

But here a murderous glance from Nair cut him short, and he mumbled the next words.

"What mare?" asked Alice, turning from the fire.

"I dunno. Just a fine chestnut. She was a free goer, I'd tell a man."

"You started out as though you knew her," said the girl. "I almost thought, from the way you started, that she was a champion."

"She had the looks," muttered Chick Logan.

"But there's nothing in the mountains to touch that Whimsy mare," added the girl thoughtfully. "You ought to know that, Chick! Why, I thought that you were out with him, making the trip?"

"Oh, him?" said Chick, still muttering and with growing confusion.

"Have you seen that mare?" broke in Nair sharply, to turn the conversation.

"Whose? Train's?"

"Yes."

"I saw her, of course, when he talked to me the day he shot poor old Jerry."

At the word, the wolf dog lifted his head in the corner of the room and growled softly, flattening his ears in token of submission to the voice which he loved.

"The hound!" exclaimed Nair. "He should have had a bullet put in himself, for that. That would teach him to——"

"You don't understand. Jerry was running a deer. And he looked enough like a lofer to fool Train. He came out and told me about it. Didn't I tell you?" replied Alice.

"No," said Nair, willing enough, so it seemed, to have the conversation follow this bent. "You didn't tell me what he said or what he did."

"He has nerve," answered the girl, looking far off with thoughtful eyes. "He went right up to Jerry and gave him his hand. Think of that—put his hand right against Jerry's nose! And Jerry sniffed it, and started wagging his tail. My blood ran cold to watch the two of them. They made me think of two wolves meeting—Train the bigger one of the pair, you know."

"You didn't like his looks, then?" said Nair with some eagerness.

"I didn't say that. At least, I liked the way he handled Jerry. Who else on Music Mountain would have the courage to come that close to Jerry, even when Jerry wasn't wounded?"

She turned with a bright smile of mischief. "Would you be brave enough for that, Jim?"

"To put my hand within an inch of his nose?"

"Yes, and take the chance of having it bitten off at one snap?"

The outlaw shuddered.

"Of course you wouldn't," said the girl. "But Train seems to have no fear of anything."

If comparisons are odious, at least this one made Nair flush with anger, as though he felt himself degraded from a high position which was his right. And Train, listening hungrily at the window, smiled to himself as he saw the pride and the envy in the face of the outlaw.

"He may have a trick with dogs," said Nair at last. "But I'd take a chance where any other man in the world would take one. Besides, I think that Jerry ought to know me. I've been around him long enough. Eh, boy?"

The last was addressed in a most conciliatory tone to the big brute in the corner, but Jerry regarded Nair with unblinking, expressionless eyes.

"Don't go near him, Jim," cautioned Curtney. He had been sitting in a corner of the room, all this time, apparently lost in the deeps of thought and paying no attention to the conversation of the others. But now he left his abstraction and cautioned Nair again.

"Even I can't do much with Jerry. He will obey Alice, but I don't think there's another person in the world who could handle him."

"Except Steve Train," said the girl.

The taunt acted like a whip to Nair. He started at once to his feet.

"We'll see about that," he declared.

"Jim!" exclaimed Curtney. "Don't be an ass! I say, you can't handle that beast."

"He's afraid of me," said Nair with great resolution. "Look at him now, cowering in front of me. Bah, Tom! If I can handle men with guns, I can handle dogs with teeth. Steady, Jerry!"

So saying, he approached the dog, holding out his hand, speaking very softly.

155

"Jim," called Curtney, "you'll make me kill the dog if he takes a jump at you."

He reached for his revolver which hung in the cartridge belt that was suspended from the back of the nearest broken chair, but Alice caught his arm.

"Hush!" she whispered. "I just want to see—"

Her curiosity, with such a creature as Jerry pitted against a man, even such a giant of a man as Nair was in strength, seemed to Train a rather horrible thing. In fact, he began to look at her with new eyes. In the meantime, Nair had come close to Jerry, and began to bring his hand slowly to the nose of the wolf dog. The latter had not moved, as though not sure that he had been picked out by this advance of Nair's, until the latter was just before him. Then he gathered himself suddenly together, crouching low, his hair bristling, a devil of green hatred coming in his eyes. A growl which seemed to be tearing his throat to shreds issued from between his bare teeth and set his body trembling. In man or beast, Train thought that he had never seen such a formidable fury.

And then he glanced to the girl. She was watching with rather a pale face, steadily, seeming to study the situation as though it were a book which she was reading. Nair stepped back, muttering an oath beneath his breath. While Jerry sank down again to his place of rest, Nair turned to the others and exposed to them a face black with anger and beaded with perspiration.

"The devil is in that brute," he said savagely. "All that I need is a little time and—my own ways with him!"

"What would you do?" asked the girl.

"Do?" exclaimed Nair. "The whip! That's what I'd use with him," he went on, mastering himself quickly.

She did not answer him directly, but she said softly: "Here, boy."

Jerry rose, displaying his immense size of shoulder and length of leg, and in spite of the weight of his body, crossed the floor with no sound other than that of a slight scratching of his nails. He couched himself at the feet of his mistress. Still his size was so great that he could lay his head upon her knee, and there he looked steadily, with the love of a slave, into her face.

"He'll do you harm, one of these days," cautioned Nair.

But she shook her head. "We understand each other—Jerry and I!" she said.

156

And she passed her slender fingertips deeply through the ruff of fur which coated his neck. The great bushy tail swept the floor rhythmically.

In the meantime, the bacon having been cooked, was eaten with the bread and a second cup of coffee all around. After that Nair rose to his feet, but he seemed to be hesitating.

"I want to talk to your father alone," he said at last to Alice. "Will you and Chick make yourselves happy in some other place."

They hastened to assure him that they would go, and so they left the room, with the huge wolf dog gliding behind them. Already the long and deep wound in the shoulder of Jerry had been almost healed by the free action of the air and the strength of a perfectly healthy body. Train noted that, as the monster went by the window.

30

When the two older men were left together, Curtney asked at once: "What's happened, Jim? No, I don't want to know. I suppose one more wild raid—one more robbery. Jim, you have changed since the old days!"

Under the steady, large voice and the hidden scorn of the other, Nair winced. "A man has to live," he said gloomily.

Curtney made a vague gesture of assent and shrugged his shoulders.

"Now," said Nair, "what does Alice say?"

"About you?"

"Of course."

"She says, against all my persuasion, that she has given her word to you and that she'll keep it."

"Against all of your persuasion?" echoed Nair bitterly.

"What else did you expect from me? I told you freely where I stood in the matter. You must have understood that when we talked together about this matter."

"I understood, or thought I did, that you knew I was working for your happiness as well as my own."

"My happiness?" said Curtney gently. "I tell you, Jim, that you are a thousand times kind to me. I believe with all my heart that you are truly a friend to me."

Nair flushed. "After these years, I hope that much is demonstrated," he said.

"It is not so simple," replied Curtney. "I'll tell you now, Nair, that I have often had my suspicions."

"Of what?"

"You have taken every step in your life for the sake of gaining an advantage for yourself against the world."

"What could I gain from you, speaking frankly?"

"The friendship of an honest man, Jim."

"Are you the only one I know? You see, we're both to speak frankly."

"By all means! Yes, Jim, I'm about the only one you know."

"Nonsense, Tom! I have adherents scattered up and down the range."

"Rascals who hope for reward; weak people who admire your strength; cowards who fear you!"

"Tom, I'd take that from no other man living."

The other frowned. "Don't tell me what you'd take. I'm talking about facts as I see them. I say that I know most of your life has been black as the night; it has made me suspect even your relations with me. You wanted, I used to think, one honest friend, because in your heart of hearts, you knew that the friendship of rascals is so much empty air and cannot be depended on. But you knew that if you could count on me, you'd have strong help without pay."

"That's hard talk, Tom," said Nair, controlling his raging temper only with the greatest exertion of his will.

"I'm opening my heart to you, my friend."

"Tom, will you say that I've had no cause to break the law?"

"You mean, because you failed in business and had hard luck, which was no fault of yours, in the East, before you came West?"

Train could have groaned, for in that sentence he heard what surely seemed the fullest possible identification of Nair as James Nair Cartwright. The money, then, belonged to him. For he knew that Cartwright had passed through exactly what Nair seemed to have undergone.

"Bad luck is a mild thing to call it. I was beaten—squeezed dry! I say, society owed me something. I couldn't get it; so I went out and took it by force."

"You've taken ten dollars for one, and you know it. For

158

every dollar society stole from you, as you'd put it, you took back ten. That's rank usury, Jim!"

"You've fixed your mind on looking at the worst side of my case."

"It isn't a case. Except for one thing. I earnestly believe that the one exception is that you've been a true friend to me, Jim. I wavered a bit when you told me that you want to marry Alice, but let that go with the rest."

"God knows, Tom, that I never thought of such a thing until quite recently. But let's talk of her."

"You'll be no better pleased by what I have to tell you of her."

"Ah?" Nair opened his eyes like one who sees a gun suddenly pointed at his heart. "Do you mean it, Tom?"

"I do."

"What has she said? I thought—I was sure, when I came in, that she'd changed toward me."

"She doesn't love you, Jim."

The big man sagged. Then he shook his head like one trying to clear one's brain after a heavy shock.

"A woman can be taught to love a man," he said slowly. "I've seen it done!"

"I've heard of it, but I've never seen it. Well, let that go. She says that she'll go through with her contract; she's given you her promise."

"Has she complained to you, Tom?"

"That's not her way. I've only guessed at the truth. I've talked to her and tried to persuade her from this marriage. Her answer has always been the same—that she has given you her word!"

"Ah!" exclaimed Nair, vastly relieved. "She has not said she did not love me, Tom? You've only guessed at that?"

"Nonsense, man! Does one have to be told such things? Did you see her face when you came in tonight? Was it the face of a girl meeting the man she loves?"

"What should she do?" answered Nair sullenly. "Run at me and throw her arms around my neck, in front of Logan? Of course she wouldn't act like that. She has too much pride!"

"The proudest woman that ever lived," said Tom Curtney, "can't help changing when the man she loves comes near her. In the name of Heaven, Jim," he cried, his voice changing until it was charged with pity and almost with horror, "have you no idea of what a good woman is like when she comes near the man she loves?"

"I haven't been interested in such things," said Nair, more gloomily than ever. "I've wasted no time around girls. I've been busy with other things."

"Nair, I watched you when you came in tonight. You're a fairly hard man; as hard as any man I've ever laid eyes upon, but when you saw Alice, you changed color, your eyes grew bigger, you could hardly speak."

Nair flushed. "I'd been coming a long distance," he said. "Besides, I've been through excitement tonight."

"Excitement never affected a man like that. It was love, Nair. Confess it! And if love changed even a man like you, what would it have done to Alice? Her heart would have been seen in her face as easily as if she were made of glass. No, no, Jim! You are a clever fellow in every other way, but with women, you are a simpleton. Forgive me if I tell you that. There was the affair of the dog, tonight. What under heaven possessed you to try to master Jerry offhand, in that fashion?"

"Why not? She challenged me to it!"

"She only told you that Train had done it."

"Am I to let another man pass me? And let her know it?"

"You let her know it in the end; you let her see you afraid."

A great oath tore from the lips of Nair. "I'll throttle the brute before I'm done with it!" he vowed.

"You throttle all chances of winning the love of Alice at the same instant," Curtney said calmly.

"In Heaven's name, Tom, are you judging me through a dog?"

"I'm telling you where you were rash. If you'd known that Alice was testing you, you wouldn't have taken such a wild gambling chance."

"Train had done the same thing," said Nair.

"Train seems to be a remarkable fellow."

"Train is—" blurted out Nair, and then checked himself.

"Train is what? I'd like to see something of him. Alice chatters about him half of every evening—how he looked—what he wore—how he rode his horse—what he said and how he swung his guns in Morriston when he fought for me and for her!"

"I wish I had been there," said the outlaw through his teeth.

"So do I. You would have seen one of the finest pieces of cool courage I've ever looked at. When we left the town, afterward, my heart was fainting in me. I felt myself going and decided that I wouldn't let Train see my weakness. I was ashamed of it, Jim. So I sent him on his way as rudely as though he were simply in my way and had never been of use to me. He took it like a man, Jim. Looked me fairly in the eye and didn't say a word. Almost any other man of spirit would have damned me as an ingrate."

"He seems to have his points," said Nair, with a dry lack of enthusiasm which Train could perfectly well understand, no matter how odd it might seem to Tom Curtney. "But let's leave him and get back to something important. When we're married, where do we start for?"

"Yes, I have a good deal to say about that. I have to tell you—"

There was so much stern decision in the voice of Curtney that Nair broke in: "You have to know the full truth, Tom. I told you I had several hundred thousand put away. But tonight has given me something more."

He raised the canvas sack and dumped the contents upon the surface of the table.

"There must be a quarter of a million there, Tom," he said. "Count it if you wish. I simply estimated it."

"I'll take your word for it. Somebody gave it to you, I suppose?"

"Of course," said Nair, smiling with sudden satisfaction as he handled the packages of money. He added: "And here's another fifty thousand in hard cash that I've just secured. Altogether, Tom, I may say that here's about three hundred thousand dollars. There you are, Tom. We're made forever No need to worry about where we go or what we do, for I imagine that half a million and well over, at six per cent, will give us enough of an income to live on!"

Curtney shook his head. "This is what I wanted to tell you, Jim. I'll never take a cent of your money. I'll never use a horse you own, a saddle you ride in; or a house that covers your head. I've thought it out carefully since we talked together last. I changed my name and came West determined on doing very much what you've done, Jim. But I found that I couldn't. There was one thing too strong for me, and that was the power of honesty that's born in a man, I suppose. And that's what will keep me from using the help you're so generous as to offer me. I can't do it, Jim. This is three hundred thousand dollars of good coin to you. To me it is so much dirt—worse than dirt. It's stolen goods, my friend, and I'll have none of it!"

31

Shooting at one target, Curtney had struck another. Every syllable he spoke went home in the heart of Train. It was as though some one had asked big Tom Curtney to sum up in a forceful manner all the vague thoughts and the drifting emotions which had been passing through the mind of the gambler during the past days. Here was the case made up neatly and presented to him for judgment. He saw before him, again, the faces of a hundred men whom he had encountered in his travels. All of them had been weaker than he in some respect, and yet he had felt in them a greater underlying power. It was this which made old Comstock so insignificant. It was that which had raised Gresham to the very threshold of success in this pursuit. It was the strength of honesty. Formidable as he knew Nair to be, the big man grew small indeed before Tom Curtney.

Like a hunted thing Nair glanced from side to side, seemed to rack his brain in the hunt for arguments, and found none worth uttering. He could only fumble at the money with his strong fingers, but though the money had a ringing voice for him, Curtney was deaf to it.

"Who is this man?" said Train to himself. "And why has he changed his name?"

There was no answer to those questions. And though he bent every nerve to follow keenly the rest of the conversation, he could not draw the clews he wanted out of what was said.

But he knew with a wonderful surety, from that instant forward, that his old self was gone. The gallant and reckless adventurer who had dealt crooked cards and drawn guns and ridden wildly up and down the mountains, taking fame and money wherever he went, was dead. There was a new self in Steve Train, and that new self was something delightfully new, unexplored, and full of strengths of which the old self had had no knowing.

Suddenly, all doubts left him. If he faced Nair again, he would not go down. He could not. For justice was now with him, and the strength of the law was his strength. A thousand shadows flickered across the corners of his brain—evil deeds of stealth and cunning which he had performed in a thousand far-off places. God give him strength to rub them all away, and out of his memory, if he could, with one large action in the cause of right.

The fiery zeal of the new convert flooded him, and the same wild confidence. It was a new religion to Train. It was an emotion and a conception greater than himself. Always, before, he had been campaigning to take swiftly and largely from the world and make no return; what he wanted to do now was to give, with all his strength, and still give more. He had passed through a great and guarded gate. He was on the inside of the wall, now, to hold the fort against the hungry marauders who prowled on the outside through the night.

"I see now," Nair was saying, "that you've hated me all these years, and simply kept back what you thought."

"Far from it. Far, far from it, Jim!" said the other. "If I haven't approved of what you have been doing, I haven't felt that I was capable of making a judgment. Your business is your own business. In the name of Heaven, live your own life according to your own lights. I simply tell you, honestly, what my feelings are."

"I suppose," said Nair darkly, "that Alice is to hear all of this?"

"Not a word. She has come of age. She can decide these matters to suit her own convenience. I may speak against her marriage with you, but I shall never speak against you."

"What is her own opinion?"

"Of your—way of making a living?"

"Yes."

"She hardly has thought much about it, I think. She simply remembers what you have told her, at some time or other, which is, that you were cheated out of certain properties when you were a younger man and that you are honestly convinced that society owes you reparation for your losses. As for what you have taken back from society already, I don't think that that subject has entered her mind. She's known you for years, Jim. I think she takes it for granted that the good in you is far greater than the evil. But—tell me how you managed to persuade her to promise you marriage?"

163

"I—we won't talk about it," said Nair shortly. "Curtney, you've hurt me more than I've ever been hurt before. Suppose I try you for the last time. When I say that I'll take this money and that all three of us will live on it, perhaps you think that I'm talking through my hat. Is it that, Tom? But I tell you, I'll deed you whatever portion of the money you want. There are three of us. I'll give you your third in cash. You can do with it what you want."

"You're a thousand times too generous. Not a cent, Jim. But tell me how you can have all of it to dispose of?"

"Why, you see it in my hands, don't you?"

"Aye, but there's your gang. You split your profits with them."

"The gang shall never see me again."

"You are breaking with them?"

"Did you think," said Nair, with something akin to honest indignation, "that I can be the husband of Alice and the leader of such a crew at one and the same time? Tom, you underrate me!"

"I was only asking. I was not accusing. But then you have forgotten another factor and an important one. What of Logan?"

"Well, what of him?"

"He helped you get that money tonight, did he not?"

"Perhaps. Perhaps a little."

"Will he let you walk off without giving him his share of the loot?"

"*Let* me? I can manage Logan and ten like him. He's had enough money. If he had more, the fool would simply gamble it away. I tell you, he's made enough working for me and under me. He can get on very well without his share of this."

Tom Curtney regarded his guest with a quiet eye, but it seemed to Train that he could read in the face of the older man the growing scorn and contempt and disgust.

"You have capacities of which I knew nothing," he said at length. "I begin to see that, Jim!"

"Would you have me rob Alice in order to line the pockets of an ordinary thief?" asked Nair, again with that same ring of generous indignation.

But Curtney raised a hand to compel silence; then he filled and lighted his pipe and returned to an earnest contemplation of the fire.

"Tell me one thing," said Nair at last, softly. "How would you get on if I took Alice away with me?"

"I? Very well! A little loneliness, but I could stand that."

"And your heart, man?"

"The sooner the better. Never a man was born more ready to die than I am now. However, I presume there'll be no hurry about your marriage with Alice?"

"I'll talk it over with her. I'll talk to her, as a matter of fact, right now!"

"Bring her in here. I'll walk out."

"No! Stay where you are; I'll find her. Stay where you are, Tom."

He swept his securities and money from the surface of the table and into the yawning mouth of the canvas bag, which he then drew shut again and slung lightly across his shoulder. Then, waving his hand to Curtney he strode away through the doorway. The latter started half from his chair, as though to call Nair back, but thinking better of it, he sank back, with an expression of the most terrible concern on his face. However, he shrugged his shoulders as though he were striving to get rid of a burden, and then settled again to a steady contemplation of the burning logs. Yet it was plain that he was tense with anxiety. For presently, when a log burned in two and fell to the hearth with a slight noise, sending up a great, bright cloud of sparks, Curtney started again so violently that the chair rocked with his bulky weight.

What impelled Train to do it, he could not tell, but as though destiny took him bodily and forced him forward, he stood up, slipped through the window, and stood inside the room. What danger he thereby invited upon his head, he could not even guess. At any moment Nair might return, and if Nair saw him, he would receive a bullet through the back. There was no doubt of that. Yet he was forced by an irresistible desire to talk with this big, quiet man.

He stood for a moment inside the window, apparently unnoticed, but then Curtney, without turning his head, removed the pipe from between his teeth and said: "Well?"

Train did not speak, and the query was repeated: "What do you wish?"

"Talk!" said Train bluntly.

At his voice, Curtney turned his head hastily and frowned at his strange visitor—frowned at his dusty, travel-stained clothes, and then at the bandage around his head, and at the dark streak which covered one side of his face.

"Do you know me?"

"I do not," said Curtney.

"I am Train."

"You're in trouble, Train?"

"Tolerable much."

"Followed?"

At that mild statement of the facts, Train could not avoid a smile, and he indulged himself broadly before he answered his questioner.

"Surrounded," he said quietly. "They're coming from Creighton behind me, most like, and Nair is in front of me."

"Nair?"

"Yes."

"What's he to you?"

"This!" And he pointed to the bandage which surrounded his head.

"Nair did that, then?"

"He did."

"When?"

"There was three men that robbed the Creighton Bank."

"Ah?" murmured Curtney. "And on the way, you quarreled?"

"Nair quarreled."

"Now you've come for what? Your share of the loot, or a gun fight? And, above all, what makes you want to talk to me?"

"Because," said Train, "as a talker you lay over any I've ever heard. When I got to that window, yonder, I was two thirds crooked and one third straight. Then I listened to you, and now, maybe, I'm two thirds straight and one third crooked." He smiled again in his peculiar way.

"Do you know that Nair is apt to come back into this room at any moment?"

"I been sort of hopin' that he might."

"You mean to fight, then?"

"If I have to."

"One beating in a night isn't enough for you?"

Train set his teeth and answered through them: "Not half, Mr. Curtney!"

He saw a faint glitter come into the eyes of the older man,

and the gleam was not one of anger or disapproval. Of that he could be sure.

"Now, Train, what do you expect from me?"

"That you'll stop that wedding."

Curtney stirred again. "Young man," he said, "you've listened at that window like a spy."

"Thank God that I did, say I. I stayed and heard you say that you'd let her pick and choose for herself, and the next minute I heard you say that she didn't know anything about Nair. Is that fair to her?"

"Listen to me, my young friend: When I was a youngster and engaged to a girl, her family undertook to stop the marriage. At that time I swore that I'd never interfere with any of the fancies of my own daughter, if I should ever have one. Now I live up to my vow. Do you understand that?"

"There's a difference between persuasion and tellin' the facts. Let her listen two minutes while you tell her nothing but the facts about Nair. Let her listen only to what he's done tonight and how he figures on double crossing Logan. Do you think she'll stand for that?"

"Do you know her, Train?"

"I do."

"How many times have you talked to her?"

"Once."

The big man twisted in his chair and squarely faced the other.

"Train, what does this mean?"

"No matter what. I seen her and I knew her at one look."

"Then tell me what she is?"

"As clean as virgin rock, Mr. Curtney, as true as the steel in the bit of a drill, and as silly as a yearling in a burning barn."

To this brief and rapid summing up, Curtney responded with a smile that lighted his face strangely and made him seem, for the instant, a full half score of years younger.

"You are an odd chap, Train," he said quietly. "You have come in here and taken a chance of having your head blown off by Nair for the sake of saving that same silly girl. Is that it?"

"That's one way of putting it."

"Will you talk with her yourself?"

"To do that, I'll have to meet Nair again."

"And you're willing to meet him?"

"When I meet him again," said Train very soberly, "I'll kill him, and there's the end."

At that Curtney became grave enough. "Very well," he said. "A fair fight is a fair fight. But—what made you join Nair?"

"I had to join him in order to meet him."

"What do you mean by that?"

"It's too long a story to tell."

"Make it a short one."

"I can, I think. There's an honest gent who gets a young friend into a bad bit of business; the friend goes broke; he won't take no help; he blows West to start things again and he leaves behind him the bum stock that he'd picked up. Some of that stock comes to life a lot of years later, and the honest man sells and cleans up fifty thousand on the shares that belong to the gent that went West. You follow the drift of that?"

"I follow you. Then the honest man pockets the money, I presume?"

"You put on the wrong brand that time. The honest man has lost track of his friend, but he hears about a crook in the mountains that has a name with part of the same run to it. He takes the fifty thousand and hunts around to find somebody who'll take that money to the crook, because the crook is outlawed and the honest man can't get at him any other way. Understand?"

"Very clearly! A strange story, Train. But who could he find to trust fifty thousand dollars in cash to?"

"Try hard to keep from laughin'. He found me!"

"Ah?"

"That's right. I wanted to laugh, too. But when I started off to put the coin in my pocket, I got to thinking the thing over. The old gent was such a good, trusting chap that I couldn't double cross him. God knows how hard I tried to, but I just nacherally couldn't persuade myself."

He paused and shook his head, still wondering at the thing he had done.

"Well," said Train, "the crook in the case was Nair."

There was an exclamation from Curtney.

"Sound queer to you? It sounded queer to me, too. But the old gent was positive, so I started on Nair's trail. Finally, I joined his gang to have a chance to meet up with him and hand over the coin, but when I met up with him, doggone me

168

if he didn't seem a long shot from being a gent that had ever been honest. I couldn't figure him that way. So I keeps that money back while I have a think about it and look things over.

"While I was still thinking, along comes this bank deal, and I thought I had to play my hand in along with the rest of 'em. Otherwise, I'd of had no chance to stay close by Nair and study him. The deal went through, as you seen tonight. But while it was going through, Nair made me feel pretty sure that he couldn't be the man that I was after and that owned that fifty thousand by rights.

"In the meantime, there was another angle to the job. A crook that had introduced me to the honest gent for the sake of trimming him thought I'd double crossed him when I didn't hand over his share of the loot. He went to Nair, it seems, and told him that *he'd* been given the coin to take to Nair, and that I'd stuck him up and grabbed it. So tonight, on the way out of Creighton, Nair accuses me and reaches for a gun. I wake up with the money gone. I patch up my head and follow him on, and here I am!"

"By the heavens," said Curtney, "the very queerest story that I've ever heard. What was the stock?"

"That the honest man sold?"

"Yes."

"Oil stock."

Curtney removed the pipe from his mouth and stared. The his eyes widened still more.

He said suddenly, "Was the name of the honest man Comstock?"

It was the turn of Train to be amazed.

"Comstock is the name," he admitted, astonished. "How did you gather that much?"

"And the man you were to take the money to was James Cartwright!"

"Look here!" gasped out Train, "have you been reading my mind? What do you know of James Nair Cartwright!"

"I can tell you more about him than any other person in the world."

"Let go with it, then!"

"You are looking at Cartwright now!"

"You?" cried Train.

They stared at one another through a long moment. Then

169

Curtney struck his hands together. "And Nair knew who the money was intended for?"

"Of course. Rainier must have told him. That's the crook I was speaking of."

"He took the money, then, knowing that it belonged to me. That was the packet he showed me and said it was fifty thousand from another source."

"He's cool enough," said Train. "I heard him say it. Now what's next?"

"To talk quietly with Mr. Nair, I presume, will be the next step," said Curtney, but his face was like iron.

"Will you tell me how that mix-up of names come about?"

"Easily. The life of my father was saved by a man named James Nair. He gave his son—that is to say, he gave me—the name of his preserver. That accounts for James Nair Cartwright. As for James Nair whom you have seen, he has the same name that his father wore. The mystery is a very simple one, after all!"

"So far it's cleared up, but how did Nair happen to land in the same part of the West that you was in?"

"He got into trouble. I'd been in touch with him on the last of my business affairs. When he left the East—and he was forced to run for it, in the end—he came out to me. That was the beginning of his career."

"Suppose you tell him some of the facts?" asked Train. "What will he do now?"

"I can't guess. I wonder what lie he will use. But at least, Alice must hear what he has to say."

At the thought of this, Train's smile was broad indeed.

"I'll be back outside the window again," he said. "If there is a gun play starting, you'll hear from me, and you'll hear pronto!"

"What a consummate and perfect rascal that fellow is, and what an abominable hypocrite!" said James Cartwright.

A step sounded at the other end of the house.

"There's Nair now," warned Cartwright. And Train was instantly outside the window.

It was Logan, however, who came to the doorway, yawning.

"All right, Mr. Curtney," he said. "I guess I'll be blowing along on my way, too. I'll take the stuff that Nair left with you for me."

"What stuff?" asked Cartwright.

"What stuff?" cried Logan. "D'you aim to beat me out of what's my own right? And what belongs to the whole gang?"

"You're talking like a madman," said Cartwright. "I have nothing for you."

The fingers of Logan dropped to the butt of his gun and fumbled it.

"Curtney," he said, "I've always treated you as good as I've treated anybody. And I've always thought that you was square. But if you try to double cross me and the rest of the boys, I'll let you know here and now that you don't get away with it!"

"Logan," said Cartwright, "you can search me and every inch of the house. Nair was joking with you. Call him in and ask him, if you wish to make sure."

"Call him back? How can I call him back when he's gone on the brown hoss?"

"What's that?" cried Train, leaping back through the window.

At the new voice, Logan turned, and threw up his arms with a yell of dismay, cowering behind his hands.

"It wasn't me that done it," he cried. "Don't bring his ghost to me—"

"I'm no ghost, Logan," said Train. "Wake up, Chick. I'm no ghost, as Nair is going to find out before morning, if I have luck. What do you mean when you say that he's gone?"

"Why, he said that he'd left my share and the share of the gang with Curtney and that him and the girl was to ride off together and that they'd planned to meet Curtney later on, some place or other in the mountains, back behind Music Mountain."

32

Here, then, was the thunderstroke which crushed both Train and Cartwright. The latter cast at the younger man a glance of agony and of despair. For the moment he could not speak.

"Did the girl leave any word behind her?" asked Train grimly of Chick Logan.

"She did," said Chick. "It was a queer thing, but she pulled me aside and she told me to tell Mr. Curtney that she was going with Jim Nair because Jim said that her father wanted her to do so, and that she'd not the strength to face Curtney right then and say good-by. But that when she met him in the morning—"

Here he was interrupted by a hoarse cry of rage from Cartwright.

"Listen," said Train swiftly to Chick. "He's double crossed all of us. He left no money with Curtney for you or for the gang. He's gone and gone for good, and you'll never clap eyes on him again unless the three of us can ride him down tonight. Do you understand? He's lied to this girl and taken her away to marry her—"

It was impossible for Train to put his rage and grief into words. He choked and then turned to Cartwright, who was saying: "How can we trail them by night?"

"We got to take our chance," said Train. "Better to start riding than to sit here and let things drift. We got one chance in a million."

They rushed from the house like men possessed, and caught horses from among those which belonged to Cartwright. But the two freshest and choicest ones were backed by the girl and Nair. There was only Cartwright's saddle left, but Train and Logan mounted bareback and prepared to make the best of it.

"Train, lead the way for us!" commanded Cartwright.

"I've only one guess. D'you know the way to the nearest minister's house?"

There was a groan from Cartwright.

"Do you think it's that, Train?"

"No doubt about it. He's told her that you want them to marry and marry quick, so's the three of you can make a jump to some other country and settle down with half a million among you split three ways. And she's going along because it makes her so plumb sick to think that you'd tell her that she couldn't wait here to face you and say good-by to you."

Another man would have raved and raged, but Cartwright merely sighed.

"Follow me," he said. "I know the way to the nearest minister's!"

He led the way at a gallop, and they fled through the forest at close to full speed, twisting this way and that among the trees, and driving across open fields, regardless of the more roundabout paths and roads which they might have followed.

For five miles they toiled on. Then they came to the softly glimmering lights of a little town, and through it they rushed madly. In front of a little gray house which nestled beside the church, Cartwright threw himself from his saddle, but it was Train who reached the door first and raised a small thundering through the house with his knock.

A woman opened the door.

"The minister!" cried Train.

"Oh—oh," she gasped out, choked with fear. "I don't know —Who are you?"

Train went by her at a bound. One glance showed him that the downstairs rooms were vacant. He leaped up the stairs, and in a little barren room which was used as a study, he found the white-haired minister, in the act of rising and closing a book. He started back at the sight of Train.

"Friend," said Train, "you married a couple tonight."

"Yes," gasped the minister. "But what's wrong in that?"

"Listen to me! A middle-aged man and a girl of twenty?"

"Who am I to say who shall and who shall not marry, young man?"

"A tall man with black eyes—and a mighty pretty girl?"

"Yes. A very striking couple," admitted the minister, growing more complacent.

"You fool!" groaned Train. "It was Jim Nair. It was Jim Nair!"

If he had fired a gun in the face of the minister the effect could not have been more terrible. By the time he had leaped through the door, that good old man had dropped upon his knees and was praying to God to undo the wrong which had been worked by his innocent hands.

Train was already downstairs with a leap, sweeping the other two along with him, and as he ran he gave them the terrible news.

"It's done!" cried Train again, as he sat on his horse, impatient for his slower companions to mount and ride again, "but God willing, we'll undo it before the morning's over!"

"We should have better horses; we might get them here in town—"

"No time! No time!" commanded Train. "Get on, in Heaven's name, while the trail is hot!"

He had already picked the course that they should follow. Speed would be the main thing in the mind of Nair, and having left the house of the minister, he would drive across the country as fast as he could put miles behind him. South and south and south he would work, toward the border. Once across the Rio Grande the law would never take him, and the girl would be lost forever; lost, indeed, if Nair were not overtaken before the day came.

"She'll understand that something is wrong when she sees him riding straight on," said Cartwright, striving to argue himself into hope as they swept out of town and drove southward, "and when she guesses at that, she'll turn back. He'll not be able to force her to go with him."

"He'll need no force," insisted Train, shattering this pleasant illusion at a stroke. "He'll have a hundred lies to tell her. Trust Nair for that. If he fooled you these years, couldn't he fool a young girl like that for one night?"

There was a stifled shout from Cartwright, and again they pushed ahead desperately through the night. But presently the horse of Cartwright began to fall back. His great weight was a handicap which it could not withstand. Logan would have pulled up for him, but Train would not listen to delay.

"We'll lose him if we turn. We'll lose him if we halt once more," he said. "He's well mounted, and we have nags. Think of the amount of time he gained on us on the ride to the town? Enough to get married in!"

"That was because I waited a while before I came into the house and told you that they were gone."

"Partly that; partly fast riding. Keep on."

He called over his shoulder: "Keep coming as you can, partner. We're going on!"

"Brave lads!" shouted Cartwright falling behind, more and more hopelessly distanced every moment. "Keep on. Ride hard. Fight hard. The fifty thousand, Train! It's for you and Logan if you win; it's for you and Logan if you come near enough to exchange shots with him—remember."

His voice died away in the rattle of the hoofs and the increasing distance and the wind in their faces. They rode on once more, two instead of three. One thing at least was in their favor. Before them the pass clove straight through the heart of the mountains. Music Mountain rose huge and cloudy to the west, bathed in the moonshine. That way, unless Nair were a fox indeed, he must be riding.

Aye, if they needed proof, now came a faint yell, wavering far before them, like the cry of a wolf hunting.

But Logan knew the call. "It's Jerry on a trail!" he cried. "and we're right, Steve."

Train said nothing. He was riding as a jockey rides, studying every inch of the way before them, easing his horse up the slopes, steadying it down the inclines, picking his path with as much care as though it were a mile race and not a cross-country drive of unknown length.

But as they pressed on, Chick Logan asked what the shout about fifty thousand dollars meant. To him, then, Train told the whole story, speaking by fits and starts, as the exigencies of the wild ride gave him opportunity, and Chick Logan answered for comment with streams of weird oaths.

He said at the end: "I only want to live for two things, partner. I want to kill Rainier; I want to help kill Nair. He's too much for me alone, but I want to get in one shot, even if he drills me clean the next second!"

To all of this, Train answered not a word, for he was holding a greater converse; he was praying as his horse swung forward with nodding head and laboring body up the incline of the pass. There might be something; there were mysteries in this world, and though he had doubted them all before, he might learn to believe them afterward. If only he could believe them now.

And he said to himself that good men and great had believed in the truth of a God. Who was he, then, to doubt? Who was he to believe in a horse and gun and the speed and the strength of his hands only? For something more than speed and strength, he told himself, must come to his aid now.

33

The wolf cry sounded far through the night again. How could he tell? That cry in itself might be the message sent by the Almighty to guide him on to the goal he had chosen. And he himself, dark though his life had been, might on this night be the hand by which God would work a good deed on earth.

And as he thought of this, he felt his heart leap and swell in him with a new strength and a calmer courage. It seemed that his very horse felt the difference in the rider, for the poor nag began to draw ahead of Logan's mount.

"Keep back with me! Pull up, Steve!" begged Logan. "You can't handle that job alone. You got to have help; Nair ain't human. Nair'll beat you if you tackle him alone—Steve. Steve! Don't you hear me?"

He did not answer. He was working with his horse, thrilling that work-wracked body of the mustang with new life, while Logan fell steadily behind him. Far behind him in the valley, a gun exploded. The sharp, barking sound rang dimly through the pass and was lost. Another gun spoke. Then he heard only the straining voice of Logan behind him and the dying rattle of the hoofs of Logan's horse, but that, too, fell away to nothing. He was alone. This great work was left to his hand only!

So said Train, gritting his teeth, and, as he spoke, he felt the mustang beneath him begin to falter and fail. He eased it down the next fall of the trail. He walked it up the farther rise. But when he called on the poor brute for a gallop, again, it responded with only a staggering and pitiful effort. The third horse, then, was spent, and the trail was lost!

Then he heard, far, far behind him, the dim roaring as of a fall of water. It was sustained. It grew and grew. It dissolved into clearer sounds, as he made out the pattering of flying hoofs of horses. Freshly mounted men were swinging his way up the trail. The noise grew and grew through the thin, clear air of the mountains. It came to him like a fresh perfume of pine trees to a lover of mountains. Help was coming from the rear. He let the beaten mustang fall back to an easier jog.

One ringing hoofbeat now advanced before the rest. Then he heard a voice shouting behind him, a sharp, high, nasal voice:

"Train! Oh-h-h, Train!"

He waited without answering. It came again, far closer: "Tra-a-ain! Oh-h-h, Train!"

It was Gresham again, Gresham the indefatigable, Gresham the hand of the law. And he who would have fled from Gresham that morning like the presence of the plague, now threw up his hands in thanksgiving to the bright sky of the mountain night and shouted an answer.

What matter if himself were taken and sent to prison—ay, even for the rest of his days? What matter that? He would let himself be put in irons and kept by a few of Gresham's men, so long as Gresham himself and enough fighting men with

176

him could be induced to take that trail through the mountains and keep on for the sake of the girl.

He called again. There was a ringing answer and a burst of clattering hoofbeats around a curve of the trail, and there came Gresham with the slender, graceful body of Whimsy beneath him, wafting him forward as easily and tirelessly as though she had been a feather blowing on a lazy wind.

"I surrender, Gresham!" cried Train, holding his hands above his head as the detective swept to his side. "I surrender, Gresham. Turn me over to your boys. Put the irons on me—make sure of me. But for God's sake ride on ahead. Keep up the path. Two riders—a big man on a brown hoss—a girl on a gray—ride, Gresham. It's Nair!"

"Shut up!" gasped out the detective. "I don't need no orders from you, Train."

"Gresham, if you let her go with that rank devil—"

Gresham drew Whimsy to a halt. Behold, her long flanks were barely disturbed by her breathing. Her head was as lightly carried and her eyes as bright in the starlight as though she had that moment stepped from her stall in the morning after a night of rest. She whinnied and danced with delight as she recognized her old master.

"Git off your horse!" snarlingly commanded Gresham.

The heart of Train sank. But it was too late to struggle. He might kill Gresham, but before he could change into the saddle on Whimsy, the rest of the posse would be swarming around him. And these were partly Gresham's hired men and partly the choice of the fighting men of the town of Creighton, mounted upon their picked horses. He would be taking a life only in order to lose his own and do no good to the girl.

"Down, down, darn you!" shouted Gresham.

He dragged a foot from the right-hand stirrup. He slumped heavily down to the road.

"Come here—quick!"

A child could have commanded him then, so broken was his spirit. He stood before Gresham with his head bowed and his hands wearily raised to his shoulders' height.

"Now get on that horse!" commanded Gresham.

"What horse?"

"Whimsy, you fool!"

But what mattered an insult or two now? He clambered slowly into the stirrups; behind him came the rush of the posse as he swung into the saddle and felt the supple, muscular body of Whimsy flexing beneath him.

"Now ride like the devil!" yelled Gresham. "Ride like the devil, Train, and get Nair for yourself and me and the rest of the world."

The stunned brain of Steven Train refused to record the words he heard. He leaned in the saddle and shouted: "What?"

"I've met up with Cartwright; he's told me everything, and—I think you're square, kid! I think you're square. Hop to it; grab the glory; beat it! You're all right!"

The last words were spoken to a whir of empty air as Whimsy leaped away into the night. No words of thanks streamed back to Gresham. Neither did he seem to wish for them, for he stood in the trail with a broad grin wreathing his face. He was not a man, to-day, he was a hand of the law, and with his hand he was striking down a criminal. No matter to Gresham if the fame descended upon the shoulders of another. He felt as though he had launched a dreadful arrow from his bow. It would strike the target, though far, far away from his sight.

In the meantime, the posse stormed around him, half composed of the men of Creighton and half composed of his own hired men. One of these Gresham caused to halt and dismount, and seated in his stead Gresham galloped ahead again. It was a good horse, this new mount of his, and though it was no second Whimsy, yet it was able to keep up with the rest of the rushing horses. But Gresham rode without enthusiasm. Far, far ahead, gaining ground at every stride, he knew the beautiful mare was running through the night. They would never catch Whimsy even with an ordinary rider on her back, but with Steve Train up, as well strive to overtake a comet. The battle with Nair would be over before they could arrive!

In the meantime Train was letting the mare extend herself, but not so far as her gallant heart bade her. She would have run herself to death in the first half dozen miles, had her rider permitted her to go ahead, but Train knew that the chase might still be long and hard before they overtook the fugitive, and when the time of the dawn came and he could catch sight of his man, he wanted ample speed and power left beneath him to carry him swiftly toward his goal.

As for the posse, he quite forgot about them. They were

banished in his wake. They would never catch sight of him until after either he or the outlaw were dead. His work lay all before him, and only a few wondering thoughts clung to the strange thing that Gresham had done.

That very morning it would have been a thing which he could not have understood, but now there was a change, and he began to grasp at the essential significance of what the detective had dared to try. He might be as ambitious as any detective who ever stepped, but on this day he forgot himself and merged himself in the good of the law, in the good of society.

Not that Train voiced the thought in such words, but he gripped the meaning firmly. It was a great power which planned and executed all of this. Perhaps all that wild and lawbreaking life of his had been ordained so that, when the great moment came, he, Train, could be fitted and equipped with every tool to perform the mission. Who else, then, could have done better? He had needed one gift only—Whimsy. That had been given to him—taken away—restored once more and now he rode with the weird certainty that fate was in him and that the life of the big outlaw was in his hand.

34

In the dawn, as he had hoped, he saw them.

They were riding against the crest of a ridge. The empty sky yawned on the farther side. Only for an instant he glimpsed them as they rose out of the shadow and were framed against the growing light.

Then he drew rein on Whimsy and put her gingerly up the slope, so slowly, so steadily, that his heart raged within him at the delay. He wanted wings to fly at the throat of Nair, but instead, he must go slowly up the slope, keeping the heels of Whimsy nimble so that she might fly like an arrow off the string when he launched her at the prey on the farther side.

She went up the incline shaking her head at the restraint, turning her large bright eyes to him as though she wondered at these tactics, as though, indeed, she had sighted the enemy and wanted to rush like a battle-trained charger to the assault. He soothed her with his voice, well knowing that, what the reins cannot do by physical force, the voice can sometimes accomplish through a far greater and more subtle power.

They gained the height. They looked down like eagles on the softly dipping hills beneath. It was the rosy light of the morning, now, indescribably bright and fresh. The keen wind blew the weariness out of his body. New life came to him from every breath he drank. And there he saw them, jogging their drooping horses through a hollow. No wonder the horses were fagged, but though they had ridden far and fast on this night of nights, they had not ridden far enough. Here was Whimsy still, dancing for freedom on the rein, filled with inextinguishable ardor for the chase.

Beneath him, the wolf dog howled, and he could see Nair turn his head and look back. At that, a pang started through the wound along the side of Train's head, but it was merely the spur which sent him down the slope like a whirlwind. Nair, too, had urged his horse to a gallop, and the girl was riding by him—yes, and ahead, for her weight in the saddle had been hardly half that of the giant's and her horse was far less exhausted. But only for a matter of a hundred yards did Nair flee. Then, looking back again and seeing how the gap between him and his pursuer had shrunk so fast, he drew rein. Train saw him wave the girl ahead, and saw her canter on, while Nair turned back to fight.

He drew his rifle from the holster; so much Train saw, before he rushed out of sight of his foe in a steep-sided little cañon. In the bottom of that little defile he turned sharply to the right and sprinted Whimsy ahead over the thick dead grasses which muffled the falling of her hoofs. Then he twitched her to the right again and darted up to the top of the slope.

Luck, glorious luck, and that little maneuver had stood him in good stead, for he had come right up behind the back of Nair, who sat in his saddle with his rifle ready, scanning the lowlands beyond him.

"Nair!" shouted Train.

And he knew, from the corner of his eye, though he could not look, that the girl had heard the cry and had reined her horse around to watch the encounter. He gripped his own revolver, bringing Whimsy to a halt with a jerk, and he heard Nair curse, saw him drop the rifle, and snatch at a revolver as he swung the brown around.

It would be fair fighting; so much for that. And if he died, he knew with utter surety that Nair must die also. There was a promise to that effect ringing out of nowhere, tolling like a bell at his ear.

He saw the flash of Nair's gun as it whipped up. Then he raised his own revolver and fired.

A heavy weight struck his left shoulder, tore it with a mangling pain, and twisted him violently in the saddle. He lost balance and crashed to the ground.

He heard a yell of triumph. There was Nair, erect in the saddle, firing again and again, thundering his exultation in the victory. Another blow struck him with sickening effect; it ripped his thigh from hip to knee. A third bullet spatted dust and gravel in his face and half blinded him. And in that way, lying on his back, half blinded, he leveled his revolver, forgot his pain, drew his bead with solemn care, and pulled the trigger.

He did not need to look in order to know that Nair was killed. The last thing he saw, before the wave of darkness washed from his feet up and across his brain, was the huge form of Nair tossing up his hands and toppling from the saddle, while his riderless, exhausted horse tried the renewed lightness of its heels in a lumbering gallop across the hilltop.

Afterward, the light broke in a sort of red lightning flash of pain across his mind. He looked up. Men were standing around him. He smelled the choking dust which their stirring feet had worked up into the air.

"More air!" he breathed.

"Keep back!" cried a small, sweet voice just above him, and he looked up into the face of Alice.

Then, as he extended his arm, the darkness rose again in a thick tide, his fingers gripped hard on nothingness, and he was lost again.

When he came to himself for a second glimpse of life, his body was supported by the softness of a bed. He wondered over it dimly before he had the strength to open his eyes. A dozen pangs of torture wrung and wrenched him, and with a groan he looked up. Cartwright was just above him; the deep voice of the big man was like a distant thunder, bidding him be of good cheer. It was a haggard face; he noted that with a sort of empty curiosity.

"He's coming to!" he heard Cartwright say, and then that voice which spoke from heaven answered: "Oh, thank God!" And he saw her running toward him through an open door—

a paler face—staring eyes of sleeplessness—then the quick curtaining blackness cut them apart once more.

He passed into a land of horror and dim dreams. He was on the ocean, in a sinking ship; he was in the salt water, which was closing at his lips. Once, though all remained in the dark and he could not open his eyes, he heard voices in his dream, clearly speaking voices.

"He'll live, doctor? He *has* to live!"

"He can't live," said the second speaker. "He's lost enough blood to kill two men. And those wounds—they'd do for two, unless he had enough deviltry in him to take the place of blood."

Then, rising out of the land of death and floating dizzily back to the warmth and the light of the living, he heard the strong bass voice of Cartwright speaking again together with another voice. It was Patrick Comstock upon whom he looked when his eyelids raised.

"Boy," said Comstock, taking his hand gently, "do you know me? Do you recollect me, Train?"

"Don't know you half so well as I thought I did once!" gasped out Train, and smiled a faint ghost of his old smile.

So he hung in a coma, starting back to life—sinking again—verging once more toward sense of the world—dropping again into the abyss which borders death. Once when his senses struggled feebly back, he heard a man who leaned above him saying: "Steven Train, have you any earthly wishes to make before you die? Have you messages and bequests to make?"

And he answered with his half-dying breath: "Make 'em feed Whimsy oats—not barley!"

But on a day, he opened his eyes and looked gravely and deliberately around him upon a ghostly circle; Comstock worn and wan, Cartwright with haggard face and sunken eyes, and a pale ghost of what had once been lovely Alice. How her eyes filled with tears when he smiled on her. And then how she laughed half hysterically with joy and dropped on her knees by the bed as he whispered her name!

That was a brief glimpse of heaven for which even death would not have been half enough to pay. But he did not die. His eyes opened once again, and this time he raised his hand and wondered at the shrunken, wan fingers which stirred at his bidding.

"We'll take no credit for this," said the doctor on this day.

182

"For this is one of those things that happen without rhyme or reason. I say that this man was dead and came to life again. He had to die; four doctors said so. But there was a miracle. God knows what."

"I think," said the grave voice of Comstock, "that that name may indeed be the answer."

On the first day thereafter, he found himself condemned to silence, and to speechlessness. He asked for many things and many people, but all they would allow him to see was a short, square-built man with pale eyes and colorless eyebrows. He sat down on the edge of a chair and grinned foolishly at Train.

"The devil, man," he said, "they couldn't kill you. You had too much to live for. She's a pippin, eh?" And he winked at Train.

The second day he was again allowed only one visitor. It was a grizzled gentleman ill at ease in Sunday clothes, with a stiff white collar chafing the bristles of his sunburned, wrinkled throat. Mr. Logan smoked a tailor-made cigarette and announced with casual interest that he had just been appointed a deputy sheriff and that a special salary had been appointed to him, and that he was in charge of certain valuable work ridding the mountains of the pests of outlaws which infested them, making them dangerous.

But on the third day he forced himself up on his elbow and vowed that he would see her if he had to climb out of bed and tear down the wall to get to her. At which they chuckled and said he was getting on. So they opened a door and led in a girl with a frightened face and great eyes and a white, thin face, as though she had passed through a great sickness.

She sat down in a chair beside the bed and looked in fear at the doctor. The doctor left the room. She looked at the nurse. The nurse departed. And then she said:

"Mr. Train, I'm very glad to see you looking so much better."

He took both her hands in his trembling one.

"Dear girl, dear Al," said Steve Train, "it was your hands that pulled me back. Tell me now that you got me here, will you take me for keeps?"

And she turned a glorious scarlet, stammering: "The doctor says you mustn't—"

"What?" said Steven Train masterfully.

"Nothing," she quavered.

"Darn the doctor," said Steve. "Only tell me, Al!"

So she leaned to his ear and whispered it.

For everyone who just misses making big money in the market.

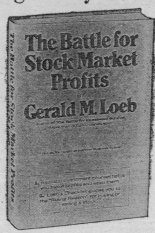

In this entirely new book,
THE BATTLE FOR STOCK MARKET PROFITS,
Gerald M. Loeb,

the celebrated "Dean of Wall Street," draws on his fifty years of experience to prepare you for the stock market of the seventies.

▼ **AT YOUR BOOKSTORE OR MAIL THIS COUPON NOW FOR FREE 10-DAY TRIAL** ▼

How to stay healthy all the time.

"*I can recommend this book for authoritative answers to questions that continually come up about health and how to live.*"—Harry J. Johnson, M.D., Chairman, Medical Board Director, Life Extension Institute.

Wouldn't it be wonderful if your whole family could stay healthy all the time?

It may now be possible, thanks to PREVENTIVE MEDICINE. This is the modern approach to health care. Its goal is to prevent illness before it even has a chance to strike!

A new book called **THE FAMILY BOOK OF PREVENTIVE MEDICINE** shows how you can take advantage of this preventive approach, and make it an everyday reality for yourself and your family. More than 700 pages long—and written in clear, simple language.

TELLS YOU ALL ABOUT THE LATEST MEDICAL ADVANCES

For example, the new knowledge of risk factors in disease is a vital tool of preventive medicine. With it, your doctor might pinpoint you as, say, a high heart attack risk *long before your heart actually gives you any trouble.* He could then prescribe certain changes in your diet and habits—perhaps very minor ones—that could remove the danger entirely. This would be preventive medicine at its ideal best! But even if a disease has already taken root, new diagnostic techniques can reveal its presence earlier than ever before. And, as a rule, the sooner a disease is discovered, the more easily it is cured.

SEND NO MONEY—10 DAYS' FREE EXAMINATION

Mail the coupon below, and **THE FAMILY BOOK OF PREVENTIVE MEDICINE** will be sent to you for free examination. Then, if you are not convinced that it can help you protect the health of your entire family, return it within 10 days and owe nothing. Otherwise, we will bill you for $12.95 plus mailing costs. At all bookstores, or write to Simon and Schuster, Dept. S-53, 630 Fifth Ave., New York, N.Y. 10020.

SIMON AND SCHUSTER, Dept. S-53
630 Fifth Ave., New York, N.Y. 10020

Please send me on approval a copy of THE FAMILY BOOK OF PREVENTIVE MEDICINE. If not convinced that this book belongs permanently in my home, I may return it within 10 days and owe nothing. Otherwise, you will bill me for $12.95, plus mailing costs.

Name...

Address..

City...State.............Zip..........

☐ SAVE. Enclose $12.95 now, and publisher pays mailing costs. Same 10-day return privilege with full refund guaranteed. (New York residents please add applicable sales tax.)

P 65/2